THE STUFF OF
DREAMS
THE WEIRD STORIES OF
EDWARD LUCAS WHITE

THE STUFF OF DREAMS

THE WEIRD STORIES OF EDWARD LUCAS WHITE

Edited & Introduced by S. T. Joshi

Dover Publications, Inc.
Mineola, New York

DOVER HORROR CLASSICS

Copyright

Copyright © 2016 by Dover Publications, Inc.
Introduction © 2016 by S. T. Joshi

Bibliographical Note

The Stuff of Dreams: The Weird Stories of Edward Lucas White, first published by Dover Publications, Inc., in 2016, is a new anthology of thirteen works reprinted from standard sources. A new Introduction has been specially prepared for the present edition by S. T. Joshi.

International Standard Book Number
ISBN-13: 978-0-486-80615-0
ISBN-10: 0-486-80615-4

Manufactured in the United States by RR Donnelley
80615401 2016
www.doverpublications.com

Contents

Introduction ix

The House of the Nightmare 1
The Flambeau Bracket 11
Amina 23
The Message on the Slate 34
Lukundoo 67
The Pig-skin Belt 81
The Song of the Sirens 110
The Picture Puzzle 141
The Snout 155
Sorcery Island 187
Azrael 206
The Ghoula 208
Edward Lucas White on Dreams 212

Introduction

PERHAPS EDWARD LUCAS White (1866–1934) would be irked if he knew that amidst the mass of his literary productions spanning more than three decades, virtually the only works that are remembered are his tales of supernatural horror, especially those contained in the scarce collection *Lukundoo and Other Stories* (1927). Such a fate has overtaken many other writers—from F. Marion Crawford to Robert W. Chambers—renowned in their own day for work of a very different sort. It is perhaps a testament to the timeless quality of so much weird fiction that it can be relished by today's readers far longer than social or political novels whose interest fades so rapidly after the circumstances engendering them have lapsed from public attention. In White's case it must be doubly frustrating in that his weird tales were in his day received so unenthusiastically that a number of them failed to find lodgment in magazines even after repeated submissions, whereas his historical novels—all ably written and several of them still compellingly readable—achieved near-bestseller status.

White was born on May 11, 1866, in Bergen, New Jersey. George T. Wetzel, for whose invaluable biographical research on White I am deeply indebted,[1] notes that White's paternal ancestors were French immigrants who settled in Pennsylvania in the 1730s, and his maternal ancestors were Irish immigrants who established themselves in Baltimore in the early nineteenth century. Shortly after his birth, White's family moved to Brooklyn,

---

[1] See Wetzel's "Edward Lucas White: Notes for a Biography," serialised in *Fantasy Commentator* 4, No. 2 (Winter 1979–80): 94–114; 4, No. 3 (Winter 1981): 178–83; 4, No. 4 (Winter 1982): 229–39; 5, No. 1 (Winter 1983): 67–70, 74; 5, No. 2 (Winter 1984): 124–27. The account proceeds only up to 1909, cut short by Wetzel's death in 1983.

where his father, Thomas Hurley White, was ruined in the "Black Friday" panic of 1869. The family was forced to separate, Edward going with his mother, Kate Butler (Lucas) White, to the town of Coxsackie, New York (on the Hudson River), while his father continued to work in the New York area. An attempt to run a farm in Ovid, New York, in the western part of the state, failed after a few years, and by 1874 Thomas had moved to Baltimore, where his side of the family now resided. The poverty that plagued the family through much of Edward's early years left a lasting impression on him.

For a variety of reasons Edward's mother was unwilling to reunite the family in Baltimore, and for five years she and her husband saw little of each other. Edward was educated largely by his parents, but in 1877 was sent to the Pen Lucy School in Baltimore. His formal schooling was somewhat sporadic, but he made up for it by poring over books at the Peabody Institute Library. It was here that he developed his lifelong fascination for ancient history, specifically the history of Rome.

In 1884 White entered Johns Hopkins University, where he impressed future president Woodrow Wilson (then an instructor in history) with his skills in a debating club. White had been plagued by migraine headaches since the age of ten, and throughout his life they caused serious disruptions in his life and work. However, the headaches that he experienced during his first year at Johns Hopkins were not migraines, but rather they were caused by overwork (another recurring problem for White), and a doctor advised him to take a long sea voyage. In June 1885 he did so, sailing on the freight vessel *Cordorus* to Rio de Janeiro. At that time he wrote the first version of his utopia, *Plus Ultra,* but on the return journey he found it unsatisfactory and threw it overboard.

White had been writing fiction and poetry since his teens, but upon his return to Baltimore he destroyed virtually every scrap of this work—which he estimated to consist of more than 1200 items. Returning to Johns Hopkins in the fall of 1886, he received his B.A. in Romance Languages in 1888 and immediately began postgraduate studies, hoping to earn a Ph.D. But, by June 1890 he was forced to withdraw, as his father no longer had the money to fund his education. It was a bitter blow to White, seemingly dashing his hopes to secure a teaching position in a university. By 1892, however, he was hired to teach freshman Latin at Dartmouth, but he taught poorly and his assignment was not renewed. He subsequently landed a teaching job at Friends High School in Baltimore, thereby beginning a lifelong career as a high school teacher that would make him a legend to generations of boys in the Baltimore area. In 1899 he was hired at the Boys Latin School, where he remained until 1915. In 1900, after a long courtship, he married Agnes Gerry, the sister of a school friend.

In the 1890s White resumed writing, and produced a great quantity of poetry. Among the products of this period were two striking poems, "The Ghoula" and "Azrael." The latter, written in 1897, was not published until White included it in his book *Matrimony* (1932). Addressed to his future bride, the poem's chief feature is its suggestion of White's recurrent nightmares. White had been a vivid dreamer since the age of five, and nearly all his weird tales are the product of dreams, in many cases being literal transcripts of them. "The Ghoula" was inspired by a chance remark in Rudyard Kipling's "Her Majesty's Servants," in *The Second Jungle Book* (1895), in which Hindu oxen are said to be instinctively afraid of the English because they know that the English will eat them. This set White to thinking of the reverse phenomenon: what if there were a creature that ate human beings? Hence "The Ghoula," a chilling poem about a female ghoul, and the clear predecessor to White's striking tale "Amina."

White published two stories in the small Baltimore magazine, *Dixie*, but the bulk of his short fiction was written in a remarkable span between 1905 and 1909. Of the tales in this volume, all but one date to this period. Among the first of them was "The House of the Nightmare," which White dated 1905 when it appeared in *Lukundoo*. Unlike many of his stories, it sold readily, appearing in *Smith's Magazine* for September 1906. "The Flambeau Bracket," written in January 1906, had a less happy fate: it was rejected by 75 magazines over a 51-month period, finally landing in *Young's Magazine* (the date of publication is uncertain; it probably appeared in late 1910 or early 1911). The story is a remarkable testament to Edgar Allan Poe's influence on White. White notes that he had been a devotee of Poe since his early teenage years, and late in life he made the confession that "I have had to banish from my home every scrap of [Poe's] printed writings, else I should waste my time and fuddle myself and reread him when I should be doing other things."[2] He also confessed that he destroyed nearly every scrap of his work that was influenced by Poe, but "The Flambeau Bracket" survived. Although based upon a dream, White admits that the dream itself was largely triggered by "The Cask of Amontillado." It is White's solitary excursion into non-supernatural horror.

"Amina," written in 1906, appeared in the *Bellman* on June 1, 1907, but several other weird tales—"The Message on the Slate" (written 1906), "The Pig-skin Belt" (written 1907), "The Picture Puzzle" (written 1909), and "The Snout" (written 1909)—did not find periodical publication and appeared for the first time in *Lukundoo*. The title story of that collection—far and away White's finest weird tale—was also written in 1907, but not published until it appeared in *Weird Tales* in November 1925—one of White's few contributions to a pulp magazine. "The Song of the Sirens" appeared in severely truncated form as "The Man Who Had Seen Them" in *Sunset Magazine* (March 1909).

White published a number of other stories around this time, but they are not weird. One, "The Little Faded Flag" (*Atlantic Monthly,* May 1908), is a fine tale of the Civil War.[3] Another, a humorous story entitled "A Transparent Nuisance" (*New York Herald,* June 17, 1906), is marginally weird in being derived from Wells' *Invisible Man.* "The Buzzards" (*Bellman,* July 25, 1908) is a melding of romance and suspense. On the whole, however, White's uncollected stories are not of high quality, and have not been included in this volume.

Wetzel describes several unpublished stories found among White's effects. Two in particular seem of interest to devotees of

---

[2] Edward Lucas White to the Poe Society (12 January 1929); quoted in Wetzel, "Notes for a Biography" [I], p. 98.

[3] It is now reprinted in my anthology, *Civil War Memories* (Nashville: Rutledge Hill Press, 2000).

the weird. The first is "Mandola." Written as early as 1890, Wetzel summarizes the plot as follows:

> Mountjoy, the narrator, is studying prehistoric man and owns a plaster cast of an ancient skeleton found at Neandertal, Germany. Later he has a nightmare in which he sees the Neandertal relic as a living being, stalking in the woods. After waking he remarks, "In dreams the nightmare effect of terror is tenfold that which one feels awake. The agony of dread, the sickness and cold sweat, and the total inability to move is made up of a torture unpaintable." (Here, of course, White is clearly describing his own reactions to nightmares.) Over a period of time the terror of this nightmare affects Mountjoy's memory. One day he decides to see how badly his memory has been affected by trying to recall details from his dreams. He evokes the Neandertal image, and sees it again as if in his nightmare—but now it strikes down with its club at a shawl near where he is sitting. Later he looks for his fiancée, Mandola, who earlier had wandered off for a walk in the wood. He finds her seated on a stone, dead from fright, at her feet her pet dog a pulp of blood and bones; and on the ground footprints bigger than any human's. His ability to visualize has actually conjured into existence the horror from his nightmare.

Wetzel describes the other story as follows:

> "The Serge Coat" is another story based on White's actual dreams. He described it as "of double location and thought-transference," but it would more accurately be termed a variation on the doppelgänger theme. Hume, the narrator, is walking in the autumnal countryside. Becoming overheated, he takes off his jacket and puts it under his arm along with a thin serge topcoat he is already carrying. Later in his walk he discovers that the serge coat is missing. The following spring he is tramping again over the same countryside, and by an accidental series of events enters a barn wherein he finds the lost coat. Several young women in the adjoining house chat with him as he passes. On arriving home, he tosses the coat in a drawer and lies down to nap. When he awakes, he believes he dreams of entering the barn and talking again to the women. And as he stirs, his landlady, who had been nursing him as he lay actually unconscious for

ten days, notices the serge coat, which she is sure was not in the house at the onset of his illness. Hume keeps his puzzlement to himself. Not long after he encounters the young women, who say they met him not on the day he believes, but during the time of his unconsciousness.[4]

It is evident that White was frustrated by the lack of commercial success of his short fiction. Other aspects of his work met a similar fate. In 1908 he published his first book, a slim volume of poetry entitled *Narrative Lyrics*. Although it appeared under the imprint of the prestigious G. P. Putnam's Sons, it was (as commonly, both then and now) issued at White's own expense, and sold only 78 copies in two years. As a result, White decided to turn to the writing of novels, and here he enjoyed markedly better success.

El Supremo: A Romance of the Great Dictator of Paraguay, which White began as early as 1910, was published in 1916 by E. P. Dutton and was both a popular and a critical success. This historical novel, set in 1815, deals with Dr. José Gaspar Rodriguez de Francia, the autocrat who ruled Paraguay from 1813 to 1840. Although more than 700 pages in length, it was reprinted at least ten times, the last in 1943. White followed this up with two superlative historical novels about his beloved Rome, *The Unwilling Vestal: A Tale of Rome under the Caesars* (1918) and *Andivius Hedulio: Adventures of a Roman Nobleman in the Days of the Empire* (1921), both published by Dutton. Both were well received by critics and readers; the former went through twelve printings by 1937, and the latter had been printed fourteen times by 1941. H. P. Lovecraft, also an ardent devotee of Rome, considered *Andivius Hedulio* the finest and most realistic novel about the Roman Empire he had ever read, far surpassing such popular works as Henryk Sienkiewicz's *Quo Vadis* (1896) and William Stearns Davis' *A Friend of Caesar* (1900). White, however, was not able to sustain his popularity. *Helen* (1925) was a lackluster novel about Helen of Troy, and the nonfiction work *Why Rome Fell* (1927)—which, in a reprise of Gibbon's *Decline and Fall of the Roman Empire*, blamed the fall

---

[4] Wetzel, "Notes for a Biography" [III], pp. 236–37.

of Rome on the spread of Christianity—received very mixed reviews, some praising the work but others condemning it for superficiality and factual errors. White's final book, *Matrimony* (1932), is a touching account of his marriage with Agnes, who had died on March 30, 1927.

White's two collections of tales, *The Song of the Sirens* (1919) and *Lukundoo*, were also accorded a mixed reception, and neither sold well. Aside from the title story and "The Flambeau Bracket," *The Song of the Sirens* is largely devoted to tales of ancient Rome. In his afterword to the book White takes pride in maintaining that these stories are "veracious glimpses of the past, without any marring anachronisms," but as stories they often drag and are weighed down with excessive historical baggage. Another story in this volume, "Disvola," is a vivid tale of the Italian Renaissance, based on a dream. As noted, most of the stories in *Lukundoo* date to 1905–09, but he did manage to write the tale "Sorcery Island" in 1922, although it too remained unpublished until its incorporation into the collection. This story is perhaps dimly related to the unpublished "Diminution Island," a work dating from as early as 1896.

For much of his adult life, however, White was at work on a variety of rewrites of his destroyed utopian novel, *Plus Ultra*. He had begun rethinking the work from as early as 1901, and in 1918–19 he produced a short novel, *From Behind the Stars,* but it remained unpublished. Then, beginning in 1928, a year after his wife's death, White devoted the next five years to *Plus Ultra*, incorporating *From Behind the Stars* as the opening "book" of the work. The result is an immense, 500,000-word novel with many science-fictional elements that might well be of interest to present-day readers; but the novel's length caused it to be rejected by several publishers, and it remains unpublished among White's effects.[5]

It is perhaps fortunate that White—who in later years sported a long white beard and came to look rather strikingly like Bernard Shaw—did not attempt to be a full-time writer, for he

---

[5] For a synopsis and analysis see A. Langley Searles, "'Plus Ultra': An Unknown Science-Fiction Utopia," *Fantasy Commentator* 4, No. 2 (Winter 1979–80): 51–59; 4, No. 3 (Winter 1981): 162–69, 176–77; 4, No. 4 (Winter 1982): 240–42; 5, No. 1 (Winter 1983): 44–49; 5, No. 2 (Winter 1984): 100–105.

would have suffered even greater poverty than he experienced as an impecunious school teacher, especially prior to his novel-writing period. Wetzel's biography is full of charming recollections by White's students, and he clearly came to love the instruction of young scholars into the mysteries of the ancient languages. From as early as 1911 he had begun teaching at the University School for Boys in Baltimore, and he started working there full-time in 1915, remaining until his retirement in 1930. Edward Lucas White died on March 30, 1934—seven years to the day after his beloved wife.

It is difficult to convey in small compass the distinctive qualities of White's weird tales, especially as I am reluctant to reveal their plots for those coming upon them for the first time. Aside from their inspiration from dreams, their most salient feature is perhaps the sheer bizarrerie of their weird manifestations. Rarely do we find the conventional ghost in White's work; instead, we come upon the female ghoul in "Amina," the hideous growth that plagues the protagonist in "Lukundoo," the monster that is Hengist Eversleigh in "The Snout," and so many others. Even when a ghost is present—as perhaps is the case in "The Message on the Slate"—it exhibits itself in a piquant and novel way.

White admitted that he had renounced all religious belief as early as the age of fourteen, and this very lack of belief may have contributed to the effectiveness of his tales. As H. P. Lovecraft noted in his essay "Supernatural Horror in Literature":

> It may be well to remark here that occult believers are probably less effective than materialists in delineating the spectral and the fantastic, since to them the phantom world is so commonplace a reality that they tend to refer to it with less awe, remoteness, and impressiveness than do those who see in it an absolute and stupendous violation of the natural order.[6]

It is this sentiment that lends poignancy to the charlatan clairvoyant's confession in "The Message on the Slate," that the

---

[6] H. P. Lovecraft, *The Annotated Supernatural Horror in Literature,* ed. S. T. Joshi (New York: Hippocampus Press, 2000), p. 58.

supernatural phenomenon he has just experienced "has demolished the entire structure of my spiritual existence."

There is perhaps a reason to complain that White's development of his narrative is at times a bit slow and drawn-out. Indeed, it would appear that several of his lengthier tales were rejected largely on the grounds of length; as noted, "The Song of the Sirens" was first published only in a heavily abridged form. But in most instances, White's leisurely narration is designed to build up an insidious atmosphere of horror by the slow accretion of bizarre details, and in the end we find that few of his tales are open to the charge of prolixity. He had learned well from his early idol Poe, and adhered fully to Poe's conceptions of the "unity of effect."

White was able to mingle his love of classical antiquity and his love of the weird only in "The Song of the Sirens"; but his tales feature other interesting bits of autobiography. The ship *Medorus* that is the setting for "The Song of the Sirens" is a clear reflection of the *Cordorus,* on which White sailed in 1885. "Sorcery Island"—a weird and ambiguously supernatural tale that uncannily foreshadows the "Prisoner" television series—may also owe something to White's travels. "The House of the Nightmare" evokes the rural setting of White's early years in New York.

White's most famous story, "Lukundoo," is worth considering in some detail. White makes the interesting comment that, although the story was based on a dream, he would never have had that dream if he had not read H. G. Wells' "Pollock and the Porroh Man," included in *The Plattner Story and Others* (1897). In this story Wells (who, like Kipling, was an occasional correspondent of White's) depicts the fate of an Englishman, Pollock, who, while on an expedition in West Africa has a violent encounter with a "Porroh man" (witch doctor), wounding him in the hand with a pistol shot. Subsequently Pollock is harassed by a variety of minor but ever intensifying annoyances—incursions of snakes, darts and arrows that narrowly miss him, an aching in his muscles, and the like. Feeling that the Porroh man is responsible, Pollock hires another African to kill him. The latter does so with alacrity, bringing the Porroh man's decapitated skull back to Pollock. But a Portuguese associate tells Pollock that he has made a grave mistake: the only way to end the "curse" is for Pollock to have killed the Porroh man himself. Pollock is now haunted by the skull, as it keeps returning to him even though he has successively buried it, tossed it into the river, and burned it. Returning to England, Pollock seems to see the skull, dripping with blood, everywhere; as his desperation and fear grow, he finally kills himself.

A supernatural explanation is not required to account for the events in "Pollock and the Porroh Man"; indeed, at the end Wells suggests that the entire scenario is largely a series of hallucinations brought on by Pollock's fear of the Porroh man's supposed powers. In "Lukundoo" White has duplicated only the barest outline of the plot of Wells' tale: the curse inflicted upon a white man by an African sorcerer. "Lukundoo" is, however, manifestly supernatural, and is still more terrifying in that the curse actually invades the explorer Ralph Stone's body. And yet, both tales are fundamentally tales of revenge, and in both tales we find the victims overcome by remorse at their mistreatment of African natives and inexorably losing their very will to live.

It is regrettable that White never wrote a full-length weird novel, for the crisp character development he displays in his historical novels could have been fused with his powerful weird conceptions to produce a stellar work in this field. Perhaps he was too wedded to Poe's restriction of weirdness to the short story (with the notable exception of *Arthur Gordon Pym*); perhaps, too, the tradition of the weird novel was not sufficiently established in his day to render it commercially feasible for White. Whatever the case, Edward Lucas White has left us a small but potent body of weird short fiction that has waited too long for a new generation of appreciative readers.

—S. T. JOSHI

A Note on the Texts

"The Song of the Sirens" and "The Flambeau Bracket" are derived from *The Song of the Sirens and Other Stories* (New York: E. P. Dutton, 1919); all the other stories are from *Lukundoo and Other Stories* (New York: George H. Doran,

1927). I have omitted two stories from *Lukundoo:* "Floki's Blade," which is more of a legend or fairy tale than a short story; and "Alfandega 49A," a tale that, although marginally weird, strikes me as not being equal in quality to White's other stories. I have arranged the tales chronologically by date of writing, not date of first publication. Of the two poems, "Azrael" (dated October 15, 1897) derives from White's *Matrimony* (Baltimore: Norman Publishing Co., 1932); "The Ghoula" is taken from *Narrative Lyrics* (New York: G. P. Putnam's Sons, 1908). Many of the stories in *Lukundoo* contained typographical and other errors; they have been silently corrected here.

THE STUFF OF DREAMS
THE WEIRD STORIES OF EDWARD LUCAS WHITE

The House of the Nightmare

I FIRST caught sight of the house from the brow of the mountain as I cleared the woods and looked across the broad valley several hundred feet below me, to the low sun sinking toward the far blue hills. From that momentary viewpoint I had an exaggerated sense of looking almost vertically down. I seemed to be hanging over the checkerboard of roads and fields, dotted with farm buildings, and felt the familiar deception that I could almost throw a stone upon the house. I barely glimpsed its slate roof.

What caught my eyes was the bit of road in front of it, between the mass of dark-green shade trees about the house and the orchard opposite. Perfectly straight it was, bordered by an even row of trees, through which I made out a cinder side path and a low stone wall.

Conspicuous on the orchard side between two of the flanking trees was a white object, which I took to be a tall stone, a vertical splinter of one of the tilted lime-stone reefs with which the fields of the region are scarred.

The road itself I saw plain as a box-wood ruler on a green baize table. It gave me a pleasurable anticipation of a chance for a burst of speed. I had been painfully traversing closely forested, semi-mountainous hills. Not a farmhouse had I passed, only wretched cabins by the road, more than twenty miles of which I had found very bad and hindering. Now, when I was not many miles from my expected stopping-place, I looked forward to better going, and to that straight, level bit in particular.

As I sped cautiously down the sharp beginning of the long descent the trees engulfed me again, and I lost sight of the valley. I dipped into a hollow, rose on the crest of the next hill, and again saw the house, nearer, and not so far below.

The tall stone caught my eye with a shock of surprise. Had I not thought it was opposite the house next the orchard? Clearly it was on the left-hand side of the road toward the house. My self-questioning lasted only the moment as I passed the crest. Then the outlook was cut off again; but I found myself gazing ahead, watching for the next chance at the same view.

At the end of the second hill I only saw the bit of road obliquely and could not be sure, but, as at first, the tall stone seemed on the right of the road.

At the top of the third and last hill I looked down the stretch of road under the overarching trees, almost as one would look through a tube. There was a line of whiteness which I took for the tall stone. It was on the right.

I dipped into the last hollow. As I mounted the farther slope I kept my eyes on the top of the road ahead of me. When my line of sight surmounted the rise I marked the tall stone on my right hand among the serried maples. I leaned over, first on one side, then on the other, to inspect my tires, then I threw the lever.

As I flew forward I looked ahead. There was the tall stone—on the left of the road! I was really scared and almost dazed. I meant to stop dead, take a good look at the stone, and make up my mind beyond peradventure whether it was on the right or the left—if not, indeed, in the middle of the road.

In my bewilderment I put on the highest speed. The machine leaped forward; everything I touched went wrong; I steered wildly, slewed to my left, and crashed into a big maple.

When I came to my senses I was flat on my back in the dry gulch. The last rays of the sun sent shafts of golden green light through the maple boughs overhead. My first thought was an odd mixture of appreciation of the beauties of nature and disapproval of my own conduct in touring without a companion—a fad I had regretted more than once. Then my mind cleared and I sat up. I felt myself from the head down. I was not bleeding; no bones were broken; and, while much shaken, I had suffered no serious bruises.

Then I saw the boy. He was standing at the edge of the cinder-path, near the ditch. He was stocky and solidly built; barefoot, with his trousers rolled up to his knees; wore a sort of butternut shirt, open at the throat; and was coatless and hatless. He was tow-headed, with a shock of tousled hair; was much freckled, and had a hideous harelip. He shifted from one foot to the other, twiddled his toes, and said nothing whatever, though he stared at me intently.

I scrambled to my feet and proceeded to survey the wreck. It seemed distressingly complete. It had not blown up, nor even caught fire; but otherwise the ruin appeared hopelessly thorough. Everything I examined seemed worse smashed than the rest. My two hampers alone, by one of those cynical jokes of chance, had escaped—both had pitched clear of the wreckage and were unhurt, not even a bottle broken.

During my investigations the boy's faded eyes followed me continuously, but he uttered no word. When I had convinced myself of my helplessness I straightened up and addressed him:

"How far is it to a blacksmith's shop?"

"Eight mile," he answered. He had a distressing case of cleft palate and was scarcely intelligible.

"Can you drive me there?" I inquired.

"Nary team on the place," he replied; "nary horse, nary cow."

"How far to the next house?" I continued.

"Six mile," he responded.

I glanced at the sky. The sun had set already. I looked at my watch: it was going—seven thirty-six.

"May I sleep in your house tonight?" I asked.

"You can come in if you want to," he said, "and sleep if you can. House all messy; ma's been dead three year, and dad's away. Nothin' to eat but buckwheat flour and rusty bacon."

"I've plenty to eat," I answered, picking up a hamper. "Just take that hamper, will you?"

"You can come in if you're a mind to," he said, "but you got to carry your own stuff." He did not speak gruffly or rudely, but appeared mildly stating an inoffensive fact.

"All right," I said, picking up the other hamper; "lead the way."

The yard in front of the house was dark under a dozen or more immense ailanthus trees. Below them many smaller trees had grown up, and beneath these a dank underwood of tall, rank suckers out of the deep, shaggy, matted grass. What had once been, apparently, a carriage-drive left a narrow, curved track, disused and grass-grown, leading to the house. Even here were some shoots of the ailanthus, and the air was unpleasant with the vile smell of the roots and suckers and the insistent odor of their flowers.

The house was of grey stone, with green shutters faded almost as gray as the stone. Along its front was a veranda, not much raised from the ground, and with no balustrade or railing. On it were several hickory splint rockers. There were eight shuttered windows toward the porch, and midway of them a wide door, with small violet panes on either side of it and a fanlight above.

"Open the door," I said to the boy.

"Open it yourself," he replied, not unpleasantly nor disagreeably, but in such a tone that one could not but take the suggestion as a matter of course.

I put down the two hampers and tried the door. It was latched, but not locked, and opened with a rusty grind of its hinges, on which it sagged crazily, scraping the floor as it turned. The passage smelt moldy and damp. There were several doors on either side; the boy pointed to the first on the right.

"You can have that room," he said.

I opened the door. What with the dusk, the interlacing trees outside, the piazza roof, and the closed shutters, I could make out little.

"Better get a lamp," I said to the boy.

"Nary lamp," he declared cheerfully. "Nary candle. Mostly I get abed before dark."

I returned to the remains of my conveyance. All four of my lamps were merely scrap metal and splintered glass. My lantern was mashed flat. I always, however, carried candles in my valise. This I found split and crushed, but still holding together. I carried it to the porch, opened it, and took out three candles.

Entering the room, where I found the boy standing just where I had left him, I lit the candle. The walls were white-washed, the floor bare. There was a mildewed, chilly smell, but the bed looked freshly made up and clean, although it felt clammy.

With a few drops of its own grease I stuck the candle on the corner of a mean, rickety little bureau. There was nothing else in the room save two rush-bottomed chairs and a small table. I went out on the porch, brought in my valise, and put it on the bed. I raised the sash of each window and pushed open the shutters. Then I asked the boy, who had not moved or spoken, to show me the way to the kitchen. He led me straight through the hall to the back of the house. The kitchen was large, and had no furniture save some pine chairs, a pine bench, and a pine table.

I stuck two candles on opposite corners of the table. There was no stove or range in the kitchen, only a big hearth, the ashes in which smelt and looked a month old. The wood in the woodshed was dry enough, but even it had a cellary, stale smell. The ax and hatchet were both rusty and dull, but usable, and I quickly made a big fire. To my amazement, for the mid-June evening was hot and still, the boy, a wry smile on his ugly face, almost leaned over the flame, hands and arms spread out, and fairly roasted himself.

"Are you cold?" I inquired.

"I'm allus cold," he replied, hugging the fire closer than ever, till I thought he must scorch.

I left him toasting himself while I went in search of water. I discovered the pump, which was in working order and not dry on the valves; but I had a furious struggle to fill the two leaky pails I had found. When I had put water to boil I fetched my hampers from the porch.

I brushed the table and set out my meal—cold fowl, cold ham, white and brown bread, olives, jam, and cake. When the can of soup was hot and the coffee made I drew up two chairs to the table and invited the boy to join me.

"I ain't hungry," he said; "I've had supper."

He was a new sort of boy to me; all the boys I knew were hearty eaters and always ready. I had felt hungry myself, but somehow when I came to eat I had little appetite and hardly relished the food. I soon made an end of my meal, covered the fire, blew out the candles, and returned to the porch, where I dropped into one of the hickory rockers to smoke. The boy followed me silently and seated himself on the porch floor, leaning against a pillar, his feet on the grass outside.

"What do you do," I asked, "when your father is away?"

"Just loaf 'round," he said. "Just fool 'round."

"How far off are your nearest neighbors?" I asked.

"Don't no neighbors never come here," he stated. "Say they're afeared of the ghosts."

I was not at all startled; the place had all those aspects which lead to a house being called haunted. I was struck by his odd matter-of-fact way of speaking—it was as if he had said they were afraid of a cross dog.

"Do you ever see any ghosts around here?" I continued.

"Never see 'em," he answered, as if I had mentioned tramps or partridges. "Never hear 'em. Sort o' feel 'em 'round sometimes."

"Are you afraid of them?" I asked.

"Nope," he declared. "I ain't skeered o' ghosts; I'm skeered o' nightmares. Ever have nightmares?"

"Very seldom," I replied.

"I do," he returned. "Allus have the same nightmare—big sow, big as a steer, trying to eat me up. Wake up so skeered I could run to never. Nowheres to run to. Go to sleep, and have it again. Wake up worse skeered than ever. Dad says it's buckwheat cakes in summer."

"You must have teased a sow some time," I said.

"Yep," he answered. "Teased a big sow wunst, holding up one of her pigs by the hind leg. Teased her too long. Fell in the pen and got bit up some. Wisht I hadn't 'a' teased her. Have that nightmare three times a week sometimes. Worse'n being burnt out. Worse'n ghosts. Say, I sorter feel ghosts around now."

He was not trying to frighten me. He was as simply stating an opinion as if he had spoken of bats or mosquitoes. I made no reply, and found myself listening involuntarily. My pipe went out. I did not really want another, but felt disinclined for bed as yet, and was comfortable where I was, while the smell of the ailanthus blossoms was very disagreeable. I filled my pipe again, lit it, and then, as I puffed, somehow dozed off for a moment.

I awoke with a sensation of some light fabric trailed across my face. The boy's position was unchanged.

"Did you do that?" I asked sharply.

"Ain't done nary thing," he rejoined. "What was it?"

"It was like a piece of mosquito-netting brushed over my face."

"That ain't netting," he asserted; "that's a veil. That's one of the ghosts. Some blow on you; some touch you with their long, cold fingers. That one with the veil she drags acrosst your face—well, mostly I think it's ma."

He spoke with the unassailable conviction of the child in "We Are Seven." I found no words to reply, and rose to go to bed.

"Good night," I said.

"Good night," he echoed. "I'll set out here a spell yet."

I lit a match, found the candle I had stuck on the corner of the shabby little bureau, and undressed. The bed had a comfortable husk mattress, and I was soon asleep.

I had the sensation of having slept some time when I had a nightmare—the very nightmare the boy had described. A huge sow, big as a dray horse, was reared up on her forelegs over the foot-board of the bed, trying to scramble over to me. She grunted and puffed, and I felt I was the food she craved. I knew in the dream that it was only a dream, and strove to wake up.

Then the gigantic dream-beast floundered over the foot-board, fell across my shins, and I awoke.

I was in darkness as absolute as if I were sealed in a jet vault, yet the shudder of the nightmare instantly subsided, my nerves quieted; I realized where I was, and felt not the least panic. I turned over and was asleep again almost at once. Then I had a real nightmare, not recognizable as a dream, but appallingly real—an unutterable agony of reasonless horror.

There was a Thing in the room; not a sow, nor any other namable creature, but a Thing. It was as big as an elephant, filled the room to the ceiling, was shaped like a wild boar, seated on its haunches, with its forelegs braced stiffly in front of it. It had a hot, slobbering, red mouth, full of big tusks, and its jaws worked hungrily. It shuffled and hunched itself forward, inch by inch, till its vast forelegs straddled the bed.

The bed crushed up like wet blotting-paper, and I felt the weight of the Thing on my feet, on my legs, on my body, on my chest. It was hungry, and I was what it was hungry for, and it meant to begin on my face. Its dripping mouth was nearer and nearer.

Then the dream-helplessness that made me unable to call or move suddenly gave way, and I yelled and awoke. This time my terror was positive and not to be shaken off.

It was near dawn: I could descry dimly the cracked, dirty window-panes. I got up, lit the stump of my candle and two fresh ones, dressed hastily, strapped my ruined valise, and put it on the porch against the wall near the door. Then I called the boy. I realized quite suddenly that I had not told him my name or asked his.

I shouted "Hello!" a few times, but won no answer. I had had enough of that house. I was still permeated with the panic of the nightmare. I desisted from shouting, made no search, but with two candles went out to the kitchen. I took a swallow of cold coffee and munched a biscuit as I hustled my belongings into my hampers. Then, leaving a silver dollar on the table, I carried the hampers out on the porch and dumped them by my valise.

It was now light enough to see to walk, and I went out to the road. Already the night-dew had rusted much of the wreck, making it look more hopeless than before. It was, however, entirely undisturbed. There was not so much as a wheel-track or a hoof-print on the road. The tall, white stone, uncertainty about which had caused my disaster, stood like a sentinel opposite where I had upset.

I set out to find that blacksmith shop. Before I had gone far the sun rose clear from the horizon, and almost at once scorching. As I footed it along I grew very much heated, and it seemed more like ten miles than six before I reached the first house. It was a new frame house, neatly painted and close to the road, with a whitewashed fence along its garden front.

I was about to open the gate when a big black dog with a curly tail bounded out of the bushes. He did not bark, but stood inside the gate wagging his tail and regarding me with a friendly eye; yet I hesitated with my hand on the latch, and considered. The dog might not be as friendly as he looked, and the sight of him made me realize that except for the boy I had seen no creature about the house where I had spent the night; no dog or cat; not even a toad or bird. While I was ruminating upon this a man came from behind the house.

"Will your dog bite?" I asked.

"Naw," he answered; "he don't bite. Come in."

I told him I had had an accident to my automobile, and asked if he could drive me to the blacksmith shop and back to my wreckage.

"Cert," he said. "Happy to help you. I'll hitch up foreshortly. Wher'd you smash?"

"In front of the gray house about six miles back," I answered.

"That big stone-built house?" he queried.

"The same," I assented.

"Did you go a-past here?" he inquired astonished. "I didn't hear ye."

"No," I said; "I came from the other direction."

"Why," he meditated, "you must 'a' smashed 'bout sunup. Did you come over them mountains in the dark?"

"No," I replied; "I came over them yesterday evening. I smashed up about sunset."

"Sundown!" he exclaimed. "Where in thunder've you been all night?"

"I slept in the house where I broke down."

"In that there big stone-built house in the trees?" he demanded.

"Yes," I agreed.

"Why," he quavered excitedly, "that there house is haunted! They say if you have to drive past it after dark, you can't tell which side of the road the big white stone is on."

"I couldn't tell even before sunset," I said.

"There!" he exclaimed. "Look at that, now! And you slep' in that house! Did you sleep, honest?"

"I slept pretty well," I said. "Except for a nightmare, I slept all night."

"Well," he commented, "I wouldn't go in that there house for a farm, nor sleep in it for my salvation. And you slep'! How in thunder did you get in?"

"The boy took me in," I said.

"What sort of a boy?" he queried, his eyes fixed on me with a queer, countrified look of absorbed interest.

"A thick-set, freckle-faced boy with a harelip," I said.

"Talk like his mouth was full of mush?" he demanded.

"Yes," I said; "bad case of cleft palate."

"Well!" he exclaimed. "I never did believe in ghosts, and I never did half believe that house was haunted, but I know it now. And you slep'!"

"I didn't see any ghosts," I retorted irritably.

"You seen a ghost for sure," he rejoined solemnly. "That there harelip boy's been dead six months."

The Flambeau Bracket

GENTLEMEN, CALM yourselves, there is no occasion for an uproar. Be seated again, be seated, all of you, I beg. Honor me with your attention for a moment. Signor Orsacchino has called me a murderer. He need not repeat the epithet. We have all heard it. Some of you gentlemen—I did not recognize the voices—so far forgot yourselves as to suggest that I should cross swords with Signor Orsacchino here and now, or that I should call him out and fight him at once. Gentlemen, I brook no suggestions as to what I should or should not do upon any point of honor. I permit no man to school me as to when or to what extent I should consider myself offended. Still less would I fail to resent any question of the propriety of my ignoring what other men dare not ignore. Signor Orsacchino has shown his courage by applying to me, before so many of you, a term of such serious import. He can incur no dishonor by hearing out in silence what I wish to say before we proceed to a final settlement. As victor in some score of duels I pray your indulgence if for once in my life I depart from my habits, and instead of fighting at once and keeping silence, talk first and fight afterwards, or not at all. You, as my friends, will do me the honor to listen to me. Signor Orsacchino, as my enemy, will do himself the honor to hearken. A young man, and one who has never yet taken part in a serious combat, he has exhibited his conscientious conviction of the justice of his views, and proved his valor and daring by bearding a master of fence who, in fifteen years, has never failed to kill his man. As a skilled swordsman I should feel myself a murderer indeed were I to take upon my soul his blood in haste. The Signor is young; the wine has passed rather freely; we are heated. If I say earnestly—let no man interrupt me—that if Signor Orsacchino tomorrow in cool daylight chooses to reiterate his words, I shall take them as a deadly insult and shall challenge, meet and slay him without compunction. If, on the other hand, after I have told my story, he does not repeat his accusations, I shall regard them, all of them, as not merely withdrawn, but as things never said at all.

Signor Orsacchino has called me a murderer because I killed in a duello his kinsman, General della Rubbalda. That was more than fifteen years ago, and it was my first formal duel. So far from being a seasoned fighter who butchered a feeble and heartbroken old man, I was then a boy, very raw, and to a great extent unpracticed, pitted against a cool, dexterous, and envenomed adversary. In the many encounters through which I have since passed I recall not one which taxed me more severely or in which I ran a greater risk. In fact, the General would assuredly have killed me had he not chosen to fight with a sword, a perfect mate of my own, which I knew and recognized—a sword the sight of which converted me from an excited lad into a being strung far beyond the reach of any personal or paltry emotions; a thing all muscle, nerve and will, perfectly co-ordinated; an infallible supernaturally accurate incarnation of unhurried, predestinate vengeance. We met in the meadow outside of the river gate. Our seconds are all alive, men of unimpeachable integrity, nobles of the loftiest traditions, of the most honorable lineage. There were other witnesses of the fight which was scrupulously fair, and which I won by mere force of right and justice. I believe that, when I have had my say, all of you and Signor Orsacchino not least, will admit that I had just cause, more than just cause, for any vengeance upon the General—that to treat him as a man of honor and meet him sword to sword was a condescension upon my part. So far from having forced him to meet me, his challenge was simultaneous with mine to him. Signor Orsacchino has insinuated what, if he were ever to put into words—no, Signor, hear me out, you may then say what you please—I should resent far more bitterly than the epithet of murderer. You will all recall the sudden and lamented death of Signora della Rubbalda, more than two years after that of her husband. You will all remember that she, the most beautiful woman of our city, who was mourned by unsuccessful suitors beyond any count, left behind her a reputation for saintliness, such as few women have ever attained to. I had, indeed, seen the Signora before my combat with her husband, but I say solemnly that until the Carnival ball I had never spoken to her, that until the morning after, just before the duel, I had not known whom I so admired. I admit that he challenged me upon her account, but his jealousy was as insensate as the spleen that drove him, whose household had escaped loss, to press an imaginary grievance upon me, whose house was most desolate of all, upon a morning of general sorrow and desolation.

If the story of my grievance—all too weak a word—against him has never before been told by me, it is not because I have any reason to be ashamed of it, but rather chiefly that I was not willing to smirch the name of della Rubbalda with a tale of villainy so cynical, and, after the custom of our family, I reserve everything involving penitence or repentance for my confessor. You shall judge whether I am right in confessing to you all. I shall detain you but a few moments longer.

Without penitence I cannot speak of my brother Ettore, at the thought of him I am convicted of ingratitude, that most universal, most unforgivable of the sins of youth. I failed to appreciate my brother Ettore. He was to me not merely a beloved comrade, he not only more than filled for me the place of the father I had lost, but also of the mother I had never known. His tenderness was as exquisite as his precepts were wise, his concern universal, his care constant. I loved him, loved him with the ardent adoration of an unproved boy for a young, handsome, accomplished cavalier who is and does all that the boy longs to be and do. Yet, although he stinted me in nothing, fulfilled for me all my reasonable desires, granted most of my wishes, humored my whims and bore with my moods, some malignant fiber of my heart drove me into perpetual opposition to him. His solicitude irked me; for, with a boy's folly I mistook stubbornness for resolution, recklessness for valor, and self-assertion for independence. I misconstrued supervision as espionage. Resenting it I began by evading perfectly natural questions as to my whereabouts and doings. From that I grew into a contemptible habit of petty and unnecessary concealment as to my outgoings, incomings and occupations. He bore this patiently, not showing any change of his affectionate and kindly bearing.

Presently my perversity drove me to run counter to his wishes in first one thing and then another. Because he had advised me to cultivate certain of my associates I drew off from them; because he had warned me against others I made cronies of them, although I liked them little or not at all. I felt myself manlier for this sort of folly. I consorted with persons of dubious character or manifestly beneath me, resorted to quarters of the town I should have avoided. When I should have been diverting and improving myself in the best company possible for a young cavalier of our part of the world, I was roistering—by no means enjoying it—with fellows I heartily despised. I lost much money gaming, yet Ettore refilled my purse without chiding me in words, his manner conveying the just disapprobation I would not heed. I came home many times so late or so early that I found our porter difficult to wake, and more than once was nearly compelled to find shelter elsewhere. Sometimes I returned so disordered that I shrank from ascending the grand staircase and slunk around the courtyard under the galleries to the servitors' stair. I became habituated to low taverns across the river, where I naturally became involved in wine-room quarrels and street brawls. I flattered myself that I comported myself well in these senseless melées. I dealt some shrewd wounds and came off unscathed. I felt all the man, the man of pleasure.

Then one night I was entrapped, I never realized how, in a street fight with several rufflers. One of my comrades fell and the rest fled, and I was left alone, my back to a barrel door, facing several blades which I barely kept off, when a tall man appeared behind my assailants, fell upon them without warning and promptly beat them off. After the sound of their fleeing feet had died away in the alleys I found myself face to face with Ettore, wearing a cap without a feather, and a plain brown cloak. He asked only:

"You are not wounded?"

"Not a scratch," I replied.

"We will walk together, if you do not object," he said. "Which way are you going?"

"Home," I answered.

As we traversed the crooked streets, crossed the bridge and made our way home, he kept silence at first and then led me into some light gossipy talk, making no remark upon my silly foolhardiness, nor saying anything relative to his sudden appearance or my rescue.

I should have been touched by his solicitude, but with a boy's folly, instead of being overwhelmed with gratitude to him for having saved my life, I was merely indignant at his having followed me and watched over me, and furious at the thought that he had felt that I, who aspired to be redoubtable, might be—as I was too headstrong to confess I had been—in need of assistance.

After this adventure my perversity was aggravated. I took the most sedulous precautions for my own hurt, doing all I could to preclude the possibility of Ettore's ever again being able to protect me from any possible consequences of the dangers into which I needlessly thrust myself.

Throughout the carnival time I fairly lived away from home, mostly, and this, with Ettore's full knowledge, at the Palazzo Forticello with wild Gianbattista and his wilder brother Lorenzo. I took perverse care that Ettore should not be able to recognize me, changing my dress often and wearing a variety of masks. Throughout the carnival I had been hoping to encounter a lady whom I had first seen the previous autumn, whom I had caught sight of but twice during winter, whom I had watched for in vain at the Cathedral, and in the search for whom I had fruitlessly haunted every church in the city. It had so happened that on each of the three times I had seen her I was alone. My descriptions had been unrecognizable to those of my friends whom I asked to enlighten me. When I had described her to Ettore he had maddened me by saying that he knew well who the lady was, but declined to tell me, advising me to think no more of her, as her husband was devoted to her and a spleenful, dangerous man. I spurned his advice, but my fevered efforts won me no success. I had no clue to her, and even during the delirium of the carnival time I had sighted no one whom I could take for her. This failure diminished my enjoyment of the week of revelry, but I had at least the satisfaction that I had not seen Ettore. No sense of his presence, of his hovering influence, dimmed the glow of my delight in feeling myself my own master and perfectly able to take care of myself, in getting into scrapes, as I did, and getting out of them as I might, untrammeled.

On the night of the great ball I was dressed as a troubadour and was very proud of my becoming costume. No sooner had Lorenzo and I entered the theater than I saw the lady of my dreams. She wore a very narrow mask, no more than an excuse for a mask, and was dressed in fanciful garb, the significance of which I did not try to guess, but with the effect of which I was enraptured. She was with a very young man, and after a word with Lorenzo, using the freedom of the festal time, we accosted them. Lorenzo engaged the attention of her escort, while I gained possession of the lady. I may say that we spent the evening together, dancing countless dances, partaking of refreshments, strolling about, or seated on one or another of the benches in the corridors or loggias. So engrossed was I that it was only occasionally that I remembered to look about for Ettore. I never saw him, nor any figure at all suggesting his. But each time I looked among the crowd, the parti-colored brightness of which was accentuated by a liberal sprinkling of cavaliers in black dominoes, all alike slender, youthful, and tall, I saw somewhere one figure that, as it were, stood out among the rest—a tallish spare man of erect carriage, stiff bearing, and moving in a way not at all suggestive of youth, most absurdly and unbecomingly habited as a buffoon, not after the manner of our theater, but in the French fashion, all in white, with a tight-fitting cap and a full false face whitened with flour, a loose, white blouse, with huge, white buttons big as biscuits, loose, wide, white trousers, and white slippers with white rosettes. This costume, odd enough on a young and plump figure, had an uncanny effect preposterously hung about the leanness of an elderly and frigid form. It was so unpleasantly weird that more than once my gaze dwelt on it for an instant before it returned to peering through my dear comrade's mask at the half-revealed wonders of her dazzling eyes. Our conversation was very innocent, witty we thought, delightful we felt. It was near the unmasking time when, as we gave ourselves to the intoxication of one of the last dances, I heard Ettore's voice whisper in my ear.

"Take care. Do not go home alone. You have been three hours with the wife of the most jealous man alive."

I turned my head, and as well as I could in whirling through the whirling crowd, I looked about for Ettore. I did not catch sight of him, nor of any costume such as he might be likely to wear. I saw only the everlasting parti-colored whirl, the iterated black dominoes, the inevitable misfit zany.

At the end of the dance the youth, whom Lorenzo had removed for me, claimed my partner so peremptorily that I could not but resign her—and she, addressing him as cousin, went off with him. They had scarcely more than disappeared when, as I stood leaning against a pilaster gazing across the press of dancers who thronged the floor at the dazzling parties which crowded every box of the seven tiers, a woman's shriek filled the hall. The next instant came the cry of "Fire," and almost before the boxes opposite me emptied the blaze ran across the ceiling. I took no part in the mad panic which ensued. I stood petrified, as did a few others, and recovered my senses only when the billows of smoke rolled to the floor. Then, from under dropping masses of blazing decorations, through doors empty save for the trampled shapes of dead or insensible victims of the rush, I made my way from the auditorium. How I so made my way out, and by which door I do not know, the spectacle of the trampled women so sickened me that I marvel I ever escaped at all. For, at the sight of a corpse not of my own making, I have always turned, I confess, utterly a coward. To gaze at a man dead by my sword does not disturb me. I see in it only the evidence that heaven's justice has made use of my hand to give a scoundrel his deserts. But a glimpse of a dead body, that of one not slain by me, makes my head swim, my eyes dazzle, my sinews loosen, my knees knock together. Before such a corpse I am—I may apply to myself what no other man would venture to hint—no better than a craven. Therefore, I shall never know how I came out of that furnace. I was delirious with horror—a mere animal driven by the primitive instinct of the dread of fire.

The corridors and passageways were almost as full of smoke as the theater itself, and, it seemed to me, more aflame. I dare not venture to say how many stairways I seemed to find ablaze. The rush of the fire drove me in frantic flight hither and thither through several narrow doors and—for down every stair I saw climbing flames—up more than one stair. I realized that I was quite out of the theater and on an upper floor of one or the other of the long-disused, deserted palazzos which flanked it. I could not guess which, and whichever it might be, it was certainly as much on fire as the theater. I recall rushing through room after room all filled with smoke, often turning back, finding no outlet and no way down. Several times I scrambled over heaps of what seemed to be old stage scenery. Once I stumbled and fell, jammed in a forest of broken laths and scantlings. I do not know how I reached the window at which I finally found myself, nor where I was joined by that sinister figure, in the white clown's dress, which I had remarked so often during the dancing. I was first aware of him beside me when I pushed vainly against the shut lattices of the window, and it was his strength, not mine, before which they gave way—not opening on their hinges, but carrying with them their crazy rotten frames, wrenched loose from the stone work of the window and falling altogether with a splintering smash upon the pavement below.

The noise of their crash struck our ears, while our eyesight was yet stunned by the impact of the hot brilliance with which, as the dislodged woodwork left the window aperture clear, we were flooded, diving upward, as it were, from the smoky obscurity of the interior into an intense ruby glare. We both scrambled upon the sill. There was no balcony outside. We were looking into a courtyard so filled with crimson radiance that not only were the walls opposite us bathed in an intense light, but the dark corners were penetrated by a weird carmine-tinted glow even in the deepest shadows. There was not a human being in sight—the court was deserted. It was of considerable size, paved with big square blocks of black-and-white stone. I could make out on the side opposite us the opening of a wagon archway, yawning like a black throat. No arcades flanked the courtyard, and every window I could see was shuttered fast. There were six stories of windows, and we were at one of the fifth story. The roof cornice beetled above us, the roofs above the court were silhouetted against the inflamed sky, and overhead poured the vast inverted cataract of sparks which streamed up from the holocaust we had not yet escaped. We spoke no word. He stood upon the left side of the window, I upon the right. My lute I had, of course, thrown away, my mask I had on no longer. I had lost both sword and poignard, my whole belt was gone. I had nothing in my hands, which were torn and bleeding. The buffoon had a naked dagger in his right hand, a piece of rope in his left. He leaned over and scrutinized the outlook, as I did. We were a frightful distance above the pavement, and even had we been lower, dropping to the pavement would have been certain destruction, for precisely beneath us was a long narrow area, about a yard wide, and how deep I could not guess, constructed to let light into some cellar. The coping along its edge, where the pavement ceased, showed as a line of dull light in the appalling illumination. There were no balconies to the windows below us, or to any of those immediately on the right or left of them. About halfway down the face of the wall, from just below the left of the window in which we were to the corner of the courtyard on that side, ran a broad stone cornice, wide enough for a lean man once standing upon it to walk along it without holding to anything. About halfway to the corner of the court a metal rainspout ran down, making a conspicuous elbow over the jutting stone shelf. Once set on his feet upon this cornice, either of us was sure of escape. The end of it was not precisely below the left side of our window, but a little to the left.

All this I took in in a moment, so, apparently, did the other man. There were many flambeau brackets projecting from the walls of the courtyard. There was one beside each lower corner of our window. The buffoon took his dagger in his teeth, kneeled down, reached over and fastened one end of his rope to the flambeau socket. He did not hurry, but made sure of his knots. Then he dropped the rope and, holding to the bracket with his left hand, shook the rope into undulations with his right, peering down to descry its end. Its end was all of ten feet above the level of the cornice, too far for a man holding the extreme end of it to set his feet on the cornice top. To jump for that cornice, or to drop upon it from even a yard above, it would have meant the certainty of going down to be dashed to pieces on the cruel flagstones below. The buffoon pulled up the rope and stood up, his dagger still between his teeth, projecting from under the false face which it thrust away from his own, and through the eyeholes of which I seemed to feel his eyes fixed upon me. We could hear, above the roar of the fire, the confused hubbub of shouts from the crowds which thronged the square and the streets round about. I had called for help when first I reached the sill, but my bawling, lost in the steady deep, rumbling note of the fire and in the confusion of voices beyond, won no response. Now I yelled again, screamed, shrieked, but no one heard. The buffoon echoed my outcries, but not as if assisting them, not as if hoping against hope for rescue, not as if, like myself, merely giving way to terror and despair, but rather with derisive mockery in his rallying halloos. I felt totally helpless. If I were to escape at all it would be through him, yet I felt him as an inimical presence and feared him almost more than the fire behind us. He stood with the rope bunched inside his fingers, it seemed to me nervously knotting and unknotting it, then he let most of it go slack, a coil of a loop or two swinging back and forth in his left hand, his face toward me and his eyes I felt steadily on me. The tiny threads of lazy smoke that had been faltering out of the window under the lintel increased from a thin trickle to a continuous stream. Through the door of the room behind us was visible a faint blush of blurred brownish light. As I looked at it I saw the door darken suddenly. A man rushed through it, incredibly alive out of the throttling reek, crossed the room in a bound, and leaped upon the sill between us. He was all in black—black cap, black mask, black domino, black hose, and his sword in a black scabbard. So swift was his rush, so impetuously did he leap, that I wondered whether he had meant to set foot on the window sill or had expected to land on a balcony outside. As it was, he planted his feet fairly on the sill, but just missed pitching forward into space. He toppled, bent double, and saved himself only by touching the outer sill with the outstretched fingers of his tense arm.

At this instant, as the masked, black domino rocked unsteadily, head and shoulders into the outer air, the zany flung the noose—for it was by no means a snarl of rope, but a cunningly knotted slip-noose, which he had held inside his closed left hand—over the newcomer's head, and, with one lightning movement, half dragged, half hurled him from the sill. In the air the victim spread out arms, legs, and cloak, like a huge bat. His hands windmilled wildly, searching for the rope, and failed to touch it. For a horrid instant, as the rope checked its headlong dive, the inverted body gave a jolted bob upward before it turned, then it lurched over, the hands making one last clutch for the rope, and again missing. The cord drew up straight as a rapier blade and held. The body was violently and convulsively agitated once or twice, and its sword, tossed out of the upturned scabbard, struck the corner of the cornice with a sharp clang, bounded up, flashing in the red glare, and shot down a long line of light to the pavement. Its owner's corpse writhed sinuously and then merely gyrated limply at the end of the rope. Its feet were not much more than a man's height above the cornice. My abomination of the sight unnerved me so that my impulse to hurl myself upon the murderer was swallowed up in a physical sickness in which I nearly fell from the sill. As I clung to the stone jamb the malignant white shape, dagger in hand, addressed me:

"Sir, I know who you are. I was about to piece my rope with your carcass. Since this intruding stranger has spared me the necessity, and since the rope is now long enough to be useful, I offer you the courtesy of the first opportunity to descend."

Speechless with horror and loathing I tottered, a helpless jelly, against the jamb. He stood, his long dagger in his right hand, eyeing me through his whitened mask.

"Ah," he went on. "You hesitate. You can pass me easily, descend by the bracket, the rope, the cornice, and the rain-spout. You will not? Then you will pardon me if I leave you. You will find it warm here before long. Nevertheless, if this place is more to your liking than the street, I do not dispute your right of choice. A good night to you. I am tempted indeed to put this dagger into you before I go. But I reflect that, though you do not look it, you might have the strength and sleight to avoid my thrust, and perhaps even throw me down. I shall not risk it. If you overcome your panic and are not burned here or killed by falling, if, in short, you get down alive and get home, you shall hear from me in the morning."

He leaned over, tore off and threw away his false face and revealed to me a countenance I did not then recognize. Next, his dagger in his teeth, he dived for the bracket, caught it with both hands, swung himself off into space, gripped the rope, first with one hand, then with both, went down it, stood on the dead man's shoulders, let himself down the rope till he clasped the corpse, wriggled down it, embracing it close, dislodging the cloak which sailed down the air like some huge bird and settled down upon the pavement far out into the court near the sword.

The escaping villain finally gripped one ankle of the corpse with each hand, swung himself and all above him gently sideways until his feet found the cornice, steadied himself by the feet of the corpse, let go and stood up, edged gingerly along the cornice to the rain-spout, and slid down it smoothly. Once on the pavement he leaped into the air, clapping his hands and crowing, scampered briskly across the court, stopped to pick up his victim's cloak and sword, turned to glance up at me, waved me a derisive farewell, and, after a hideous caper of joy, vanished into the black throat of the wagon archway, running like a fiend.

My eyes came back to the dangling body, revolving slowly now. Its mask hung beside the neck and the back of the head was toward me. I felt myself doomed. I knew I could never summon up resolution to escape by that road. In fact, I am sure that from losing my hold, as I actually later descended, and being dashed to pieces on the pitiless stones, nothing saved me but the set fixed purpose of vengeance, which made me not a man, but an automaton.

I looked behind me. The glare of the fire was bright through the smoke, dense volumes of which poured out of the window above my head, and the heat of which I could feel.

At that instant came a terrific dragging crash, a brief darkness, and an agonized wail of groaning shouts. The roof of the theater had fallen in. The smoke sucked back through the window above me, and momentarily I felt cool air on my face. The next instant the volume and intensity of the light redoubled as the overarching stream of sparks became a firmament of fire. The court grew bright to the deepest, darkest corner, eddies of air swept past me, the corpse swung round, its mask blew away wholly. Hideously bowed the head was, the chin driven into the bosom. But I knew the face of my brother Ettore.

Amina

WALDO, BROUGHT face to face with the actuality of the unbelievable—as he himself would have worded it—was completely dazed. In silence he suffered the consul to lead him from the tepid gloom of the interior, through the ruinous doorway, out into the hot, stunning brilliance of the desert landscape. Hassan followed, with never a look behind him. Without any word he had taken Waldo's gun from his nerveless hand and carried it, with his own and the consul's.

The consul strode across the gravelly sand, some fifty paces from the southwest corner of the tomb, to a bit of not wholly ruined wall from which there was a clear view of the doorway side of the tomb and of the side with the larger crevice.

"Hassan," he commanded, "watch here."

Hassan said something in Persian.

"How many cubs were there?" the consul asked Waldo.

Waldo stared mute.

"How many young ones did you see?" the consul asked again.

"Twenty or more," Waldo made answer.

"That's impossible," snapped the consul.

"There seemed to be sixteen or eighteen," Waldo asserted. Hassan smiled and grunted. The consul took from him two guns, handed Waldo his, and they walked around the tomb to a point about equally distant from the opposite corner. There was another bit of ruin, and in front of it, on the side toward the tomb, was a block of stone mostly in the shadow of the wall.

"Convenient," said the consul. "Sit on that stone and lean against the wall, make yourself comfortable. You are a bit shaken, but you will be all right in a moment. You should have something to eat, but we have nothing. Anyhow, take a good swallow of this."

He stood by him as Waldo gasped over the raw brandy.

"Hassan will bring you his water-bottle before he goes," the consul went on; "drink plenty, for you must stay here for some time. And now, pay attention to me. We must extirpate these vermin. The male, I judge, is absent. If he had been anywhere about, you would not now be alive. The young cannot be as many as you say, but, I take it, we have to deal with ten, a full litter. We must smoke them out. Hassan will go back to camp after fuel and the guard. Meanwhile, you and I must see that none escape."

He took Waldo's gun, opened the breech, shut it, examined the magazine and handed it back to him.

"Now watch me closely," he said. He paced off, looking to his left past the tomb. Presently he stopped and gathered several stones together.

"You see these?" he called.

Waldo shouted an affirmative.

The consul came back, passed on in the same line, looking to his right past the tomb, and presently, at a similar distance, put up another tiny cairn, shouted again and was again answered. Again he returned.

"Now you are sure you cannot mistake those two marks I have made?"

"Very sure indeed," said Waldo.

"It is important," warned the consul. "I am going back to where I left Hassan, to watch there while he is gone. You will watch here. You may pace as often as you like to either of those stone heaps. From either you can see me on my beat. Do not diverge from the line from one to the other. For as soon as Hassan is out of sight I shall shoot any moving thing I see nearer. Sit here till you see me set up similar limits for my sentry—go on the farther side, then shoot any moving thing not on my line of patrol. Keep a lookout all around you. There is one chance in a million that the male might return in daylight—mostly they are nocturnal, but this lair is evidently exceptional. Keep a bright lookout.

"And now listen to me. You must not feel any foolish sentimentalism about any fancied resemblance of these vermin to human beings. Shoot, and shoot to kill. Not only is it our duty, in general, to abolish them, but it will be very dangerous for us if we do not. There is little or no solidarity in Mohammedan communities, but on the comparatively few points upon which public opinion exists it acts with amazing promptitude and vigor. One matter as to which there is no disagreement is that it is incumbent upon every man to assist in eradicating these creatures. The good old Biblical custom of stoning to death is the mode of lynching indigenous hereabouts. These modern Asiatics are quite capable of applying it to anyone believed derelict against any of these inimical monsters. If we let one escape and the rumor of it gets about, we may precipitate an outburst of racial prejudice difficult to cope with. Shoot, I say, without hesitation or mercy."

"I understand," said Waldo.

"I don't care whether you understand or not," said the consul, "I want you to act. Shoot if needful, and shoot straight." And he tramped off.

Hassan presently appeared, and Waldo drank from his water-bottle as nearly all of its contents as Hassan would permit. After his departure Waldo's first alertness soon gave place to mere endurance of the monotony of watching and the intensity of the heat. His discomfort became suffering, and what with the fury of the dry glare, the pangs of thirst and his bewilderment of mind, Waldo was moving in a waking dream by the time Hassan returned with two donkeys and a mule laden with brushwood. Behind the beasts straggled the guard.

Waldo's trance became a nightmare when the smoke took effect and the battle began. He was, however, not only not required to join in the killing, but was enjoined to keep back. He did keep very much in the background, seeing only so much of the slaughter as his curiosity would not let him refrain from viewing. Yet he felt all a murderer as he gazed at the ten small carcasses laid out in a row, and the memory of his vigil and its end, indeed of the whole day, though it was the day of his most marvelous adventure, remains to him as the broken recollections of a phantasmagoria.

On the morning of his memorable peril Waldo had waked early. The experiences of his sea-voyage, the sights at Gibraltar, at Port Said, in the canal, at Suez, at Aden, at Muscat, and at

Basrah had formed an altogether inadequate transition from the decorous regularity of house and school life in New England to the breathless wonder of the desert immensities.

Everything seemed unreal, and yet the reality of its strangeness so besieged him that he could not feel at home in it, he could not sleep heavily in a tent. After composing himself to sleep, he lay long conscious and awakened early, as on this morning, just at the beginning of the false-dawn.

The consul was fast asleep, snoring loudly. Waldo dressed quietly and went out; mechanically, without any purpose or forethought, taking his gun. Outside he found Hassan, seated, his gun across his knees, his head sunk forward, as fast asleep as the consul. Ali and Ibrahim had left the camp the day before for supplies. Waldo was the only waking creature about; for the guards, camped some little distance off, were but logs about the ashes of their fire. Meaning merely to enjoy, under the white glow of the false-dawn, the magical reappearance of the constellations and the short last glory of the star-laden firmament, that brief coolness which compensated a trifle for the hot morning, the fiery day and the warmish night, he seated himself on a rock, some paces from the tent and twice as far from the guards. Turning his gun in his hands he felt an irresistible temptation to wander off by himself, to stroll alone through the fascinating emptiness of the arid landscape.

When he had begun camp life he had expected to find the consul, that combination of sportsman, explorer and archæologist, a particularly easy-going guardian. He had looked forward to absolutely untrammelled liberty in the spacious expanse of the limitless wastes. The reality he had found exactly the reverse of his preconceptions. The consul's first injunction was:

"Never let yourself get out of sight of me or of Hassan unless he or I send you off with Ali or Ibrahim. Let nothing tempt you to roam about alone. Even a ramble is dangerous. You might lose sight of the camp before you knew it."

At first Waldo acquiesced, later he protested. "I have a good pocket-compass. I know how to use it. I never lost my way in the Maine woods."

"No Kourds in the Maine woods," said the consul.

Yet before long Waldo noticed that the few Kourds they encountered seemed simple-hearted, peaceful folk. No semblance of danger or even of adventure had appeared. Their armed guard of a dozen greasy tatterdemalions had passed their time in uneasy loafing.

Likewise Waldo noticed that the consul seemed indifferent to the ruins they passed by or encamped among, that his feeling for sites and topography was cooler than lukewarm, that he showed no ardor in the pursuit of the scanty and uninteresting game. He had picked up enough of the several dialects to hear repeated conversations about "them." "Have you heard of any about here?" "Has one been killed?" "Any traces of them in this district?" And such queries he could make out in the various talks with the natives they met as to what "they" were he received no enlightenment.

Then he had questioned Hassan as to why he was so restricted in his movements. Hassan spoke some English and regaled him with tales of Afrits, ghouls, specters and other uncanny legendary presences; of the jinn of the waste, appearing in human shape, talking all languages, ever on the alert to ensnare infidels; of the woman whose feet turned the wrong way at the ankles, luring the unwary to a pool and there drowning her victims; of the malignant ghosts of dead brigands, more terrible than their living fellows; of the spirit in the shape of a wild-ass, or of a gazelle, enticing its pursuers to the brink of a precipice and itself seeming to run ahead upon an expanse of sand, a mere mirage, dissolving as the victim passed the brink and fell to death; of the sprite in the semblance of a hare feigning a limp, or of a groundbird feigning a broken wing, drawing its pursuer after it till he met death in an unseen pit or well-shaft.

Ali and Ibrahim spoke no English. As far as Waldo could understand their long harangues, they told similar stories or hinted at dangers equally vague and imaginary. These childish bogy-tales merely whetted Waldo's craving for independence.

Now, as he sat on a rock, longing to enjoy the perfect sky, the clear, early air, the wide, lonely landscape, along with the sense of having it to himself, it seemed to him that the consul was merely innately cautious, over-cautious. There was no danger.

He would have a fine leisurely stroll, kill something perhaps and certainly be back in camp before the sun grew hot. He stood up.

Some hours later he was seated on a fallen coping-stone in the shadow of a ruined tomb. All the country they had been traversing is full of tombs and remains of tombs, prehistoric, Bactrian, old Persian, Parthian, Sassanian, or Mohammedan, scattered everywhere in groups or solitary. Vanished utterly are the faintest traces of the cities, towns, and villages, ephemeral houses or temporary huts, in which had lived the countless generations of mourners who had reared these tombs.

The tombs, built more durably than mere dwellings of the living, remained. Complete or ruinous, or reduced to mere fragments, they were everywhere. In that district they were all of one type. Each was domed and below was square, its one door facing eastward and opening into a large empty room, behind which were the mortuary chambers.

In the shadow of such a tomb Waldo sat. He had shot nothing, had lost his way, had no idea of the direction of the camp, was tired, warm and thirsty. He had forgotten his water-bottle.

He swept his gaze over the vast, desolate prospect, the unvaried turquoise of the sky arched above the rolling desert. Far reddish hills along the skyline hooped in the less distant brown hillocks which, without diversifying it, hummocked the yellow landscape. Sand and rocks with a lean, starved bush or two made up the nearer view, broken here and there by dazzling white or streaked, grayish, crumbling ruins. The sun had not been long above the horizon, yet the whole surface of the desert was quivering with heat.

As Waldo sat viewing the outlook a woman came round the corner of the tomb. All the village women Waldo had seen had worn yashmaks or some other form of face-covering or veil. This woman was bareheaded and unveiled. She wore some sort of yellowish-brown garment which enveloped her from neck to ankles, showing no waist line. Her feet, in defiance of the blistering sands, were bare.

At sight of Waldo she stopped and stared at him as he at her. He remarked the un-European posture of her feet, not at all turned out, but with the inner lines parallel. She wore no anklets, he observed, no bracelets, no necklace or earrings. Her bare arms he thought the most muscular he had ever seen on a human being. Her nails were pointed and long, both on her hands and feet. Her hair was black, short and tousled, yet she did not look wild or uncomely. Her eyes smiled and her lips had the effect of smiling, though they did not part ever so little, not showing at all the teeth behind them.

"What a pity," said Waldo aloud, "that she does not speak English."

"I do speak English," said the woman, and Waldo noticed that as she spoke, her lips did not perceptibly open. "What does the gentleman want?"

"You speak English!" Waldo exclaimed, jumping to his feet. "What luck! Where did you learn it?"

"At the mission school," she replied, an amused smile playing about the corners of her rather wide, unopening mouth. "What can be done for you?" She spoke with scarcely any foreign accent, but very slowly and with a sort of growl running along from syllable to syllable.

"I am thirsty," said Waldo, "and I have lost my way."

"Is the gentleman living in a brown tent, shaped like half a melon?" she inquired, the queer, rumbling note drawling from one word to the next, her lips barely separated.

"Yes, that is our camp," said Waldo.

"I could guide the gentleman that way," she droned; "but it is far, and there is no water on that side."

"I want water first," said Waldo, "or milk."

"If you mean cow's milk, we have none. But we have goat's milk. There is to drink where I dwell," she said, sing-songing the words. "It is not far. It is the other way."

"Show me," said he.

She began to walk, Waldo, his gun under his arm, beside her. She trod noiselessly and fast. Waldo could scarcely keep up with her. As they walked he often fell behind and noted how her swathing garments clung to a lithe, shapely back, neat waist and firm hips. Each time he hurried and caught up with her, he scanned her with intermittent glances, puzzled that her waist, so well-marked at the spine, showed no particular definition in front; that the outline of her from neck to knees, perfectly shapeless under her wrappings, was without any waistline or suggestion of firmness or undulation. Likewise he remarked the amused flicker of her eyes and the compressed line of her red, her too red lips.

"How long were you in the mission school?" he inquired.

"Four years," she replied.

"Are you a Christian?" he asked.

"The Free-folk do not submit to baptism," she stated simply, but with rather more of the droning growl between her words.

He felt a queer shiver as he watched the scarcely moved lips through which the syllables edged their way.

"But you are not veiled," he could not resist saying.

"The Free-folk," she rejoined, "are never veiled."

"Then you are not a Mohammedan?" he ventured.

"The Free-folk are not Moslems."

"Who are the Free-folk?" he blurted out incautiously.

She shot one baleful glance at him. Waldo remembered that he had to do with an Asiatic. He recalled the three permitted questions.

"What is your name?" he inquired.

"Amina," she told him.

"That is a name from the 'Arabian Nights'," he hazarded.

"From the foolish tales of the believers," she sneered. "The Free-folk know nothing of such follies." The unvarying shutness of her speaking lips, the drawly burr between the syllables, struck him all the more as her lips curled but did not open.

"You utter your words in a strange way," he said.

"Your language is not mine," she replied.

"How is it that you learned my language at the mission school and are not a Christian?"

"They teach all at the mission school," she said, "and the maidens of the Free-folk are like the other maidens they teach, though the Free-folk when grown are not as town-dwellers are. Therefore they taught me as any townbred girl, not knowing me for what I am."

"They taught you well," he commented.

"I have the gift of tongues," she uttered enigmatically, with an odd note of triumph burring the words through her unmoving lips.

Waldo felt a horrid shudder all over him, not only at her uncanny words, but also from mere faintness.

"Is it far to your home?" he breathed.

"It is there," she said, pointing to the doorway of a large tomb just before them.

The wholly open arch admitted them into a fairly spacious interior, cool with the abiding temperature of thick masonry. There was no rubbish on the floor. Waldo, relieved to escape the blistering glare outside, seated himself on a block of stone midway between the door and the inner partition-wall, resting his gun-butt on the floor. For the moment he was blinded by the change from the insistent brilliance of the desert morning to the blurred gray light of the interior.

When his sight cleared he looked about and remarked, opposite the door, the ragged hole which laid open the desecrated mausoleum. As his eyes grew accustomed to the dimness he was so startled that he stood up. It seemed to him that from its four corners the room swarmed with naked children. To his inexperienced conjecture they seemed about two years old, but they moved with the assurance of boys of eight or ten.

"Whose are these children?" he exclaimed.

"Mine," she said.

"All yours?" he protested.

"All mine," she replied, a curious suppressed boisterousness in her demeanor.

"But there are twenty of them," he cried.

"You count badly in the dark," she told him. "There are fewer."

"There certainly are a dozen," he maintained, spinning round as they danced and scampered about.

"The Free-people have large families," she said.

"But they are all of one age," Waldo exclaimed, his tongue dry against the roof of his mouth.

She laughed, an unpleasant, mocking laugh, clapping her hands. She was between him and the doorway, and as most of the light came from it he could not see her lips.

"Is not that like a man! No woman would have made that mistake."

Waldo was confused and sat down again. The children circulated around him, chattering, laughing, giggling, snickering, making noises indicative of glee.

"Please get me something cool to drink," said Waldo, and his tongue was not only dry but big in his mouth.

"We shall have to drink shortly," she said, "but it will be warm."
Waldo began to feel uneasy. The children pranced around him, jabbering strange, guttural noises, licking their lips, pointing at him, their eyes fixed on him, with now and then a glance at their mother.

"Where is the water?"

The woman stood silent, her arms hanging at her sides, and it seemed to Waldo she was shorter than she had been.

"Where is the water?" he repeated.

"Patience, patience," she growled, and came a step near to him.

The sunlight struck upon her back and made a sort of halo about her hips. She seemed still shorter than before. There was something furtive in her bearing, and the little ones sniggered evilly.

At that instant two rifle shots rang out almost as one. The woman fell face downward on the floor. The babies shrieked in a shrill chorus. Then she leapt up from all fours with an explosive suddenness, staggered in a hurled, lurching rush toward the hole in the wall, and, with a frightful yell, threw up her arms and whirled backward to the ground, doubled and contorted like a dying fish, stiffened, shuddered and was still. Waldo, his horrified eyes fixed on her face, even in his amazement noted that her lips did not open.

The children, squealing faint cries of dismay, scrambled through the hole in the inner wall, vanishing into the inky void beyond. The last had hardly gone when the consul appeared in the doorway, his smoking gun in his hand.

"Not a second too soon, my boy," he ejaculated. "She was just going to spring."

He cocked his gun and prodded the body with the muzzle.

"Good and dead," he commented. "What luck! Generally it takes three or four bullets to finish one. I've known one with two bullets through her lungs to kill a man."

"Did you murder this woman?" Waldo demanded fiercely.

"Murder?" the consul snorted. "Murder! Look at that."

He knelt down and pulled open the full, closed lips, disclosing not human teeth, but small incisors, cusped grinders, wide-spaced; and long, keen overlapping canines, like those of a greyhound: a fierce, deadly, carnivorous dentition, menacing and combative.

Waldo felt a qualm, yet the face and form still swayed his horrified sympathy for their humanness.

"Do you shoot women because they have long teeth?" Waldo insisted, revolted at the horrid death he had watched.

"You are hard to convince," said the consul sternly. "Do you call that a woman?"

He stripped the clothing from the carcass.

Waldo sickened all over. What he saw was not the front of a woman, but more like the underside of an old fox-terrier with puppies, or of a white sow, with her second litter; from collarbone to groin ten lolloping udders, two rows, mauled, stringy and flaccid.

"What kind of a creature is it?" he asked faintly.

"A Ghoul, my boy," the consul answered solemnly, almost in a whisper.

"I thought they did not exist," Waldo babbled. "I thought they were mythical; I thought there were none."

"I can very well believe that there are none in Rhode Island," the consul said gravely. "This is in Persia, and Persia is in Asia."

The Message on the Slate

Mrs. Llewellyn had always held—in so far as she ever thought about the subject at all—that to consult a clairvoyant was not merely an imbecile folly, but a degrading action, nearly akin to crime. Now that she felt herself overmasteringly driven to such an unconscionable unworthiness she could not bring herself to do it openly. Anything underhand or secretive was utterly alien to her nature. She was a tall woman, notably well shaped, with unusual dignity of demeanor. The poise of her head would have appeared haughty but for the winning kindliness of her frequent smile. Her dark hair, dark eyes and very white skin accorded well with that abiding calm of her bearing which never seemed mere placidity in a face habitually lighted with interested comprehension. Like a cloudless springtime sunrise over limitless expanses of dewy prairies, she was enveloped in an atmosphere of spacious serenity of soul, and her appearance was entirely in consonance with her character. She was still a very beautiful woman, high-souled as she was beautiful and exceedingly straightforward. Yet to drive in open day to a house bearing the displayed sign of a spirit-medium was more than she could do. Bidding her footman call for her later, much later, at her hairdresser's, she dismissed her carriage at the main entrance of a department store. Leaving it by another entrance, she took a street car for the neighborhood she sought. The neighborhood was altogether different from what she had anticipated; the houses, by no means small, were even handsome; not least handsome that of the clairvoyant. And it was very well kept, the pavement and the steps clean, the plate glass window panes bright, the shades and curtains new and tasteful, the silver doorknobs and door-bell fresh polished. There was a sign, indeed, but not the flaming horror her imagination had constructed from memories of signs seen in passing. This was a bit of glass set inside the big, bright pane of one of the parlor windows. It bore in small gold letters only the name, SALATHIEL VARGAS, and the word, CLAIRVOYANT.

A neat maid opened the door. Yes, Mr. Vargas was in; would she walk into the waiting room? The untenanted waiting room was a dignified parlor, furnished in the costliest way, but with a restraint as far as possible from ostentation. The rug was Persian, each piece of furniture different in design from any other, yet all harmonizing, while the ten pictures were paintings by well-known artists. Before Mrs. Llewellyn had time for more than one comprehensive and surprised glance about, when she had barely seated herself, the retreating maid struck two sharp notes on a silvery gong. Almost immediately the door leading to the rear room was opened. In it appeared a man under five feet tall, not dwarfish, but deformed. His patent-leather shoes were boyish, his trousers hung limp about the legs shriveled to mere skeletal stems, and his left knee was bent and fixed at an unchanging angle, so that his step was a painful hobble. Above the waist he was well made; a deep chest; broad, square shoulders; a huge head with a vast shock of black, curly hair. He had the look of a musician or artist; with a wide forehead; delicately curved eyebrows; nose hooked, sharp and assertive; eyes, wide apart, large, dark brown with sparkles of red and green; and a mouth whose curled upper lip was almost too short. The mouth and eyes held Mrs. Llewellyn at first glance, and the instant change in them startled her. He had appeared with a suave mechanical smile, with a look of easy expectancy. As his gaze met hers his lips set and their redness dulled; his eyes were full of so poignant a dismay that she would not have been surprised had he abruptly retreated and slammed the door between them. Without a word he clung to the knob, staring at her. Then he drew the door to after him and leaned against it, still holding to the knob with one hand behind his back. When he spoke it was in a dry whisper.

"You here, of all women!"

"You know me!" she exclaimed; "I have never seen you."

"You are seen of many thousands you never note," he replied. "Everyone knows Mrs. David Llewellyn. Everyone knew Constance Palgrave."

"You flatter me," she said coldly, with the air of one resenting an unwelcome familiarity.

"Flattery is part of my trade," he replied. "But I do not flatter you. So little that I have forgotten my manners. I should have asked you to step into my consulting room. Pray, enter it."

She passed him as he held the door open for her. The inner room was not less seemly than the outer. Except for three doors and one broad window looking out on an area, it was walled with bookcases some eight feet high, broken only where there were set into them two small cabinets with drawers below. The glass doors of the bookcases were of small panes, and the books within were in exquisite bindings. Topping the cases were several splendid bronze busts. The furniture was completed by a round mahogany center-table, several small chairs and three tapestried armchairs. When Mrs. Llewellyn had seated herself in one the clairvoyant took another. His agitation was so extreme that had she been capable of fear it would almost have frightened her; her curiosity it greatly piqued. He was as pale as a swarthy man can be, his lips bloodless and twitching, dry and moistening themselves one against the other as he mechanically swallowed in his nervousness. She herself was perturbed in soul, but an eye less practised than his would have discerned no signs of emotion beneath her easy exterior. They faced each other in silence for some breaths; then he spoke:

"For what purpose have you come here?"

"To consult you," she answered. "Is it astonishing? Do not all sorts of persons come to consult you?"

"All sorts," he replied. "But none such as you. Never any such as you."

"I have come, it seems," she said simply, "and to consult you."

"In what way do you mean to consult me?" he queried. "People consult me in various ways."

"I had in mind," she said, "the answers you give by writing on the inside of a shut slate."

"You have come to the wrong man," he said harshly, with an obvious effort that made his voice unnatural. "Go elsewhere," and he rose.

She gazed at him in astonishment without moving.

"Why do you say that?" she demanded.

He opened each of the three doors, looked outside and then made sure that each was latched. He looked out of the window, glancing at each of the other windows visible from it. He hobbled once or twice up and down the room, mopping his forehead and face with his handkerchief; then he seated himself again.

"Mrs. Llewellyn," he said, "I must request your promise of entire and permanent secrecy for what I am about to tell you."

"Anyone would suppose," she said, "that you were the client and I the clairvoyant."

"Acknowledging that," he replied, "let it pass, I beg of you. I have told you that you have come to the wrong man. I bade you go elsewhere. You ask for an explanation. But I must have your pledge of silence if you desire an explanation."

"I do desire it and you have my promise."

He looked around the room with the movement of a rat in a cage. His eyes met hers, but shifted uneasily, and his shame-faced gaze fell to the floor. His hands clutched each other upon his lame knee.

"Madame," he said, "I tell you to go elsewhere because I am a charlatan, an impostor. My trances are mere pretense, the method of my replies a farcical mummery, the answers transparent concoctions from the hints I extract from my dupes."

"You say this to try me," she cried; "you are subjecting me to some sort of test."

"Madame," he said, "look at me. Am I like a man playing a part? Do I not look in earnest?"

She regarded him, convinced.

"But," she wondered. "Why do you thrust this confession upon me?"

"I fear," he hesitated, "that a truthful answer to that question would displease you."

"Your behavior," she said, "and your utterances are so unexpected and amazing to me, coming here as I have, that I must request an explanation."

Vargas straightened himself in his chair and looked her in the eyes, not aggressively, but timidly. He spoke in a low voice.

"Madame," he said solemnly, "I have told you the truth about myself because you are the one human being whom I am unwilling to harm, wrong or cheat."

"You mean,"—she broke off, bridling.

"Ah, Madame," he cried, "I mean nothing that has in it any tinge of anything that might offend you. What does the north star know or care how many frail, storm-tossed barks struggle to steer by it? Is it any the less radiant, pure, high because so many to whom it is and shall remain forever unattainable strive to win from its rays guidance towards havens of safety? A woman such as you cannot guess, much less know, to how many she is the one abiding heavenly beacon. How could you, who need no such help from without, realize what the mere sight of you afar off must mean to natures not blest with such a heritage of goodness? How many have been strengthened at sight of your face, wherein they could not but see the visible outward expression of that inward peace and serenity that comes from right instincts unswervingly adhering to noble ideals? You have been to me the incarnate token of the existence of that righteousness to which I might not attain."

Mrs. Llewellyn had borne his torrent of verbiage with a look of intolerant toleration, of haughty displeasure curbed by astonishment. When he paused for breath she said, in a voice half angry, half repressed:

"I quite understand you, I have heard enough, I have heard altogether too much of this; we will change the subject, if you please."

"I spoke at your command," Vargas apologized, abashed, "and only to convince you of my sincerity in telling you that I am not worthy of being consulted by you."

"But," she protested, carried away by her surprise, "you are called the greatest clairvoyant on earth."

"I have schemed, advertised lavishly, spent money like water, bribed reporters, bought editors, cajoled managers, hoodwinked owners and won over their wives and daughters through laborious years to produce that impression. It is no growth of accident, no spontaneous recognition of self-evident merit."

"But," she argued, "are you a fiend doing all this for the delight of deceiving for deception's sake? Are you a man wealthy by inheritance and choosing this form of activity for the pleasure it gives you?"

"By no means, Madame," he denied, "I live by my wits."

"Your surroundings tell me that you live well," she suggested.

"Better than my surroundings reveal," he rejoined.

"Then your wits are good wits," she ventured.

"None better of their kind on earth," he naïvely admitted, wholly off his guard.

"And they are not overtaxed?" she asked.

"Deception is not hard," he told her. "The world is full of fools and even the sensible are easy to deceive."

"From what I have read," she continued, "you do not deceive. Your advice is good. Your precepts guide your clients right. Your suggestions lead to success. Your predictions come to pass, your conjectures are verified."

"All that is true enough," he allowed.

"Then how can you call your clients dupes, your methods mummeries, your answers lies?" she wound up triumphantly.

"I did not call my answers lies," he disclaimed. "Mummeries I deal in and to dupes. Dupes they are all. They pour gold into my lap to tell them what they already knew if they but reasoned it out calmly with themselves. They babble to me all they need to know and pay me insensately for it when I fling back to them a patchwork of the fragments I have extracted from their stories of expectations, apprehensions and memories."

"But if you do all that you must be a real judge of human nature, a genuine reader of hearts, a keen-brained counsellor."

"I am all that and more," he bragged. He had lost every trace of agitation and bore himself with a dashing self-confidence of manner, extremely engaging. "I cannot minister to a mind diseased; but I am called on to prescribe for all sorts of delusions, follies, blunders, miseries and griefs. I could count by thousands the men and women I have saved, the lives I have made happy, the difficulties I have annihilated, the aspirations I have guided aright."

"Then you must have an immense experience of human frailties and human needs."

"Vast, enormous, incalculable," he declared.

"Your advice then should be valuable."

"It is valuable," he boasted.

"Then advise me, I am in extreme distress. I have felt that no one could help me. The belief that you might has given me a ray of hope. You have expressed a regard for me altogether extraordinary. Will it not lead you to help me?"

"Any advice and help, any service in my power you may be sure shall be yours," he said earnestly. "But let me ask you first, how was it that you did not seek the advice of some businessman, lawyer or clergyman? You are not at all of the light-headed type of those frivolous women who flock to me and to others like me. You have common sense, unalterable principles, rational instincts and personal fastidiousness; why did you not go to one of the recognized, established, honored advisers of humanity? Tell me that if you please?"

"It was because of the dream," she faltered.

"The dream!" he exclaimed. "A dream sent you to me? What sort of a dream?"

"I had come to feel that there could be no hope for me," she said. "But about a month ago I had a dream in which I was told 'The seventh advertisement in the seventh column of the seventh newspaper in the seventh drawer of the linen room will point for you the way to escape from your miseries and win what you desire.' There should have been no papers in my linen-room and it made me feel foolish to want to go and look. Also the servants knew I never went there, so I had to watch until the housekeeper was out and no maids were on that floor. Sure enough I found seven old newspapers in the seventh drawer, and on the seventh page of the lowermost paper, on the seventh column, the seventh advertisement was yours."

"And you came to me because of that dream?"

"Yes:—and;—" she hesitated.

"Well," he interrupted, "the reasons why you came are not so important. What I want to be sure of is this. Even if you were led to come by a mere coincidence acting on your feelings, are you now, from cool, deliberate reflection, determined to consult me? Would it not be better to take my advice at this point and go to one of the world's regular, accredited dispensers of wisdom?"

"I have made up my mind to consult you," she said. "It is not a passing whim, but a settled resolve."

"Then, Madame," he said, his manner wholly changing, "you must tell me all your troubles without any reservation of any kind. If I am to help you I must know your case as completely as a physician would have to know your symptoms in an illness. Tell me plainly what your trouble is."

She began to pluck at her veil with her gloved hands.

"Oh," she gasped, "let me moisten my lips. Just a swallow of water."

For all his lameness he was surprisingly agile, as he wrenched himself up, tore open the rear door and almost instantly hobbled back with a glass and silver pitcher on a small silver tray.

She took off her veil and one glove. Several swallows were required to compose her. When she was calm again he sat looking at her with a face full of inquiry, but without uttering any questions.

"You do not know," she said, "how hard it is to begin."

"For the third time, Madame," he said, "I advise you not to consult me, to go elsewhere."

"Are you not willing to help me?" she asked, softly.

"Utterly willing," he said, "but timid, timid as a doctor would be about prescribing for his own child. Yours is the first case ever brought to me in which I feared the effect of personal bias dimming my insight or deflecting my judgment. I have a second confession to make to you. Before you married, a man desperately in love with you came to me for help. Among other things he gave me the day, hour and minute of your birth and of his and asked me to cast both horoscopes and infer his chances of success. I had and have no faith in astrology, yet I had cast my own horoscope long before from mere curiosity. When I cast yours I was amazed at the clear indications of a connection between your fate and mine. I did not believe anything of the Babylonian absurdities, yet the coincidence struck me. Perhaps I am influenced by it yet. Under such an influence, even more than under that of my feeling for yourself, my acumen is likely to be impaired. I again advise you to go elsewhere."

"I am all the more determined to consult you and you only."

He bowed without any word and waited in silence for her to go on.

She stared at him with big melting eyes, her face very pale.

"My husband does not love me," she said.

"Not love you?" Vargas exclaimed, startled. "Do you mean seriously to tell me that, you who have been loved by hundreds, been adored, worshipped, courted by so many, for despair of gaining whom men have gone mad, who have had your choice of so many lovers, are not prized by the man who succeeded in winning you?"

"Yes," she barely breathed. "He does not prize me, nor love me at all."

"Does he love anyone else?"

Out of her total paleness she flushed rose pink from throat to hair.

"Yes," she admitted.

"Who is she?" Vargas demanded.

"His first wife."

Vargas staggered to his feet. "I did not so much as know that your husband had been married before," he gasped, "let alone that he was divorced."

"He was not divorced," she stated.

"Not divorced," he quavered.

"No, he was a widower when I married him."

Vargas collapsed back into his chair.

"I do not understand," he told her. "Does he love a dead woman?"

"Just that," she asseverated.

"This will not do," the clairvoyant told her. "I cannot come nearer to helping you at this rate. Try to give me the information you think necessary, not by splinters and fragments, but as a whole. Make a connected exposition of the circumstances. Begin at the beginning!"

"That is harder," she mused, "I always want to begin anything at the last chapter."

"Woman fashion," he commented. "You are above that in most things, I know. Try a straight story from the beginning."

She reflected:

"The beginning," she said, "was before I began to remember. David and I were playmates before we could talk. Boy and girl, lad and lass, we always belonged to each other, there was no love-making between us, I think, for it was all love-living. I do not believe he ever asked me to marry him or promised to marry me, or so much as talked marriage. But we had a clear understanding that we were to marry as soon as we could, at the earliest possible day. He did not merely seem wrapped up in me, he was. God knows he was all my life. Then he had no more than seen Marian Conway when he fell in love with her. There is no use in dwelling on what I suffered. He married almost at once and I gave myself up to that empty life of frivolity which made me a reigning beauty and brought me scores of suitors for none of whom I cared anything and which gave me not a particle of satisfaction. Then after they had lost both their children Marian died. David was frightfully overcome by his loss. He had loved her inconceivably and he showed his grief in the most heart-rending ways. He had the coffin opened over and over after it had been closed. He had it even lifted out of the grave and opened yet once more for one more look at her face. He spent every moment from her death to her burial in a sort of adoration of her corpse, and he did stranger things. I do not know whether it was Mr. Llewellyn's valet who told, but at any rate the story got out among the servants. The night before she was buried he had her laid out in her coffin and a second coffin exactly like it set beside hers. He stayed locked in the room all night. They believed he lay in the other coffin. At any rate in the morning it was closed, and he did not allow it to be opened. What he had placed in it no one knew. They said it was as heavy as the other. Two hearses, one behind the other, carried the coffins to the graveyard. Her grave is not under the monument—you have seen the monument?"

"No," he said, "only a picture of it."

"Well, she is not buried under it, and the second coffin was placed on hers."

She stopped.

"Go on," he said.

"Oh," she cried, "it is so hard to go on. But it is true. As soon as David was free I felt I had an object in life. I—I followed him,

I might almost say pursued him all over the world, and when we met I courted him, and it seems strange, but I asked him to marry me. And—" she hesitated—"he refused twice."

"He did not want to marry you?" Vargas asked incredulously.

"He refused. It was at Cairo, that first time. He said he could not love anyone any more, all his love, his very self, was buried in Marian's grave. The second time was at Hongkong. Then he said he always had cared for me and still cared for me, but that affection was as nothing compared to his passion for Marian, that he would never marry, and especially he would not marry me because of his regard for me, that I would not be contented or happy with him, that I was thinking of the lad he had been and that boy was buried in his wife's grave, that he was nothing more than a walking ghost, a wraith of what he had been, a spirit condemned to wander its allotted time on earth until his hour should come and he be called to join Marian.

"The third time was in Paris. He said he was indifferent to everything, to anything, to love or hate or death or life; that he cared nothing whether he married me or not. If I cared as much as I seemed to he would marry me to please me. I told him that what I had always wanted was to be with him, that what I most wanted was to spend with him as much as possible of my time until death parted us. He said if that was what I wanted I could have it, but he was nothing more than a shadow of his old self and I was sure to be unhappy. And I am unhappy. He is generosity, gentleness, kindness and consideration itself, but he does not care. I hoped, of course, that his grief for Marian would soften, fade away and vanish, that he would cease to mourn for her, that his interest in life would reawaken, that I could win his love and that we would both be happy. But I am not. His utter indifference to me, to anything, to everything is preying on my feelings, I must do something. I shall lose my mind."

"Is that all?" Vargas asked.

"It is enough," she asserted, "and more than enough. Do you think it a small matter?"

"Not in the least," he declared. "I comprehend your disappointment in respect to your hopes, your chagrin at your baffled efforts to win him back to be his old self, your pain at his inertness. But by your own showing you have no grievance against your husband."

"That I have not," she maintained. "Not a shadow of a grievance against him. My grievance is for him as much as for myself and against—against the way the world is made."

Vargas looked at her for some little time.

"You do not say what you are thinking," she interrupted.

"I am considering how to express it," he said. "However I express it I am sure to offend you."

"Not a bit," she replied. "Say it at once."

"You must realize that if I am to advise you truly I must speak plainly," he hesitated.

"I do realize it," she told him.

"You will then pardon what I have to say?" he ventured.

"I will pardon anything except beating about the bush," she rapped out.

"Well," he said slowly, "it seems to me that your coming to me, your state of mind, your trouble, as you have related it all turns upon a piece of femininity to which you should be altogether superior, to which I should have imagined you were altogether superior. You look, and I have always imagined you, free from any trace of the eternal feminine. Here it crops out. Men in general find that women in general have no feeling for the mutuality of a contract. Some women may be exceptions, but women habitually ignore the other side of a contract and see only their own side. Here you display the same defect. Mr. Llewellyn practically proposed a contract to you: on his side he to marry you, on your side, you to put up with his complete indifference to you, to everything, and be content with his actual companionship such as he is. He has fulfilled and is fulfilling his part of the contract, you seek to escape from yours."

"I think," she snapped, "you are insufferably brutal."

"The eternal feminine again," he retorted. "Worse and more of it. I told you I should offend you."

"You do offend me. I have confidence in you, but I did not come here to be scolded or to be preached at. I do not want criticism, I want advice. Don't tell me my shortcomings, real or imaginary, think over my troubles and my needs and tell me what to do."

"That is plain enough," he asserted. "Do your obvious duty. Keep your part of your contract with your husband. Give no sign that you suffer from the absence of feeling of which he warned you. Make the most of your life with him. Hope for a change in him but do not try to force it, do not rebel if it does not come."

"I know I ought to endure," she wailed. "But I cannot, I must do something. I must act. I must."

"You have asked for my advice," he said, "and you have it."

"And what good is it to me?" she objected. "I ask for help and you string out platitudinous precepts like a snuffy, detestable old-fashioned evangelical dominie. Is this all the help you can give me?"

"All," said Vargas humbly. "If I knew of any other it should be at your service."

"You could consult your slate for me, as I proposed," she suggested.

"Great heavens above!" he cried. "I have told you that all that is imposture."

"It might turn out genuine for once," she persisted. "Don't people have real trances? Don't many people believe in the answers from slates and planchettes and ouija boards?"

"Perhaps they do," Vargas admitted. "But I never had a real trance, never saw one, never knew of one. And to my knowledge no slate or other such device ever gave any answer or wrote anything unless I or some other shuffler made it write or answer."

"But could you not try just once for my sake," she implored.

"Why on earth," he demanded, "are you, so sane and sensible in appearance, so set on this mummery?"

"Because of the other dream," she faltered.

"The other dream!" he exclaimed. "You had another dream?"

"Yes," she said, "I was going to tell you but you interrupted me. The dream about the advertisement did not convince me. I felt it might be coincidence after all. That was more than a month ago and I disregarded it. But night before last I dreamed I was told, 'The message on the slate will be true.' I fought against it all day yesterday, all last night. Today I gave up and came. I want you to consult your slate for me."

"Madame," he said, "this is dreadful. Can nothing make you see the truth? There is not anything supernatural about this trade of mine. It is as simple as a Punch and Judy show. There the puppets do nothing save as the showman controls them; so of my slate and of my trances."

"But it might surprise you," she persisted. "It might come true once. Won't you try for me?"

"I know," he mused, "that there is such a thing as auto-hypnotism. To humor you I might try to put myself into a genuine trance. But there would be nothing about it to help you, just a mere natural sleep, artificially induced. If I babbled in it the words would have no significance, and no writing would appear on the slate unless I put it there."

"Just try," she pleaded, "for my sake, to quiet me. If there is nothing, then I shall believe you."

"There will be nothing on the slate," he maintained. "But suppose I should mumble some fragments of words. You might take those accidental vocables for a revelation, they might become an obsession upon you, they might warp your judgment and do you great harm. I feel we should be running a foolish risk. Give up this idea of the trance and the slate, I beg of you."

"And I beg of you to try it. You said you would do anything for me. This is what I want and nothing else."

He shook his head, his expression crestfallen, baffled, puzzled, even alarmed.

"If you insist—" he faltered.

"I do insist," she said.

"You wish," he inquired, "to proceed exactly as I usually do with my simulated trance and pretended spirit replies?"

"Precisely," she affirmed.

He opened a drawer below one of the cabinets and took out a hinged double slate. It was made like a child's school-slate, but the rims instead of being wood, were of silver, the edges beaded and the flat of each rim chased in a pattern of pentacles, swastikas and pentagrams; a pentacle, a right-hand swastika, a pentagram, a left-hand swastika and so on all round. In the drawer was a box of fresh slate-pencils. This he held out to her and told her to choose one. At his bidding she broke off a short fragment and put it between the two leaves of the slate, the four faces of which were entirely blank.

"Settle yourself in your chair," he instructed her, "hold the slate in your lap. Hold it fast with both hands. First take off your other glove."

As she did this he settled himself into the armchair opposite her, took a silver paper-knife from the table and held it upright, gazing at its point.

"You are not to move or speak until I tell you," he directed her.

So they sat, she holding in her lap the slate shut fast upon the pencil within, her fingers enforcing its closure; he gazing intently at the point of the scimitar-shaped paper-knife. She became aware of the slow, pompous tick of a tall clock in the hallway; of faint noises, as of activity in a pantry, proceeding from somewhere in the rear of the house and barely audible through the closed window. She had expected to see him stiffen, his eyes roll up or some such manifestation appear. Nothing of the kind happened. For a long time, a very long time, she watched him staring fixedly at the sharp end of the paper-cutter. Then she saw it waver, saw his eyes close and his head, propped against the back of the armchair, move ever so little sideways, as the neck-muscles relaxed. His hands opened, the knife dropped on his knee and he was to all appearances peacefully asleep. Presently his even, regular breathing was a sound more apparent than the tick of the clock outside.

All of a sudden Mrs. Llewellyn felt herself ridiculous. Here she was, holding a childish toy, facing a strange man with whom she was entirely alone and who was apparently enjoying a needed snooze. She had an impulse to laugh and was on the point of rising, disembarrassing herself from her burden and leaving the house.

At that instant she felt a movement between the fast-shut slates. They lay level upon her lap, firmly set. She had not jarred or tilted them, yet she felt the pencil move. Felt it move and heard it too. Her mood of impatient self-contempt and irritated derision was instantly obliterated under a wave of terrified awe. She controlled a spasm of panic, an impulse to let go her hold upon her frightful charge, to scream, to run away.

Rigid, trembling, breathing quick, her heart hammering her ribs, she sat, her fingers gripping the slates, listening for another movement. It came. Faintly at first, she felt and heard it, then more distinctly. Slowly, very slowly, with intervals of silence, the bit of pencil crawled, tapped and scratched about. While listening to it, and still more while listening for it, she was under so terrific a tension that she felt if nothing happened to relieve her, she must faint or shriek. When she continued listening for a long, an interminable, an unbearable time and heard nothing but the clock in the hall and Vargas' breathing in the room, she felt she was about to do both.

Then the clairvoyant uttered a choked sound, the incipience of that feeble wailing groan or groaning wail of a sleeper in a nightmare. His feet moved, his undeformed leg stiffened, his hands clenched, his head rolled from side to side, he writhed, the effort expended at each successive groan was more and more excessive, each sound feebler and more pitiful.

Then Mrs. Llewellyn did scream.

Instantly Vargas struggled into a sitting posture, his face contorted, his eyes bulging, staring at her.

"Did I speak, did I speak?" he gasped.

Mrs. Llewellyn was past articulation, but she shook her head.

"I passed into a real trance, a real trance," he babbled.

She could only cling to the slate and gaze.

"I had a frightful dream," Vargas panted. "I dreamed there was a message on the slate. It frightened me, but what it was has escaped me."

"There is a message on the slate," she managed to utter. "I heard the pencil writing."

Vargas, holding to the back of his chair, assisted himself to his feet. From her fingers, mechanically clenched on it, he gently disengaged the slate and put it on the table. Opening one of the cabinets he took out a decanter and two glasses; half filling one he placed it in her numb grasp.

"Drink that," he dictated, draining the other full glass as he spoke.

Half dazed she obeyed him. Her face flushed angrily and the glass broke as she set it down.

"You have given me brandy!" she cried in indignation.

"You needed it," he asserted. "It will steady you, but you will not feel it. Compose yourself and we will look at the slate."

She stood up beside him and he laid the slate open. There was writing on each leaf of it, on one side legible, on the other reversed.

"Oh," she said and sat down heavily. He brought a small chair, set it beside hers and seated himself upon it, the slates open in his hands, before them both. Fine-lined, legible, plainly made by the point of the pencil, was the writing on one leaf of the slates; on the other reversed writing with coarse strokes, plainly made by the splintered end, which was worn slightly at one place. All the writing was in the same individual script.

"This is not my handwriting," said Vargas.

"It is my husband's," she gasped.

The words on the slate were:

"That which is buried in that coffin is alive. If disinterred it will die."

Vargas opened the other cabinet. The inside of its door was a mirror. Before this he held the slates. On the other leaf the broad-stroked script showed the same words.

"What does it mean?" she pleaded, "oh! what does it mean?"

"It doesn't mean anything," said Vargas, roughly.

"How can that be?" she moaned. "It must mean something. It does mean something. I feel it does."

"That is just the point," he said. "That is what I feared before, and warned you of. Here are some chance words. They mean nothing, except that you or I or both of us have been intensely strung up with emotion. But if you cannot see that or be made to see that, you are lost. If you feel that they mean something, then they do mean that something to you, that that is your danger. Do not yield to it."

"Do you mean to tell me, to try to convince me that those words, twice written, in the same handwriting, in my husband's hand of all hands, formed upon those slates while I held them myself, came there by accident?"

"Not by accident," he argued. "By some operation of unguessed forces set in motion by your excitement or mine or both; but blind forces, meaningless as the voices in dreams."

"Am I to believe meaningless," she demanded, "the voices in my dreams that sent me to that advertisement and to you and told me to expect an answer from the slates, a true answer?"

"Madame," he reasoned, "the series of coincidences is startling, but it is nothing but a series of coincidences. Try to rise superior to it."

"And you won't help me," she wailed. "You won't tell me what this message means?"

"I have told you my belief as to how it originated," he said. "I have told you that I do not attach any other significance to it."

"Oh," she groaned, "I must go home."

"Your carriage is at the door," he said.

"My carriage!" she exclaimed. "How did it get there?"

"Not your own carriage," he explained, "but one for you. I telephoned for it."

"You have not left me an instant," she asserted incredulously.

"When I brought you a glass of water I told the maid to telephone for a carriage and tell it to wait. It will be there."

"I thank you," she said, "and now, what do I owe you? What is your fee?"

Vargas flushed all over his face and neck, a deep brownish-red.

"Mrs. Llewellyn," he said with great dignity, "I take pay from my dupes for my fripperies of deception. But no money, not all the money on earth could pay me to do what I have done for you today, no sum could induce me to go through it again for anyone else. For you I would do anything. But what I have done was not done for payment, nor will anything I may do be done except for you, for whom I would do any service in my power."

"I ask your pardon," she said. "Where is the carriage? I shall faint if I stay here."

Some weeks later, in the same room, the clairvoyant and the lady again faced each other.

"I had hoped never to see you again," he said.

"Did you imagine that I could escape from the compulsion of all that series of manifestations?" she asked.

"I tried to believe that you might," he answered.

"Have you been able to shake off its hold on you?" she demanded.

"Not entirely," he confessed. "But dazing as the coincidences were, the effect on my emotions will wear off, like the smart of a burn; and, as one forgets the fury of past sufferings, I shall forget the turmoil of my feelings. There was no clear intelligibility, no definite significance in it at all."

"Not in that message!" she exclaimed.

"Certainly not," he asseverated.

"Yes there was," she contradicted.

"Madame," he said earnestly, "if you fancy you perceive any genuine coherence in those fortuitous words you have put the meaning there yourself, your imagination is riveting upon your soul fetters of your own forging."

"My imagination and my soul have nothing to do with my insight into the spirit of that message," she said calmly. "My heart cries out for help and my intellect has pondered at leisure upon what you call a fortuitous series of coincidences, a chance string of meaningless words. I see no incoherence, rather convincing coherence, in the sequence of your reading of horoscopes, my dreaming of dreams, leading up to the imperative behest given me from your slate."

"Madame," he cried, "this is heart-rending. I told you I dreaded the effect upon you of any sort of mummery. You forced me to it. I should have had strength to refuse you. I yielded. Now my cowardice will ruin you."

"Was not your trance genuine?" she queried.

"Entirely genuine, entirely too genuine."

"Did not the writing appear upon the slate independent of your will or of mine?" she demanded.

"It did," he admitted.

"Can you explain how it came there?" she wound up.

"Alas, no," he confessed, shaking his head.

"You can scarcely reproach me for accepting it as a message," she concluded triumphantly.

"I do not reproach you," he said, "I reproach myself as culpable."

"I rather thank you for what you have done for me," she almost smiled at him. "It gives me hope. I have meditated carefully upon the message and I am convinced that I comprehend its meaning."

"That is the worst possible state of mind you could get into," he groaned. "Can I not make you realize the truth? It is not as you think you see it."

"I do not think," she said. "I know. I am convinced, and I mean to act on my convictions."

"This is terrible," he muttered. Then he controlled himself, shifted his position in his chair and asked: "And what are your convictions? What do you mean to do?"

"My conviction," she said, "is that David's love for Marian is in some way bound up with whatever he had buried in that coffin. I mean to have the coffin disinterred."

"Madame," he said, "this thing gets worse the more you tell me of it. You are in danger of coming under the domination of a fixed idea, even if you are not already under its sway. Fight against it. Shake it off."

"There is no use in your talking that way to me," she said. "I mean to do it. I shall do it."

"Has your husband consented?" Vargas asked.

"He has," she replied.

"Do you mean to tell me that he has agreed to your opening his wife's grave?"

"He has agreed," she asserted.

"But did he make no demur?" the clairvoyant inquired.

"He said he did not care what I did, I could do anything I pleased."

"Was that all he said?" Vargas persisted.

"Not all," she admitted. "He asked me if I had not told him that what I wanted in this life was to spend as much as possible of my time on earth with him, for us two to be together as much as circumstances would allow, and as long as death would permit. I told him of course I had said it, not once but over and over. He asked me if I still felt that way. I told him I did. He said it made no difference to him, he was past any feelings, but if that was what I really wanted he advised me to let that grave alone."

"Take his advice, by all means," Vargas exclaimed. "It is good advice. You let that grave alone."

"I am determined," she told him.

"Madame," he said, "will you listen to me?"

"Certainly," she replied. "If you have anything to say to the purpose. But not to fault-findings or scoldings."

"Mrs. Llewellyn," Vargas began, "what happened during your former visit to me has demolished the entire structure of my spiritual existence. I had the sincerest disbelief in astrology, in prophecy, in ghosts, in apparitions, in superstitions, each and all, in supernaturalism in general, in religions, individually and collectively, in the idea of future life. Upon the most materialistic convictions my intellectual life was placid and unruffled, and my soul-life, if I had any, undisturbed by anything save occasional and very evanescent twinges of conscience over the contemptible duplicity of my way of livelihood. Intermittently only I despised myself. Mostly I only despised my dupes and generally not even that. Rather I merely smiled tolerantly at the childishness of their profitable credulity. Never did I have the remotest approach to any shadow of belief that there could be anything occult beneath or behind any such jugglery as I continually made use of. The matter of your horoscope and mine I took as mere coincidence. It might affect my feelings, never my reason; my heart, never my head. My head is involved now, my reason at fault. In the writing on that slate I am face to face with something, if not supernatural, at least preternatural. The thing is beyond our ordinary experience of the ordinary operation of those forces which make the world go. It depends upon something not yet understood, not necessarily inexplicable, but unexplained. It is uncanny. I don't like it. Yet I do not yield to its influence. I am not swept away. If I dwell upon it, I know it will unsettle my reason. I do not mean to dwell upon it, I mean to get away from it, to ignore it, to forget it, and I counsel you to do likewise."

"Your counsel," she said, "has a long-winded preamble, but is entirely unacceptable."

"I have more to say," he went on. "Mere bewilderment of mind is not an adequate ground for action. There is a fine old proverb that says, 'When in doubt, do nothing.' Take its advice and your husband's: do nothing."

"But I am not in doubt," she protested. "I am convinced that I was meant to come to you, that the message was meant for me, and that I know what it means. I am determined to act upon it."

He shook his head with a gesture of despair, but continued: "I have more yet to say and on another point. I advise you to go away from all this. You should and you can. You have your own wealth and your husband's opulence at your disposal. You have one of the finest steam-yachts on the seas awaiting your pleasure. Much as you have traveled, the globe has many fascinating regions still new to you. Your husband and you have practically not traveled at all since your marriage. You should still hope for your husband's recovery of his spirits by natural means. Travel is the most obvious prescription. Try that. Because your husband had not emerged from his brooding upon his loss and grief during two years of wandering alone with a valet; because he has not recovered his spirits after two years of matrimony spent in the neighborhood of his first wife's grave, in mansions full of memories of her, is no reason for not hoping that his elasticity will revive during months or years spent with you among delightful scenes of novelty, far from anything to recall his mind to old associations."

"I have no hope in any such attempt," she said wearily. "When I cannot bear my life here with a mate who is no more than a likeness of the man I loved, why drag this soulless semblance about the oceans of the earth in the hope of seeing it awake to love me? Shall I expect a miracle from salt air or the rays of the Southern cross?"

"Mrs. Llewellyn," Vargas said, "I have taken the liberty of making inquiries, quite unobtrusively, concerning your husband's treatment of you. I find that it is the general impression that he is a very uxorious, a very loverly husband. Except the barest minimum required for his affairs, he spends his entire time with you. His best friends, his boyhood's chums, his life-long cronies he never converses with, never chats with, hardly talks to, and for all his genial cordiality and courtesy, barely more than greets in passing. He is seldom seen at his clubs and very briefly. To all appearances he devotes himself to you wholly. You have all the external trappings of happiness: health, beauty, a devoted husband, the most desirable intimates, countless friends, luxurious surroundings, and unlimited affluence. It is for you to put life into all this, it is your duty to recall to it what you miss. You should leave no natural means untried turning to what you propose."

"My determination is irrevocably taken," she said.

"But what do you expect to find in the coffin?" he queried.

"I have no expectations, not even any anticipations," she said. "We may find keepsakes of some kind; there cannot be love-letters, for they scarcely separated a day after they met, or an hour after they married. There may be nothing in the coffin. But I am convinced that whatever it does or does not contain, David's love for Marian is bound up with the closure of that coffin. I believe that if it is opened he will be released from his passion of grief and be free to love me."

"You mean practically to resort to an incantation, a sort of witchcraft. The notion is altogether unworthy of you, especially while so natural a device as travel remains untried."

"You do not understand," she said, "that I feel compelled to do something."

"Is not going for a cruise doing something?" he asked.

"Practically doing nothing," she replied. "Just being with David and watching for the change that never comes. You don't know how that makes me feel forced to take some action."

"I do not know," he said, "because you have not told me."

"I cannot tell you," she said, "because I cannot find any words to express what I feel. I could not convey it to you, the loneliness that overwhelmed me when I am alone with David. It is worse than being alone; I cannot imagine feeling so lonely lost in a wilderness, solitary in the desert, adrift on a raft in mid-ocean. Being with David, as he is, makes me feel—" (her voice sank to a whisper and her face grew pale, her lips gray) "oh, it makes me feel as if I were worse than with nobody. It makes me feel as if I were with nothing, with nothing at all."

"I sympathize with you deeply," said Vargas. "But all you say only deepens my conviction that your one road to safety lies in striving to overcome these feelings; your best hope is change of scene and travel. Above all let that grave alone."

"My determination is irrevocably taken," she repeated.

"Mrs. Llewellyn," Vargas asked, "how, in your belief, did the writing you saw upon the slate come there?"

"I have no conception at all as to how it came there," she replied.

"None at all?" he probed.

"None definitely," she said. "Vaguely I suppose I conceive it came there by the power of some consciousness and will beyond our ken."

"Do you mean," he queried, "by the intervention of a ghost, or spirit of some such disembodied entity?"

"Perhaps," she admitted, "but I have not thought it out at all."

"Granted a spirit," he suggested, "might it not be a malignant sprite, an imp bent on doing you harm, upon entrapping you to your destruction?"

"I don't credit such an idea for a moment," she said. "The message has given me hope. Your innuendoes seek to rob me of my hope."

"I seek to save you," Vargas said, "to dislodge you from your fortalice of resolve."

"For the third time," she said, "I tell you that my determination is irrevocably taken."

Vargas awkwardly stood up. He clung to the back of a chair and gazed at her steadily. His face, from a far-off solemn look of resigned desperation, gradually took on an expression of prophetic resolve.

"Pardon me," he said, "if I must shock you. I wish to put to you a question."

"Put it," she said coldly.

"Mrs. Llewellyn," the clairvoyant asked in a deep, slow voice, "have you kept your marriage vows?"

"Sir," she said angrily, rising. "You are insulting me."

"Not a particle," he persisted. "You have not answered my question."

"To answer it is superfluous," she said, facing him in trembling wrath. "Of course I have kept them. You know how utterly I love my husband."

"You regard your vows as sacred?" he asked relentlessly.

"Of course," she said wearily.

"Why, then," he demanded, "do you attach less sanctity to your verbal compact with your husband? Your duty as a wife is to keep one compact as well as the other. Keep both. Do not be recalcitrant against the terms of your agreement. Endure his indifference and strive patiently to win his love. It is your duty, as much as it is your duty to keep your marriage vows."

"You assume a rôle," she said, "very unsuitable for you. Preaching misfits you, and it has no effect on me. I know and feel all this. But there is the plain meaning of that message. I shall open that grave."

"I have done all I can," he said dispiritedly. "I cannot dissuade you."

"You cannot," she said.

"How then can I serve you?" he asked. "I have not yet discovered to what I owe the honor of this second visit. Why are you here?"

"I wish you to be present at the opening of the coffin," she said.

"Are you sure," he demanded, "that that would not be most unseemly? The first Mrs. Llewellyn, I believe, left no near relatives. But would not even her cousins resent such an intrusion as my presence there? Would not your husband still more resent it? Would it not be in very bad taste?"

"I do not make requests," she said, "that are in bad taste. As for my husband, he resents and will resent nothing, as he approves and will approve of nothing. My brother will be there and he will not find anything unseemly in your presence."

"Nevertheless I hesitate to agree," said Vargas.

"You have expressed," said she, "a very deep regard for me, will you not do this since I ask it?"

"I will," he said with an effort.

"Then whenever I write you and send a carriage for you, you will be there at the time named?"

"I promise," he said.

Sometime before the appointed hour, at that spot where a driveway approached nearest to the Llewellyn monument, Vargas painfully emerged from a closed carriage, the blue shades of which were drawn down. He spoke to someone inside and shut the door. He had taken but two or three hobbling steps, when another carriage closely following his stopped where his had stopped. Its shades were also drawn down. When its door opened a well-dressed man got out. As Vargas had done he spoke to someone inside and closed the door. When he turned Vargas saw a man of usual, very conventional appearance, the sort of man visible by scores in fashionable clubs. His build and carriage were those of a man naturally jaunty in his movements. His well-fleshed, healthy face, smooth shaven except for a thick brown mustache, was such a face as lends itself naturally to expressions of good fellowship and joviality. His brown eyes were prone to merriment. But there was no sparkle in them, no geniality in his air, no springiness in his movements. He wore his brown derby a trifle, the merest trifle, to one side, but his expression was careworn, he looked haggard. He had the air of a man used to having his own way, but he held himself now without any elasticity. He looked the deformed clairvoyant up and down with one quick glance, fixed him with a direct gaze as he approached and greeted him with an engaging air of easy politeness, neither stiff nor familiar.

"My name is Palgrave," he said. "I presume you are Mr. Vargas."

"The same," said the clairvoyant, with not a little constraint.

"Pleased to meet you," said the other, holding out his hand and diminishing Vargas' embarrassment by the heartiness of his handshake. "Glad to have a chance for a talk with you. My sister has told me of her visits to you."

Vargas controlled his expression, but shot one lightning glance at the other's face, reading there instantly how much Mrs. Llewellyn had told her brother and how much she had not told him.

There was something very taking about Mr. Palgrave's manner, which put Vargas completely at his ease. It was more than conciliatory; it was almost friendly, almost sympathetic. It not so much expressed readiness to admit to a confidential understanding, as gave the impression of continuing a well-established natural attitude of entire trust and complete comprehension. It had an unmistakable tinge, as unexpected as gratifying, of level esteem and unspoken gratitude.

There was a rustic seat by the path and by a common impulse both moved toward it. At the clubman's courteous gesture, the cripple, with his unavoidable wrenching jolt, lowered himself painfully to the level of the bench. Mr. Palgrave seated himself beside him, crossed his knees and half turned toward him. He rested his left elbow on the back of the bench. His other hand held his cane, which he tapped against the side of his foot. The waiting carriages, one behind the other, were under a big elm some distance off; their drivers lay on the grass beside them. No one else was in sight except where, rather farther off in another direction, six laborers, their coats off, sat with a superintendent near them, in the shade of a Norway maple, near the Llewellyn monument; which dominated the neighborhood from its low, broad knoll.

The brief silence Mr. Palgrave broke.

"If you will pardon my saying it, you don't look at all like my idea of a clairvoyant."

Vargas smiled a wan smile. The tone of the words was totally disarming.

"I don't feel like my idea of a clairvoyant," he said. "I am usually clear-sighted in any matter I take up; usually so clear-sighted in respect to any personality that my advice, as it often is, seems to my clients a mere echo of their own thoughts, a mere confirmation of their own judgments, a mere additional reason for what they would have done anyhow. I am used to touching unerringly the strongest springs of action. So far I have utterly failed to gain that clue to Mrs. Llewellyn's character necessary to make my advice acceptable."

"In every other respect you seem to have been as clear-sighted as possible," Mr. Palgrave told him. "No advice could have been better nor more judiciously urged, nor more entirely disinterested."

"Rather utterly interested," said Vargas.

"In an altogether different sense," said the other. "She told me. Until I saw you I was astonished that she had not resented it."

"She did resent it, and of course," said the cripple.

"Not as she would from any other man," said Mr. Palgrave.

"There are some things—" Vargas began. His voice thinned out and he broke off.

"Yes, I understand," said her brother, "and I want to say that I feel under much obligation to you for the way you behaved and for the manliness and the straightforwardness of your whole attitude."

"I am greatly complimented," Vargas replied.

"You deserve complimenting," said Mr. Palgrave. "You acted admirably. Your consideration, I might say your gentleness shows that you really have her best interests at heart."

"I truly have," said Vargas fervently, "and I am more disturbed in mind than I can express."

"That must be a great deal," said the clubman, a momentary gleam of his usual self, fading instantly from his eyes. "I certainly cannot express how much I am upset. I hate worry or anxiety and always put such troubles away and forget them. I can't forget this. I have idolized my sister since we were babies. I have hardly slept since she talked to me. She won't hear of a doctor. She don't admit that there could be any pretext for her consulting a doctor, and I can't talk to anyone about her. I can talk to you. You seem a very sensible man. I should like to hear your opinion of her condition. Do you think her mind is unsettled?"

"Not as bad as that," Vargas told him.

"This grave-opening idea seems to me out and out lunacy," said the other.

"Not as bad as that," Vargas repeated. "It shows a trend of thought which may develop into something worse, but in itself it is only a foolish whim. The worst of it is that it produces a situation of great delicacy and high tension which may have almost any sort of bad result."

"I can't imagine," said Palgrave, "any rational or half rational basis for her whim. I can't conceive what she thinks she will accomplish by opening that coffin or why she wants it opened. I was at Marian's funeral and the two coffins made a precious lot of talk, I can tell you. I assumed that Llewellyn had some wild, sentimental notion of the second coffin waiting for him. Constance declares it was not empty, but she won't say what she expects to find in it and I believe she don't say because she has no idea at all."

"You are right," said the clairvoyant, "she hasn't."

"Well," said the other, "what do *you* think she will find in it?"

"I have no opinions whatever," said Vargas, "as to whether it is empty or not or as to what may be in it. I have no basis of conjecture. But whether empty or not or whatever may be in it, I dread the effect upon her. She is sure to be baffled in her hopes. Her present state of mind is a sort of reawakening in a civilized, educated, cultured woman of the primitive, childish, savage faith in sorcery, almost in rudimentary fetishism. She would not acknowledge it, but her attitude is very like that of a fetish-worshipper. Her mind does not reason. She is possessed of a blind, vague feeling that her welfare is implicated with whatever is in that coffin, and a compelling hope in the efficiency of the mere act of opening it, as a sort of magic rite. She is buoyed up with uncertainty. Whether she finds something or nothing she will be brought face to face with final unmistakable disappointment. I dread the moment of that realization."

"I felt something like that," said her brother. "Anyhow I brought a doctor with me, but she must not suspect that as long as we don't need him."

"That is why your carriage has the shades down," Vargas hazarded.

"Is that the reason yours has its shades down?" the other inquired.

"That is it," Vargas confessed. "I brought a doctor too."

"Two doctors," commented Palgrave. "Like a French duel. Hope it will end as harmlessly as the average French duel."

"That is almost too much to hope for," said Vargas. "She may pass the critical instant safely. But even if she does she will be thrown back into brooding over her troubles."

"Her troubles seem to me largely imaginary," said the clubman.

"All the more danger in that," said Vargas, "if merely subjective."

"In this case they ought to evaporate," said her brother, "if she acted sensibly, and yet they are not wholly imaginary. I don't wonder that she is troubled. David Llewellyn is not himself at all. His dead-and-alive demeanor is enough to prey on anybody's mind. Moping about here with him makes it worse. But going for a cruise might cure both of them and would be likely to wake him up and certain to clear her head. She ought to take your advice."

"She will not," said Vargas dejectedly, "and I scarcely wonder at her determination. Her dreams were enough to affect anybody. And the message on that slate was enough to influence anyone. Believing it addressed directly to her she is irresistibly urged to act upon it. I myself, merely a spectator, have been thrown by it into a terrible confusion of my whole mentality. I have believed in no real mystery in the universe. I am confronted by an unblinkable, an insoluble puzzle. My reliance upon the laws of space and time, as we think we know them, is, for the time being, wrenched from its foundations. My faith in the indestructibility of matter, in the continuity of force, in the fundamental laws of motion, is shaken and tottering. My belief in the necessary sequence of cause and effect, in causation and causality in general, is totally shattered. I could credit any marvel, could accept any monstrous portent as altogether to be expected. The universe no longer seems to me a scene, at least in front of the great, blank curtain of the unknowable, filled by an orderly progress of more or less cognizable and predictable occurrences, depending upon interrelated causes; it seems the playground of the irresponsible, prankish, malevolent somethings, productive of incalculabilities. I am in a delirium of dread, in a daze of panic."

"I hardly follow your meaning," said the other, "but I feel we can do nothing."

"No," said Vargas, "we can only hope for the best and fear the worst."

"And what will be the worst?" her brother demanded.

"I conceive," said Vargas, "that upon the opening of the coffin she will suffer some sort of shock, whether it be from disappointment, surprise, or whatever else. At the worst she might scream and drop dead before our eyes or shriek and hopelessly lose her reason."

"Yes," said Mr. Palgrave, "that would be the worst, I suppose."

"And yet," said Vargas, "I cannot escape from the feeling that the worst, in some incalculable, unpredictable, inconceivable way, will be something a great deal worse than that; something unimaginably, unutterably, ineffably worse than anything I can definitely put into words or even vaguely think."

"I cannot express myself as fluently as you can," her brother responded, "but I have had much the same sort of feeling. I have it now. I feel as if I were not now in a cemetery for the purpose of being present at the opening of a grave; but far away, or long ago, about to participate in some uncanny occurrence fit to make Saul's experience at Endor or Macbeth's with the witches seem humdrum and commonplace."

"I feel all that," said Vargas, "and more; as if we were not ourselves at all, but the actors in some vast drama of wretchedness, apocalyptically ignorant of an enormous shadow of unescapable doom steadily darkening over our impotence. We cannot modify, we cannot alter, we cannot change, we cannot ward off, we cannot even postpone what is about to happen."

"What is about to happen," said his companion, "is going to happen now. Here they come."

The two men rose and watched the Llewellyn carriage draw up where theirs had stopped. Its door opened and a large man stepped down.

Vargas had previously seen David Llewellyn only momentarily at a distance, and now scrutinized him with much attention. He was a tall man, taller than his brother-in-law, and was solidly and very compactly made. His manner, as he turned to the carriage, was solicitous and deferential as he helped his wife out. As they approached, walking side by side, Vargas eyed the man. He was powerfully built and showed an immense girth of chest. His close-cut beard did not disguise the type of his countenance, the face belonged to an athletic college-bred man, firm chin, set lips, straight nose and clear gray eyes. He was very handsome and reminders of what had been downright beauty in his boyhood were manifest not only in the face but in the general effect of his presence.

Without any word, barely nodding to the two men, he halted some steps away, leaving his wife to advance alone. She greeted Vargas and, slipping her hand through the bend of her brother's arm, passed on along the path with him. Vargas remained where he was, waiting for Mr. Llewellyn to go first. He seemed, by a subtle and intangible something in his look and attitude, to signify that he disclaimed any participation in what was to take place. By an almost imperceptible nod of negation and a barely discernible gesture of affirmation he indicated that the clairvoyant was to precede him. Vargas complied and hobbled after the brother and sister. The superintendent came forward to meet them, and walked beside Mrs. Llewellyn, listening to her instructions, and then going toward his assistants.

The space around their monument which was occupied by the Llewellyn graves was encircled by a low hedge, not more than knee-high. It had an opening facing the monument and through this Mrs. Llewellyn and her brother passed, Vargas some steps behind them. They stopped a pace or two from the foot of the grave, and turned about. Vargas, keeping his distance, stopped likewise and likewise turned. Mr. Llewellyn, treading noiselessly, had stepped aside from the path and took his stand just inside the hedge. The workmen straggled past him, the superintendent convoying them. When they had begun to dig, Vargas, like the rest, watched them. Presently he began to look about him and survey the cemetery, of which the knoll afforded an extensive view. The weather gave the prospect an unusual quality, the late spring or early summer warmth was unrelieved by any positive breeze, the light air stirred aimlessly, the cloudiness which completely overcast the sky was too thin to cut off the heat of the sun-rays, the foliage was dusty and the landscape a sickly yellowish green in the weak tepid sunshine. This eerie quality of the scene Vargas felt rather than saw. While the time taken up with digging postponed the all-important moment, his attention was divided between the monument and Mr. Llewellyn. He stood with his weight nearly all on one foot, leaning on the cane his left hand held, the other gloved hand, holding his hat, hanging at his side. Gazing straight in front of him toward the monument, rather than at it, there was about him the look of something inanimate, of something made, not grown, of an object immovably planted in carven, expressionless impassivity. The monument, which Vargas saw for the first time, gave from the perfectly coördinated harmonies of its architectural design, its delicate reliefs, and its exquisite statuary, an impression of individuality striking enough to anyone at any time and all the more now by contrast. Any one of its figures seemed instinct with more life than the man facing it. That member of the little gathering who should have been most moved, showed no emotion and Vargas himself felt much. As the digging proceeded, he mostly gazed back as she stood clinging to her brother's arm, leaning against him. When the workmen began to raise the coffin, he found the emotions of his strained forebodings overmastering him. His breath quickened and came hard, his heart thumped at his ribs, his eyes were unexpectedly, inexplicably moist. Glancing back at the immobile man behind him, through the iridescent film upon his lashes, he saw but a blurred, vague shape. He strove to regain his composure, conning the outline of his own barely discernible shadow.

The outer box containing the raised coffin was now supported upon two pieces of wood thrust under it across the grave. The men unscrewed the lid and laid it aside. The coffin was of ebony and as fresh as if just made.

The men, at the superintendent's bidding, shambled away round the monument and through the opening in the hedge behind it to the tree they had left.

The superintendent began to take out the silver screws which held down the lid over the glass front of the coffin-head. As they were removed one by one, Vargas again glanced behind him. He saw worse than ever. The outline of the big figure was almost indefinite, its bulk almost hazy.

As he turned his gaze again to the coffin his sight seemed to clear entirely. He saw even the silver rims round the screw-holes and the head of the last screw. As the superintendent lifted the lid, Mrs. Llewellyn, now at the foot of the coffin, leaned forward, and her brother and Vargas, now just behind her, leaned even more. Through the glass they saw a face, David Llewellyn's face. Mrs. Llewellyn screamed. All three turned round. Save themselves and the superintendent and the distant workmen there was no human shape in sight anywhere. The big, solid presence had vanished.

Again screaming Mrs. Llewellyn threw herself on the coffin, the two men, scarcely less frantic than she, close by her. Through the glass they could see the face working, the eyelids fluttering. The superintendent toiled furiously at the catches of the glass front. When he lifted it away the eyes opened, gazing straight into Mrs. Llewellyn's. Almost at once they glazed, and a moment later the jaw dropped.

Lukundoo

"IT STANDS to reason," said Twombly, "that a man must accept the evidence of his own eyes, and when eyes and ears agree, there can be no doubt. He has to believe what he has both seen and heard."

"Not always," put in Singleton, softly.

Every man turned toward Singleton. Twombly was standing on the hearth-rug, his back to the grate, his legs spread out, with his habitual air of dominating the room. Singleton, as usual, was as much as possible effaced in a corner. But when Singleton spoke he said something. We faced him in that flattering spontaneity of expectant silence which invites utterance.

"I was thinking," he said, after an interval, "of something I both saw and heard in Africa."

Now, if there was one thing we had found impossible it had been to elicit from Singleton anything definite about his African experiences. As with the Alpinist in the story, who could tell only that he went up and came down, the sum of Singleton's revelations had been that he went there and came away. His words now riveted our attention at once. Twombly faded from the hearth-rug, but not one of us could ever recall having seen him go. The room readjusted itself, focused on Singleton, and there was some hasty and furtive lighting of fresh cigars. Singleton lit one also, but it went out immediately, and he never relit it.

I

We were in the Great Forest, exploring for pigmies. Van Rieten had a theory that the dwarfs found by Stanley and others were a mere cross-breed between ordinary negroes and the real pigmies. He hoped to discover a race of men three feet tall at most, or shorter. We had found no trace of any such beings.

Natives were few; game scarce; food, except game, there was none; and the deepest, dankest, drippingest forest all about. We were the only novelty in the country, no native we met had even seen a white man before, most had never heard of white men. All of a sudden, late one afternoon, there came into our camp an Englishman, and pretty well used up he was, too. We had heard no rumor of him; he had not only heard of us but had made an amazing five-day march to reach us. His guide and two bearers were nearly as done up as he. Even though he was in tatters and had five days' beard on, you could see he was naturally dapper and neat and the sort of man to shave daily. He was small, but wiry. His face was the sort of British face from which emotion had been so carefully banished that a foreigner is apt to think the wearer of the face incapable of any sort of feeling; the kind of face which, if it has any expression at all, expresses principally the resolution to go on through the world decorously, without intruding upon or annoying anyone.

His name was Etcham. He introduced himself modestly, and ate with us so deliberately that we should never have suspected, if our bearers had not had it from his bearers, that he had had but three meals in the five days, and those small. After we had lit up he told us why he had come.

"My chief is ve'y seedy," he said between puffs. "He is bound to go out if he keeps this way. I thought perhaps . . ."

He spoke quietly in a soft, even tone, but I could see little beads of sweat oozing out on his upper lip under his stubby mustache, and there was a tingle of repressed emotion in his tone, a veiled eagerness in his eye, a palpitating inward solicitude in his demeanor that moved me at once. Van Rieten had no sentiment in him; if he was moved he did not show it. But he listened. I was surprised at that. He was just the man to refuse at once. But he listened to Etcham's halting, diffident hints. He even asked questions.

"Who is your chief?"

"Stone," Etcham lisped.

That electrified both of us.

"Ralph Stone?" we ejaculated together.

Etcham nodded.

For some minutes Van Rieten and I were silent. Van Rieten had never seen him, but I had been a classmate of Stone's, and Van Rieten and I had discussed him over many a camp-fire. We had heard of him two years before, south of Luebo in the Balunda country, which had been ringing with his theatrical strife against a Balunda witch-doctor, ending in the sorcerer's complete discomfiture and the abasement of his tribe before Stone. They had even broken the fetish-man's whistle and given Stone the pieces. It had been like the triumph of Elijah over the prophets of Baal, only more real to the Balunda.

We had thought of Stone as far off, if still in Africa at all, and here he turned up ahead of us and probably forestalling our quest.

II

Etcham's naming of Stone brought back to us all his tantalizing story, his fascinating parents, their tragic death; the brilliance of his college days; the dazzle of his millions; the promise of his young manhood; his wide notoriety, so nearly real fame; his romantic elopement with the meteoric authoress whose sudden cascade of fiction had made her so great a name so young, whose beauty and charm were so much heralded; the frightful scandal of the breach-of-promise suit that followed; his bride's devotion through it all; their sudden quarrel after it was all over; their divorce; the too much advertised announcement of his approaching marriage to the plaintiff in the breach-of-promise suit; his precipitate remarriage to his divorced bride; their second quarrel and second divorce; his departure from his native land; his advent in the dark continent. The sense of all this rushed over me and I believe Van Rieten felt it, too, as he sat silent.

Then he asked:
"Where is Werner?"
"Dead," said Etcham. "He died before I joined Stone."
"You were not with Stone above Luebo?"
"No," said Etcham. "I joined him at Stanley Falls."
"Who is with him?" Van Rieten asked.
"Only his Zanzibar servants and the bearers," Etcham replied.
"What sort of bearers?" Van Rieten demanded.
"Mang-Battu men," Etcham responded simply.

Now that impressed both Van Rieten and myself greatly. It bore out Stone's reputation as a notable leader of men. For up to that time no one had been able to use Mang-Battu as bearers outside of their own country, or to hold them for long or difficult expeditions.

"Were you long among the Mang-Battu?" was Van Rieten's next question.

"Some weeks," said Etcham. "Stone was interested in them and made up a fair-sized vocabulary of their words and phrases. He had a theory that they were an offshoot of the Balunda and he found much confirmation in their customs."

"What do you live on?" Van Rieten inquired.

"Game, mostly," Etcham lisped.

"How long has Stone been laid up?" Van Rieten next asked.

"More than a month," Etcham answered.

"And you have been hunting for the camp!" Van Rieten exclaimed.

Etcham's face, burnt and flayed as it was, showed a flush.

"I missed some easy shots," he admitted ruefully. "I've not felt ve'y fit myself."

"What's the matter with your chief?" Van Rieten inquired.

"Something like carbuncles," Etcham replied.

"He ought to get over a carbuncle or two," Van Rieten declared.

"They are not carbuncles," Etcham explained. "Nor one or two. He has had dozens, sometimes five at once. If they had been carbuncles he would have been dead long ago. But in some ways they are not so bad, though in others they are worse."

"How do you mean?" Van Rieten queried.

"Well," Etcham hesitated, "they do not seem to inflame so deep nor so wide as carbuncles, nor to be so painful, nor to cause so much fever. But then they seem to be part of a disease that affects his mind. He let me help him dress the first, but the others he has hidden most carefully, from me and from the men. He keeps his tent when they puff up, and will not let me change the dressings or be with him at all."

"Have you plenty of dressings?" Van Rieten asked.

"We have some," said Etcham doubtfully. "But he won't use them; he washes out the dressings and uses them over and over."

"How is he treating the swellings?" Van Rieten inquired.
"He slices them off clear down to flesh level, with his razor."
"What?" Van Rieten shouted.
Etcham made no answer but looked him steadily in the eyes.
"I beg pardon," Van Rieten hastened to say. "You startled me. They can't be carbuncles. He'd have been dead long ago."
"I thought I had said they are not carbuncles," Etcham lisped.
"But the man must be crazy!" Van Rieten exclaimed.
"Just so," said Etcham. "He is beyond my advice or control."
"How many has he treated that way?" Van Rieten demanded.
"Two, to my knowledge," Etcham said.
"Two?" Van Rieten queried.
Etcham flushed again.
"I saw him," he confessed, "through a crack in the hut. I felt impelled to keep a watch on him, as if he was not responsible."
"I should think not," Van Rieten agreed. "And you saw him do that twice?"
"I conjecture," said Etcham, "that he did the like with all the rest."
"How many has he had?" Van Rieten asked.
"Dozens," Etcham lisped.
"Does he eat?" Van Rieten inquired.
"Like a wolf," said Etcham. "More than any two bearers."
"Can he walk?" Van Rieten asked.
"He crawls a bit, groaning," said Etcham simply.
"Little fever, you say," Van Rieten ruminated.
"Enough and too much," Etcham declared.
"Has he been delirious?" Van Rieten asked.
"Only twice," Etcham replied; "once when the first swelling broke, and once later. He would not let anyone come near him then. But we could hear him talking, talking steadily, and it scared the natives."
"Was he talking their patter in delirium?" Van Rieten demanded.
"No," said Etcham, "but he was talking some similar lingo. Hamed Burghash said he was talking Balunda. I know too little Balunda. I do not learn languages readily. Stone learned more Mang-Battu in a week than I could have learned in a year. But I seemed to hear words like Mang-Battu words. Anyhow the Mang-Battu bearers were scared."
"Scared?" Van Rieten repeated, questioningly.

"So were the Zanzibar men, even Hamed Burghash, and so was I," said Etcham, "only for a different reason. He talked in two voices."

"In two voices," Van Rieten reflected.

"Yes," said Etcham, more excitedly than he had yet spoken. "In two voices, like a conversation. One was his own, one a small, thin, bleary voice like nothing I ever heard. I seemed to make out, among the sounds the deep voice made, something like Mang-Battu words I knew, as *nedru, metebaba,* and *nedo,* their terms for 'head,' 'shoulder,' 'thigh,' and perhaps *kudra* and *nekere* ('speak' and 'whistle'); and among the noises of the shrill voice *matomipa, angunzi,* and *kamomami* ('kill,' 'death,' and 'hate'). Hamed Burghash said he also heard those words. He knew Mang-Battu far better than I."

"What did the bearers say?" Van Rieten asked.

"They said, '*Lukundoo, Lukundoo!*'" Etcham replied. "I did not know that word; Hamed Burghash said it was Mang-Battu for 'leopard.'"

"It's Mang-Battu for 'witchcraft,'" said Van Rieten.

"I don't wonder they thought so," said Etcham. "It was enough to make one believe in sorcery to listen to those two voices."

"One voice answering the other?" Van Rieten asked perfunctorily.

Etcham's face went gray under his tan.

"Sometimes both at once," he answered huskily.

"Both at once!" Van Rieten ejaculated.

"It sounded that way to the men, too," said Etcham. "And that was not all."

He stopped and looked helplessly at us for a moment.

"Could a man talk and whistle at the same time?" he asked.

"How do you mean?" Van Rieten queried.

"We could hear Stone talking away, his big, deep-chested baritone rumbling along, and through it all we could hear a high, shrill whistle, the oddest, wheezy sound. You know, no matter how shrilly a grown man may whistle, the note has a different quality from the whistle of a boy or a woman or little girl. They sound more treble, somehow. Well, if you can imagine the smallest girl who could whistle keeping it up tunelessly right along, that whistle was like that, only even more piercing, and it sounded right through Stone's bass tones."

"And you didn't go to him?" Van Rieten cried.

"He is not given to threats," Etcham disclaimed. "But he threatened, not volubly, nor like a sick man but quietly and firmly, that if any man of us (he lumped me in with the men) came near him while he was in his trouble, that man should die. And it was not so much his words as his manner. It was like a monarch commanding respected privacy for a death-bed. One simply could not transgress."

"I see," said Van Rieten shortly.

"He's ve'y seedy," Etcham repeated helplessly. "I thought perhaps . . ."

His absorbing affection for Stone, his real love for him, shone through his envelope of conventional training. Worship of Stone was plainly his master passion.

Like many competent men, Van Rieten had a streak of hard selfishness in him. It came to the surface then. He said we carried our lives in our hands from day to day just as genuinely as Stone; that he did not forget the ties of blood and calling between any two explorers, but that there was no sense in imperiling one party for a very problematical benefit to a man probably beyond any help; that it was enough of a task to hunt for one party; that if two were united, providing food would be more than doubly difficult; that the risk of starvation was too great. Deflecting our march seven full days' journey (he complimented Etcham on his marching powers) might ruin our expedition entirely.

III

Van Rieten had logic on his side and he had a way with him. Etcham sat there apologetic and deferential, like a fourth-form schoolboy before a head master. Van Rieten wound up.

"I am after pigmies, at the risk of my life. After pigmies I go."

"Perhaps, then, these will interest you," said Etcham, very quietly.

He took two objects out of the sidepocket of his blouse, and handed them to Van Rieten. They were round, bigger than big plums, and smaller than small peaches, about the right size to enclose in an average hand. They were black, and at first I did not see what they were.

"Pigmies!" Van Rieten exclaimed. "Pigmies, indeed! Why, they wouldn't be two feet high! Do you mean to claim that these are adult heads?"

"I claim nothing," Etcham answered evenly. "You can see for yourself."

Van Rieten passed one of the heads to me. The sun was just setting and I examined it closely. A dried head it was, perfectly preserved, and the flesh as hard as Argentine jerked beef. A bit of a vertebra stuck out where the muscles of the vanished neck had shriveled into folds. The puny chin was sharp on a projecting jaw, the minute teeth white and even between the retracted lips, the tiny nose was flat, the little forehead retreating, there were inconsiderable clumps of stunted wool on the Lilliputian cranium. There was nothing babyish, childish or youthful about the head, rather it was mature to senility.

"Where did these come from?" Van Rieten inquired.

"I do not know," Etcham replied precisely. "I found them among Stone's effects while rummaging for medicines or drugs or anything that could help me to help him. I do not know where he got them. But I'll swear he did not have them when we entered this district."

"Are you sure?" Van Rieten queried, his eyes big and fixed on Etcham's.

"Ve'y sure," lisped Etcham.

"But how could he have come by them without your knowledge?" Van Rieten demurred.

"Sometimes we were apart ten days at a time hunting," said Etcham. "Stone is not a talking man. He gave me no account of his doings and Hamed Burghash keeps a still tongue and a tight hold on the men."

"You have examined these heads?" Van Rieten asked.

"Minutely," said Etcham.

Van Rieten took out his notebook. He was a methodical chap. He tore out a leaf, folded it and divided it equally into three pieces. He gave one to me and one to Etcham.

"Just for a test of my impressions," he said, "I want each of us to write separately just what he is most reminded of by these heads. Then I want to compare the writings."

I handed Etcham a pencil and he wrote. Then he handed the pencil back to me and I wrote.

"Read the three," said Van Rieten, handing me his piece.

Van Rieten had written:

"An old Balunda witch-doctor."

Etcham had written:

"An old Mang-Battu fetish-man."

I had written:

"An old Katongo magician."

"There!" Van Rieten exclaimed. "Look at that! There is nothing Wagabi or Batwa or Wambuttu or Wabotu about these heads. Nor anything pigmy either."

"I thought as much," said Etcham.

"And you say he did not have them before?"

"To a certainty he did not," Etcham asserted.

"It is worth following up," said Van Rieten. "I'll go with you. And first of all, I'll do my best to save Stone."

He put out his hand and Etcham clasped it silently. He was grateful all over.

IV

Nothing but Etcham's fever of solicitude could have taken him in five days over the track. It took him eight days to retrace with full knowledge of it and our party to help. We could not have done it in seven, and Etcham urged us on, in a repressed fury of anxiety, no mere fever of duty to his chief, but a real ardor of devotion, a glow of personal adoration for Stone which blazed under his dry conventional exterior and showed in spite of him.

We found Stone well cared for. Etcham had seen to a good, high thorn *zareeba* round the camp, the huts were well built and thatched and Stone's was as good as their resources would permit. Hamed Burghash was not named after two Seyyids for nothing. He had in him the making of a sultan. He had kept the Mang-Battu together, not a man had slipped off, and he had kept them in order. Also he was a deft nurse and a faithful servant.

The two other Zanzibaris had done some creditable hunting. Though all were hungry, the camp was far from starvation.

Stone was on a canvas cot and there was a sort of collapsible camp-stool-table, like a Turkish tabouret, by the cot. It had a water-bottle and some vials on it and Stone's watch, also his razor in its case.

Stone was clean and not emaciated, but he was far gone; not unconscious, but in a daze; past commanding or resisting anyone. He did not seem to see us enter or to know we were there. I should have recognized him anywhere. His boyish dash and grace had vanished utterly, of course. But his head was even more leonine; his hair was still abundant, yellow and wavy; the close, crisped blond beard he had grown during his illness did not alter him. He was big and big-chested yet. His eyes were dull and he mumbled and babbled mere meaningless syllables, not words.

Etcham helped Van Rieten to uncover him and look him over. He was in good muscle for a man so long bedridden. There were no scars on him except about his knees, shoulders and chest. On each knee and above it he had a full score of roundish cicatrices, and a dozen or more on each shoulder, all in front. Two or three were open wounds and four or five barely healed. He had no fresh swellings except two, one on each side, on his pectoral muscles, the one on the left being higher up and farther out than the other. They did not look like boils or carbuncles, but as if something blunt and hard were being pushed up through the fairly healthy flesh and skin, not much inflamed.

"I should not lance those," said Van Rieten, and Etcham assented.

They made Stone as comfortable as they could, and just before sunset we looked in at him again. He was lying on his back, and his chest showed big and massive yet, but he lay as if in a stupor. We left Etcham with him and went into the next hut, which Etcham had resigned to us. The jungle noises were no different there than anywhere else for months past, and I was soon fast asleep.

V

Sometime in the pitch dark I found myself awake and listening. I could hear two voices, one Stone's, the other sibilant and wheezy. I knew Stone's voice after all the years that had passed since I heard it last. The other was like nothing I remembered. It had less volume than the wail of a new-born baby, yet there was an insistent carrying power to it, like the shrilling of an insect. As I listened I heard Van Rieten breathing near me in the dark, then he heard me and realized that I was listening, too. Like Etcham I knew little Balunda, but I could make out a word of two. The voices alternated with intervals of silence between.

Then suddenly both sounded at once and fast, Stone's baritone basso, full as if he were in perfect health, and that incredibly stridulous falsetto, both jabbering at once like the voices of two people quarreling and trying to talk each other down.

"I can't stand this," said Van Rieten. "Let's have a look at him."

He had one of those cylindrical electric night-candles. He fumbled about for it, touched the button and beckoned me to come with him. Outside of the hut he motioned me to stand still, and instinctively turned off the light, as if seeing made listening difficult.

Except for a faint glow from the embers of the bearers' fire we were in complete darkness, little starlight struggled through the trees, the river made but a faint murmur. We could hear the two voices together and then suddenly the creaking voice changed into a razor-edged, slicing whistle, indescribably cutting, continuing right through Stone's grumbling torrent of croaking words.

"Good God!" exclaimed Van Rieten.

Abruptly he turned on the light.

We found Etcham utterly asleep, exhausted by his long anxiety and the exertions of his phenomenal march and relaxed completely now that the load was in a sense shifted from his shoulders to Van Rieten's. Even the light on his face did not wake him.

The whistle had ceased and the two voices now sounded together. Both came from Stone's cot, where the concentrated white ray showed him lying just as we had left him, except that he had tossed his arms above his head and had torn the coverings and bandages from his chest.

The swelling on his right breast had broken. Van Rieten aimed the center line of the light at it and we saw it plainly. From his flesh, grown out of it, there protruded a head, such a head as the dried specimens Etcham had shown us, as if it were a miniature of the head of a Balunda fetish-man. It was black, shining black as the blackest African skin; it rolled the whites of its wicked, wee eyes and showed its microscopic teeth between lips repulsively negroid in their red fullness, even in so diminutive a face. It had crisp, fuzzy wool on its minikin skull, it turned malignantly from side to side and chittered incessantly in that inconceivable falsetto. Stone babbled brokenly against its patter.

Van Rieten turned from Stone and waked Etcham, with some difficulty. When he was awake and saw it all, Etcham stared and said not one word.

"You saw him slice off two swellings?" Van Rieten asked.

Etcham nodded, chokingly.

"Did he bleed much?" Van Rieten demanded.

"Ve'y little," Etcham replied.

"You hold his arms," said Van Rieten to Etcham.

He took up Stone's razor and handed me the light. Stone showed no sign of seeing the light or of knowing we were there. But the little head mewled and screeched at us.

Van Rieten's hand was steady, and the sweep of the razor even and true. Stone bled amazingly little and Van Rieten dressed the wound as if it had been a bruise or scrape.

Stone had stopped talking the instant the excrescent head was severed. Van Rieten did all that could be done for Stone and then fairly grabbed the light from me. Snatching up a gun he scanned the ground by the cot and brought the butt down once and twice, viciously.

We went back to our hut, but I doubt if I slept.

VI

Next day, near noon, in broad daylight, we heard the two voices from Stone's hut. We found Etcham dropped asleep by his charge. The swelling on the left had broken, and just such another head was there miauling and spluttering. Etcham woke up and the three of us stood there and glared. Stone interjected hoarse vocables into the tinkling gurgle of the portent's utterance.

Van Rieten stepped forward, took up Stone's razor and knelt down by the cot. The atomy of a head squealed a wheezy snarl at him.

Then suddenly Stone spoke English.

"Who are you with my razor?"

Van Rieten started back and stood up.

Stone's eyes were clear now and bright, they roved about the hut.

"The end," he said; "I recognize the end. I seem to see Etcham, as if in life. But Singleton! Ah, Singleton! Ghosts of my boyhood come to watch me pass! And you, strange specter with the black beard, and my razor! Aroint ye all!"

"I'm no ghost, Stone," I managed to say. "I'm alive. So are Etcham and Van Rieten. We are here to help you."

"Van Rieten!" he exclaimed. "My work passes on to a better man. Luck go with you, Van Rieten."

Van Rieten went nearer to him.

"Just hold still a moment, old man," he said soothingly. "It will be only one twinge."

"I've held still for many such twinges," Stone answered quite distinctly. "Let me be. Let me die my own way. The hydra was nothing to this. You can cut off ten, a hundred, a thousand heads, but the curse you can not cut off, or take off. What's soaked into the bone won't come out of the flesh, any more than what's bred there. Don't hack me any more. Promise!"

His voice had all the old commanding tone of his boyhood and it swayed Van Rieten as it always had swayed everybody.

"I promise," said Van Rieten.

Almost as he said the word Stone's eyes filmed again.

Then we three sat about Stone and watched that hideous, gibbering prodigy grow up out of Stone's flesh, till two horrid, spindling little black arms disengaged themselves. The infinitesimal nails were perfect to the barely perceptible moon at the quick, the pink spot on the palm was horridly natural. These arms gesticulated and the right plucked toward Stone's blond beard.

"I can't stand this," Van Rieten exclaimed and took up the razor again.

Instantly Stone's eyes opened, hard and glittering.

"Van Rieten break his word?" he enunciated slowly. "Never!"

"But we must help you," Van Rieten gasped.

"I am past all help and all hurting," said Stone. "This is my hour. This curse is not put on me; it grew out of me, like this horror here. Even now I go."

His eyes closed and we stood helpless, the adherent figure spouting shrill sentences.

In a moment Stone spoke again.

"You speak all tongues?" he asked thickly.

And the emergent minikin replied in sudden English:

"Yea, verily, all that you speak," putting out its microscopic tongue, writhing its lips and wagging its head from side to side. We could see the thready ribs on its exiguous flanks heave as if the thing breathed.

"Has she forgiven me?" Stone asked in a muffled strangle.

"Not while the moss hangs from the cypresses," the head squeaked. "Not while the stars shine on Lake Pontchartrain will she forgive."

And then Stone, all with one motion, wrenched himself over on his side. The next instant he was dead.

When Singleton's voice ceased the room was hushed for a space. We could hear each other breathing. Twombly, the tactless, broke the silence.

"I presume," he said, "you cut off the little minikin and brought it home in alcohol."

Singleton turned on him a stern countenance.

"We buried Stone," he said, "unmutilated as he died."

"But," said the unconscionable Twombly, "the whole thing is incredible."

Singleton stiffened.

"I did not expect you to believe it," he said; "I began by saying that although I heard and saw it, when I look back on it I cannot credit it myself."

The Pig-skin Belt

I

Be it noted that I, John Radford, always of sound mind and matter-of-fact disposition, being entirely in my senses, here set down what I saw, heard and knew. As to my inferences from what occurred I say nothing, my theory might be regarded as more improbable than the facts themselves. From the facts anyone can draw conclusions as well as I.

The first letter read:

"San Antonio, Texas,
"January 1st, 1892.

"My dear Radford:

"You have forgotten me, likely enough, but I have not forgotten you nor anyone (nor anything) in Brexington. I saw your advertisement in the New York *Herald* and am glad to learn from it that you are alive and to infer that you are well and prosperous.

"I need a lawyer's help. I want to buy real estate and I mean to return home, so you are exactly the man I am looking for. I am writing this to ask that you take charge of any and all of my affairs falling within your province, and to learn whether you are willing to do so.

"I am a rich man now, and without any near ties of kin or kind. I want to come home to Brexington, to live there if I can, to die there if I must. Along with other matters which I will explain if you accept I want to buy a house in the town and a farm near-by, if not the Shelby house and estate then some others like them.

"If willing to act for me please reply at once care of the Hotel Menger. Remember me to any cousins of mine you may see.

"Faithfully yours,
"Cassius M. Case."

The name I knew well enough, of course, but my efforts to recall the individual resulted only in a somewhat hazy recollection of a tall, thin, red-cheeked lad of seventeen or so. It was almost exactly twenty-eight years since Colonel Shelby Case had left Brexington taking with him his son. Colonel Shelby had died some six years later. I remembered hearing of his death, in Egypt, I thought. Since his departure from Brexington I had never heard of or from Cassius.

My reply I wrote at once, professing my readiness to do anything in my power to serve him.

As soon as the mails made it possible, I had a second letter from him:

"MY DEAR RADFORD:
"Your kind letter has taken a load off my mind. I am particular about any sort of arrangements I make, exacting as to the accurate carrying out of small details and I feared I might have difficulty in finding a painstaking man in a community so easygoing as Brexington. I remember your precise ways as a boy and am basking in a sense of total relief and complete reliance on you.

"I should buy the Shelby house and estate on your representations, but I must see for myself first. If they are the best I can get I shall take them anyhow. But please be ready to show me over every estate of five hundred acres or more, lying within ten miles of the Court House. I wish to examine every one which is now for sale or which you can induce the owners to consider selling. I want the best which is to be had. Also I want a small place of fifty acres or so, two miles or more from the larger place I buy. Money is no object to me and the condition of the buildings on the places will not weigh with me at all.

"So with the town house: I may tear it down entirely and rebuild from the cellar up. What I want in the town is a place of half an acre to two acres carrying fine, tall trees, with well-developed trunks. I want shade and plenty of it, but no limbs or branches growing or hanging within eight feet of the ground. I do not desire shrubbery, but if there is any I can have it removed, while I cannot create stout trees. Those I must have on the place when I buy it, for I will have the shade and I will have a clear sweep for air and an unobstructed view all round.

"I am not at the Menger as you naturally suppose. I merely have my mail sent there. I am living in a tent half a mile or more from the town. At Los Angeles I had the luck to fall in with a Brexington nigger, Jeff Twibill. He knew of another, Cato Johnson, who was in Frisco. I have the two of them with me now, Jeff takes care of the horses and Cato of me and I am very comfortable.

"That brings me to the arrangements I want you to make for me. Buy or lease or rent or borrow a piece of a field, say four acres, free of trees or bushes and sloping enough to shed the rain. Be sure there is good water handy. Have four tents; one for me, one for the two niggers (and make it big enough for three or four); one to cook in and one for my four horses, they are luxurious beasts and live as well as I do. Have the tents pitched in the middle of the field so I shall have a clear view all around. The field must be clear of bushes or trees, must be at least four acres and may be any size larger than that: forty would be none too big for me. I want no houses too close to me.

"You see I am at present averse to houses, hotels and public conveyances. I mean to ride across the continent camping as I go. And in Brexington I mean to tent it until I have my own house ready to live in. I am resolute to be no man's guest nor any man's lodger, nor any company's passenger.

"I am coming home, Radford, coming home to be a Colonel with the rest of them. And I shall be no mere colonel-by-courtesy: I have won my right to the title, I won it twice over, years ago in Egypt and later in Asia.

"Thank you for all the news of the many cousins, I did not realize they were so very numerous. I am sorry that Mary Mattingly is dead, of all the many dear people in Brexington I loved her best.

"I shall keep you advised of my progress across the continent. And as questions come up about the details of the tent-equipment you can confer with me by letter.

"Gratefully yours,
CASSIUS M. CASE."

I showed the letters to one and another of my elder acquaintances, who remembered Cassius.

Dr. Boone said:

"I presume it is a case of advanced tuberculosis. He should have remained in that climate. Of course, he may live a long time here, tenting in the open or living with the completest fresh air treatment. His punctiliousness in respect to self-isolation does him credit, though he carries it further than is necessary. We must do all we can for him."

Beverly said:

"Poor devil. 'Live if he can, die if he must.' He'll die all right. They'd call him a 'lunger' out there and he had better stay there."

The minister said:

"The lode-star of old sweet memories draws him homeward. 'Mary Mattingly,' yes we all remember how wildly he loved Mary Mattingly. While full of youth he could find forgetfulness fighting in strange lands. Now he must be near her although she lies in her grave. The proximity even of her tomb will be a solace to his last days."

We were prepared to do all that sympathy could suggest. Mr. Hall and Dr. Boone gravely discussed together the prolongation of Case's life and the affording of spiritual support. Beverly I found helpful on my line of finances and creature comforts. As Case's leisurely progress brought him nearer and near our interest deepened. When the day came on which he was to arrive Beverly and I rode out to meet him.

II

Language has no words to picture our dumbfounded amazement. And we were astonished in more ways than one. Chiefly, instead of the lank invalid we expected to see, we beheld a burly giant every characteristic of whom, save one, bespoke rugged health. He was all of six foot three, big boned, overlaid with a surplus of brawn, a Samsonian musculature that showed plain through his negligent, loose clothing; and withal he was plump and would have been sleek but for the roughness of his weather-beaten skin.

He wore gray; a broad-brimmed felt hat, almost a sombrero; a flannel shirt, a sort of jacket, and corduroy trousers tucked into his boots. It was before the days of khaki.

His head was large and round, but not at all a bullet head, rather handsome and well set. His face was round too, and good-natured, but not a particle as is the usual round face, vacuous and like a full-moon. His was agreeable, but lit with character and determination. His neck was fat but showed great cords through its rotundity. He had a big barrel of a chest and his voice rumbled out of it. He dominated the landscape the moment he entered it.

Even in our astonishment three things about him struck me, and, as I afterwards found out, the same three similarly struck Beverly.

One was his complexion. He had that build which leads one to expect floridity of face, a rubicund countenance or, at least, ruddy cheeks. But he was dead pale, with a peculiar tint I never had seen before. His face showed an abundance of solid muscle and over it a skin roughened by exposure, toughened, even hardened by wind and sun. Yet its color was not in agreement with its texture. It had the hue which belongs to waxy skin over suety, tallowy flesh, an opaque whiteness, a pallidity almost corpse-like.

The second was his glance: keen, glittering, hard, blue-gray eyes he had, gallant and far younger than himself. But it was not the handsome eyes so much as their way of looking that whetted our attention. They pierced us through and through, they darted incessantly here and there, they peered to right and left, they kept us generally in view, indeed, and never let us feel that his attention wandered from us, yet they incessantly swept the world about him. You should say they saw all they looked at, looked at everything seeable.

The third was his belt, a mellowed old belt of pig-skin, with two capacious holsters, from each of which protruded the butt of a large-calibre revolver.

He greeted us in the spirit of old comradeship renewed. Behind him Jeff and Cato grinned from their tired mounts. He sat his big horse with no sign of fatigue and surveyed the landscape from the cross-roads' knoll where we had met him.

"I seem to recall the landmarks here," he said. "The left hand road by which you came, would take me through to Brexington."

Beverly confirmed his recollection.

"The one straight ahead," he went on, "goes past the big new distillery you wrote me about."

"Right again," I said.

"The road to the right," he continued, "will take us by the old mill, and I can swing round to my camp without nearing town."

"You could," Beverly told. "But it is a long way round."

"Not too far from me," he announced positively. "No towns or distilleries for me. I go round. Will you ride with me, gentlemen?"

We rode with him.

On the way I told him I expected him to supper that evening.

"With all my writing, Radford," he said, "you don't seem to get the idea. I flock by myself for the present and eat alone. If you insist I'll explain tomorrow."

Beverly and I left him to his camp supper.

Dr. Boone and Mr. Hall were a good deal taken aback upon learning that their imagined invalid had no existence and that the real Colonel Case needed neither medical assistance nor spiritual solace. We four sat for some time expressing our bewilderment.

Next morning I drove out to Case's camp. I found him sitting in his tent, the flaps of which were looped up all around. He was as pale as the day before. As I approached I saw him scrutinize me with a searching gaze, a gaze I found it difficult to analyze.

He wore his belt with the holsters and the revolver-butts showed from those same holsters. I was astonished at this. When I saw it on him the day before I had thought the belt a piece of bad taste. It might have been advisable in portions of his long ride, might have been imperatively necessary in some districts; but it seemed a pose or a stupidity to wear it so far east. Pistols were by no means unknown in our part of the world, but they were carried in the seclusion of the hip-pocket or inside the breast of one's coat, not flaunted in the face of the populace in low-hung pig-skin holsters.

Case greeted me cheerily.

"I got up too early," he stated. "I've had my breakfast and done my target practice twice over. Apparently you expect me to go with you in that buggy?"

I told him that I did.

"Come in and sit down a moment," he said in a somewhat embarrassed way. "This suggestion of our driving together is in line with your kind invitation for last night. I see I must explain somehow."

He offered me a cigar and though I seldom smoke in the morning, I took it, for I thought smoking would fill up the silences I anticipated.

He puffed a while, in fact.

"Have you ever been among feudists in the mountains?" he queried.

"More than a little," I told him.

"Likely enough then," he went on, "you know more about their ways than I do. But I saw something of them myself, before I left America. Did you ever notice how a man at either focus of a feud, the king-pin of his end of it so to speak, manifests the greatest care to avoid permitting others to expose themselves to any degree of the danger always menacing him; how such men, in the black shadow of doom, as it were, are solicitous to prevent outsiders from straying into the penumbra of the eclipse which threatens themselves?"

"I have observed that," I replied.

"Have you noticed on the other hand," he continued, "that they never show any concern for acquaintances who comprehend the situation, but pay them the compliment of assuming that they have sense enough to know what they are doing and to take care of themselves?"

"I have observed that same too," I affirmed.

He puffed again for a while.

"My father," he returned presently, "used to say that there are two ends to a quarrel, the right end and the wrong end, but that either end of a feud is the wrong end. I am one end of a feud. Wherever I am is one focus of that feud. The other focus is local and I have removed myself as far as may be from it. But I am not safe here, should not be safe anywhere on earth; doubt if I should be safe on the moon, or Mars, or a planet of some other sun, or the least conspicuous satellite of the farthest star. I am obnoxious to the hate of a power as far-reaching" . . . he took off his broad felt hat, and looked up at the canvas of the tent-roof . . . "as far-reaching as the displeasure of God.

"And as implacable," he almost whispered, "as the malice of Satan."

He looked sane, healthy and self-possessed.

"I am nowhere safe," he recommenced in his natural voice, "while my chief adversary is alive. My enemies are many and malignant enough, but their power is negligible, and their malignancy vicarious. Without fomenting their hostility would evaporate. Could I but know that my chief enemy were no more I should be free from all alarm. But while that arch-foe survives I am liable to attack at any moment, to attacks so subtle that I am at a loss to make you comprehend their possible nature, so crude that I could not make you realize the danger you are in at this instant."

I looked at him, unmoved.

"I shall say no more to you," he said. "You must do as you please. If you regard my warnings as vapors, I have at least warned you. If you are willing to share my danger, in such degree as my very neighborhood is always full of danger, you do so at your own risk. If you consider it advisable to have no more to do with me, say so now."

"I see no reason," I told him without even a preliminary puff, "why your utterances should make any difference in my treatment of you."

"I thought you would say that," he said. "But my conscience is clear."

"Shall we proceed to business?" I asked.

"There is one point more," he replied. "Have you ever been in mining camps or amid other frontier conditions?"

"Several times," I answered, "and for some time at that."

"Have you ever noticed that when two men have been mutually threatening to shoot each other at sight, pending the final settlement, neither will expose women or children to danger by being in their neighborhood or permitting them in his, if he can prevent such nearing them?"

"Such scrupulosity can be observed," I told him dryly, "nearer home than mining camps or frontier towns."

"So I have heard," he replied stiffly. "When I left America the personal encounter had not yet taken the place of the formal duel in these regions."

He puffed a bit.

"However," he continued, "it makes no difference from what part of the world you draw the illustration; it is equally in point.

The danger of being near me is a hundred times, a thousand times greater than that of running the risk of stopping a wild or random bullet. I cannot bring myself to expose innocent beings to such danger."

"How about Jeff and Cato?" I asked.

"A nigger," declared Colonel Case (and he looked all the colonel as he spoke it), "is like a dog or a horse, he shares his master's dangers as a matter of course. I speak of women and children and unsuspecting men. I am resolute to sit at no man's table, to enter no man's house, uninvited or invited. All who come to know me knowingly I shall welcome. When you bring anyone with you I shall assume that he has been forewarned. But I shall intrude upon no one."

"How then are you to inspect," I queried, "the properties I expected to show you?"

"Business," said Colonel Case, "is different. When people propose to do business they assume any and all risks. Are you afraid to assume the risk of driving me about in that buggy of yours?"

"Not a particle," I disclaimed. "Are you willing to expose the people of Brexington to these dangers on which you descant so eloquently and which I fail to comprehend?"

Colonel Case fixed me with a cold stare. He looked every inch a warrior, accustomed to dominate his environment, to command and be obeyed, impatient of any opposition, ready to flare up if disbelieved in the smallest trifle.

"Radford," he said, slowly and sternly, "I am willing to take any pains to avoid wronging anyone, I am unwilling to make myself ridiculous by attempting impossibilities."

"I see," I concluded. "Let us go."

III

As we drove through the town he said:

"This is like coming back to earth from another world. It is like a dream too. Some streets are just as they were, only the faces are unfamiliar. I almost expect to see the ghosts of thirty years ago."

I made some vague comment and as we jogged along talked of the unchanged or new owners of the houses. Then I felt him make a sudden movement beside me, and I looked round at him. He could not turn any paler than he was, yet there had been a change in his face.

"I do see ghosts," he said slowly and softly.

I followed his glance as he gazed past me. We were approaching the Kenton homestead and nearly opposite it. It had an old-fashioned classic portico with four big white columns. At the top of the steps, between the two middle columns, stood Mary Kenton, all in pink with a rose in her jetty hair. She was looking intently at us, but not at me. Case stared at her fixedly.

"Mary Kenton is the picture of her mother," I told him.

"Her very image," he breathed, his eyes steadily on her.

She continued gazing at us. Of course she knew whom I was driving. My horses were trotting slowly and when we were opposite her, she waved her hand.

"Welcome home, Cousin Cassius," she called cheerily.

Colonel Case waved his hat to her and bowed, but said nothing.

The Shelby mansion did not suit Colonel Case. What he wanted, he said, was a house at the edge of the town. When he had made his selection he bought it promptly. He had the outbuildings razed, the shrubbery torn up and the trees trimmed so that no limb hung within ten feet of the ground; above they were left untouched, tall and spreading as they were and almost interlacing with each other. The house he practically rebuilt. Its all-round veranda he had torn down and replaced by one even broader, but at the front only, facing the entrance, the only entrance he left. For he entirely closed the backway to the kitchen and side-gate to the stable, cutting instead a loop-drive around the house from the one front entrance.

Except for this stone-posted carriage-gate with the little foot-path gate beside it, he had the whole place surrounded with a fence the like of which Brexington had never seen. The posts were T-beams, of rolled steel, eight feet tall above ground, reaching six feet below it and bedded down in rammed concrete. To these was bolted a four-foot continuous, square-mesh wire fencing, the meshes not over six inches at its top and as small as two inches at the bottom, which was sunk a hand's breadth below the surface and there held by close-set clamps upon sections of gas-pipe, extending from post to post and bolted to them. Inside this mesh-fencing, as high as it reached, and above it to the top of the posts, were strung twenty strands of heavy barbed wire, the upper wires six inches apart, the lower strands closer. Inside the fence he had set a close hedge. As the plants composing it were large and vigorous when they arrived from the nursery-man, this was soon thick and strong. It was kept clipped to about three feet high. The flower-beds he abolished and from house to drive and drive to hedge soon had the whole place in well-kept turf.

Behind the house he had two outbuildings erected; at one corner a small carriage-house and stable, capable of holding two vehicles and three horses; at the other a structure of about the same size as the stable, half wood-shed and half hen-house.

Watching the carpenters at work on this and regarding the nine-days-wonder of a fence, several negroes stood in talk one day as I passed. They were laughing and I overheard one say:

"Mahs'r Case shuah ain' gwine tuh lose no hains awf he roos'. Mus be gwine tuh be powerful fine hains he gwine raise. He sutt'nly mus' sot stoah by he hains. He sutt'nly dun tuk en' spain' cunnsdd'ble money awn he faince."

The interior of the house was finished plainly and furnished sparingly. The very day it was ready for occupancy he moved into it and ceased his camp life. Besides Cato, an old negro named Samson acted as cook, and another named Pompey as butler. These three made up all his household. Jeff was quartered in a room over the carriage-house.

Before his residence was prepared and while he was still camping he bought Shelby Manor.

"Nothing like obliging one's cousins," he said. He also bought two adjoining farms, forming a property of over a thousand acres. This he proceeded to equip as a stud farm, engaging a competent manager; refitting the house for him and the two smaller houses for his assistants, the overseer and farmer; abolishing the old outbuildings; putting up barns and stables in the most lavish fashion. He bought many blooded mares and created an establishment on a large scale.

* * *

About two miles out of town on the road past his house, nearly half way to Shelby Manor, he bought a worthless little farm of some forty acres. This he had fenced and put in grass, except a small garden-patch by the house, which he had made snug and where he had installed an elderly negro couple as caretakers. The old man had formerly belonged to the Colonel's father, and was named Erastus Everett. All the other buildings he had removed, except a fair-sized hay barrack standing on a knoll near the middle of the largest field. This he had new roofed and repaired and given two coats of shingle stain, moss green on the roof and weather gray on the sides. In it he had ranked up some forty cords of fat pine wood. Near the house was built a small stable, which harbored the two mules Case allowed uncle Rastus.

Besides his he had built a number of low sheds, opening on spaces enclosed with wire netting. Soon the enclosures swarmed with dogs, not blooded dogs, but mere mongrel curs. Not a small dog among them, all were big or fairly large. Uncle Rastus drove about the country in his big close-covered wagon, behind his two mules. Wherever he found an utterly worthless dog of some size he bought it, if it could be had cheap, and turned it in with the rest. Before a year had passed uncle Rastus had more than a hundred no-account brutes to feed and care for.

Colonel Case was not a man to whom anyone, least of all a stranger, would put a direct unsolicited question. Uncle Rastus was more approachable. But the curious gained little information from him.

"Mahs'r Cash ain' tole muh wuff'r he keepin' awl dees yeah houns. He ain' spoke nuffin. He done tole muh tur buy 'um, he done tole muh to feed 'um. Ahze buyed 'um en' Ah feeds 'um."

Once he had established himself Case lived an extremely regular life. He rose early, breakfasted simply, and whatever the weather, drove out to Shelby Manor. He never rode in the forenoon. At his estate he had a pistol-range and a rifle-range. He spent nearly an hour each morning in pistol and rifle practice. He never used a shot-gun, but shot at targets, running marks, and trap-sprung clay-pigeons with both repeating rifle and revolver. He always carried his two repeating rifles with him, and brought them back with him. Several times, when I happened to accompany him, I watched him shoot.

The first time I was rather surprised. He emptied the chambers of one revolver, made some fifty shots with it, cleaned it, replaced the six cartridges which had been in it, and put it in its holster. Then he did the like with the other. Then he similarly emptied the magazines of one of his rifles, made some fifty shots with that, cleaned it and reloaded it with the original cartridges. So with the second rifle.

I asked him why he did so.

"The cartridges I go about with," he said, "are loaded with silver bullets. I can't afford to fire away two or three pounds of silver every day. Lead keeps my hand in just as well as silver, and the silver bullets are always ready for an emergency."

Against such an imaginary emergency, I conceived he wore his belt and kept his two rifles always at hand.

After his target practice he talked with his manager, looked over the place, discussed his stock or watched his jockeys exercising their mounts, for an hour or two. Once a week or so on his way back to town he stopped to inspect uncle Rastus' charges, and investigate his doings. His early lunch was almost as simple as his breakfast. After his lunch he slept an hour or more. Later he took a long ride, seldom toward Shelby Manor. Always, both in going and in returning, he rode past Judge Kenton's mansion. At first his hour of starting on his ride varied. Before many days he so timed his setting forth as to pass the Kenton house when Mary was likely to be at her window, and his riding homeward when she was likely to be on the portico. After a time she was sure to be at her window when he passed and on the portico when he repassed, and his departure and return occurred with clock-work regularity. When she was at her window, they never gave any sign of mutual recognition, but when she was on the portico she waved her hand to him and he his hat to her.

Towards dusk in summer, after lamp-light in winter, he ate a deliberate dinner. It never seemed to make a particle of difference to him how early he went to bed or how late, or whether he went to bed at all. He was quite capable of sitting all night at cards if the game was especially interesting. Yet he never made a habit of late hours. He was an inveterate card-player, but play at his house generally ceased before midnight and often much earlier. He could drink all night long, four fingers deep and often, and never seem the worse for it. Yet it was very seldom he did so. Habitually he drank freely after dinner, but no effects of liquor were ever visible on him. His liquors were the best and always set out in abundance. His cigars were as good as his liquors and spread out in similar profusion. His wines at dinner were unsurpassable and numerous. The dinners themselves could not have been beaten. Uncle Samson was an adept at marketing and a superlative cook. Pompey was an ideal butler. They seemed always ready to serve dinner for their master alone without waste or for a dozen more also without any sign of effort or dismay. As Case made welcome to his dinner table as to his card table anyone who happened to drop in, he had no lack of guests. All the bachelors of Brexington flocked to him as a matter of course. The heads of families were puzzled. One after another they invited him to their houses. His refusals were courteous but firm: for explanations he referred them to me. Most of them accepted my dilution of his utterances and acquiesced in his lopsided hospitality. One or two demurred and laid special siege on him. Particularly Judge Kenton would not be denied. When he was finally convinced that Colonel Case would not respond to any invitation, he declared his resolution not to cross Case's threshold until his several visits there were properly acknowledged by a return call at his house. Intercourse between him and Case thereupon ceased. Judge Kenton, however, was alone in his punctilious attitude. Everybody else frequented Case's house and table. His house indeed became a sort of informal club for all the most agreeable men of the town and neighborhood. It was not mere creature comforts or material attractions which drew them there, but the very real charm of the host. Even while he was tenting, before the house was ready for occupancy, he had made friends, according to their degree, with every man in and about Brexington, white or black. Everybody knew him, everybody liked him, everybody wondered at him.

IV

Case was in fact the most discussed man in our region of the world. Some called him a lunatic, dwelling especially on his dog-ranch, as he called it, and his everlasting pig-skin belt with the holstered revolvers, without which he was never seen at any hour of the day, by anyone. It was difficult for his most enthusiastic partisans to assign any colorable reason why he should maintain a farm for the support of some two hundred totally worthless dogs. Their worthlessness was the main point which uncle Rastus made in buying them. Often he rejected a dog proffered for little or almost nothing.

"No seh," he would say. "Dat ar dawg ain' no 'count enuff. Mah'sr Cash he dun awdah muh dat Ah ain' buy no dawg wut ain' pintedly no 'count. Dey gotter be no 'count. Ah ain' buyin' um lessen dey's wuffless en' onery."

Scarcely less easy was it to defend his wearing his twin revolvers even with dinner-dress, for he put on evening dress for dinner, with the punctiliousness of an Englishman in the wilderness, put it on as often as he dined and yet wore it so naturally and unobtrusively, that no more than the incongruous belt did it embarrass the guests he made at home in any kind of clothes they happened to be wearing. His admirers pointed to this as a kind of exploit, as something of which only a perfectly sane and exceptionally fine man could be capable. They adduced his clear-headed business sense, his excellent judgment on matters pertaining to real estate, his knowledge of horseflesh, his horsemanship, his coolness, skill and exceptional good temper at cards, as cumulative proofs of his perfect sanity. They admitted he was peculiar on one or two points but minimized these as negligible eccentricities. They were ready to descant to any extent on his personal charm, and this indeed all were agreed upon. To attract visitors by good dinners, good liquors, good cigars and endless card playing was easy. To keep his visitors at their ease and entertained for hours with mere conversations while seated on his veranda, was no small feat in itself and a hundred times a feat when their host obtruded upon them the ever visible butts of his big revolvers and kept a repeating rifle standing against each jamb of his front door. This tension of perpetual preparedness for an imminent attack might well have scared away everybody and left Case a hermit. It did nothing of the kind. It was acquiesced in at first, later tacitly accepted and finally ignored altogether. With it was ignored his strange complexion. I had myself puzzled over this: after long groping about in my mind I had realized what it reminded me of, and I found others who agreed with me in respect to it. It was like the paleness one sees for the half of a breath on the face of a strong, healthy man when in sudden alarm, astonishment or horror his blood flows momently back to his heart. Under such stress of unforeseen agitation a normal countenance might exhibit that hue for a fraction of a second; on Case's visage it was abiding, like the war paint on an armor-clad, drab-gray and dreary. Yet it produced no effect of gloom in his associates. He not only did not put a damper upon high spirits but diffused an atmosphere of gaiety and good fellowship.

And he did so not only in spite of his ever-visible weapons and of his uncanny, somber complexion, but also in spite of the strange and daunting habit of his eyes. I had seen something like it once and again in a frontiersman who knew that his one chance of surviving his enemy was to shoot first and who expected the crucial instant at any moment. I had watched in more than one town the eyes of such an individual scan each man who approached with one swift glance of inquiry, of keen uncertainty dying instantly into temporary relief. Such was the look with which Case invariably met me. It had in it hesitation, doubt, and, as it were, an element of half-conscious approach to alarm. It was as if he said to himself:

"Is that Radford? It looks like him. If it is Radford, all right. But is it really Radford after all?"

I grew used in time to this lightning scrutiny of me every time he caught sight of me. His other friends grew used to it. But it was the subject of endless talk among us. His eyes had an inexplicable effect on every one. And not the least factor in their mystery was that he bestowed this glance not only upon all men, but upon women, children, animals, birds, even insects. He regarded a robin or a butterfly with the same flash of transient interest which he bestowed upon a horse or a man. And his eyes seemed to keep him cognizant of every moving thing before, behind and above him. Nothing living which entered his horizon seemed to escape his notice.

Beverly remarked:

"Case is afraid of something, is always looking for something. But what the devil is it he is looking for? He acts as if he did not know what to expect and suspected everything."

Dr. Boone said:

"Case behaves somewhat as if he were suffering from a delusion of persecution. But most of the symptoms are conspicuously absent. I am puzzled like the rest of you."

The effect upon strangers of this eerie quality of Case's vision was by no means pleasant. Yet his merest acquaintances soon became used to it and his intimates ceased to notice it at all. His personal charm made it seem a trifle. Night after night his card room was the scene of jollity. His table gathered the most desirable comrades the countryside afforded. Evening after evening his cronies sat in the comfortable wicker chairs on his broad veranda, little Turkish tables bearing decanters and cigars set among them, Colonel Case the center and life of the group.

He talked easily and he talked well. To start him talking of the countries he had seen was not easy, but, once he began, his stories of Egypt and Abyssinia, of Persia and Burmah, of Siam and China were always entertaining. Very seldom, almost never did he tell of his own experiences. Generally he told of having heard from others the tales he repeated, even when he spoke so that we suspected him of telling events in which he had taken part.

It was impossible to pin him down to a date, almost as hard to elicit the definite name of a locality. He gave minute particulars of incidents and customs, but dealt in generalities as to place and time. Especially he was strong in local superstitions and beliefs.

He told countless tales, all good, of crocodiles and ichneumons in Egypt, gazelles and ghouls in Persia, elephants and tigers in Burmah, deer and monkeys in Siam, badgers and foxes in China and sorcerers and enchanters everywhere. He spoke of the last two in as matter-of-fact a tone as of any of the others.

He told legends of the contests of various Chinese sages and saints, with magicians and wizards; of the malice and wiles of these wicked practitioners of somber arts; of the sort of supersense developed by the adepts, their foes, enabling them to tell of the approach or presence of a sorcerer whatever disguise he assumed, even if he had the power of making himself invisible.

Several legendary anecdotes turned on this point of the invisibility of the wicked enemy and the prescience of his intended victim.

One was of a holy man said to have lived in Singan Fu about the time of the crusades. Knowing that he was threatened with the vengeance of a wizard, he provided himself with a sword entirely of silver, since the flesh of a wizard was considered proof against all baser metals. He likewise had at hand a quantity of the ashes of a sacred tree.

While seated in his study he felt an inimical presence. He snatched up his silver blade, stood upon the defensive and shouted a signal previously agreed upon. Hearing it his servants locked the doors of the house and rushed in with boxes of the sacred ashes. Scattering it on the floor, they could see on the fresh ashes the footsteps of the wizard. One of the servants, according to his master's instructions, had brought a live fowl. Slicing off its head he waved the spouting neck towards the air over the footprints. According to Chinese belief fowls' blood has the magical property of disclosing anyone invisible through incantation. In fact where the blood drops fell upon the wizard, they remained visible, there appeared a gory eye and cheek. Slashing at his revealed enemy the sage slew him with the silver sword, after which his body was with all speed burned to ashes. This was the invariable ending of all his similar tales.

Stories like this Case delighted in, but beyond this penchant for the weird and occult, for even childish tales of distant lands, his conversation in general showed no sign of peculiarity or eccentricity. Only once or twice did he startle us. Some visitors to town were among the gathering on his veranda and fell into a discussion of the contrasting qualities of Northerners and Southerners. Inevitably the discussion degenerated into a rather acrimonious and petty citation of all the weak points of each section and a rehash of all the stale sneers at either. The wordy Alabamian who led one side of the altercation descanted on the necessary and inherited vileness of the descendants of the men who burnt the Salem witches. Case had been listening silently. Then he cut in with an emphatic, trenchant directness unusual to him.

"Witches," he announced, "ought to be burned always and everywhere."

We sat a moment startled and mute.

The Alabamian spoke first.

"Do you believe in witches, Sir?" he asked.

"I do," Case affirmed.

"Ever been bewitched?" the Alabamian queried. He was rather young and dogmatically assertive.

"Do you believe in Asiatic cholera?" Case queried in his turn.

"Certainly, Sir," the Alabamian asserted.

"Ever had it?" Case inquired meaningly.

"No," the Alabamian admitted. "No, Sir, never."

"Ever had yellow fever?" Case questioned him.

"Never, Sir, thank God," the Alabamian replied fervently.

"Yet I'll bet," Case hammered at him, "that you would be among the first to join a shot-gun quarantine if an epidemic broke out within a hundred miles of you. You have never had it, but you believe in it with every fiber of your being.

"That's just the way with me. I've never been bewitched, but I believe in witchcraft. Belief in witchcraft is like faith in any one of a dozen fashionable religions, not a subject for argument or proof, but a habit of mind. That's my habit of mind. I won't discuss it, but I've no hesitation about asserting it.

"Witchcraft is like leprosy, both spread among nations indifferent to them, both disappear before unflinching severity. The horror of both among our ancestors abolished both in Europe and kept them from gaining a foothold in this country. Both exist and flourish in other corners of the world, along with other things undreamed of in some complacent philosophies. Leprosy can be repressed only by isolation, the only thing that will abolish witchcraft is fire, fire, Sir."

That finished that discussion. No one said another word on the subject. But it started a round of debates on Case's mental condition, which ran on for days, everywhere except at Case's house, and which brought up all that could be said about personal aloofness, pensioned dogs, exposed revolvers and pig-skin belts.

V

The mellow fall merged into Indian Summer. The days were short and the afternoons chill. The weather did not permit the evening gatherings on Case's veranda. No more did it allow

Mary Kenton to sit in her rocker between the two left-hand columns of the big white portico. Yet it was both noticeable and noticed that she never failed to step out upon that portico, no matter what the weather, each afternoon; that in the twilight or in the late dusk the wave of her hand and the sweep of the horseman's big, broad-brimmed felt hat answered each other unfailingly.

The coterie of Case's chums, friends and hangers-on gathered then mostly around the generous log-fire in his ample drawing-room, when they were not in the card-room, the billiard-room or at table. I made one of that coterie frequently and enjoyed my hours there with undiminished zest. When I dined there I habitually occupied the foot of the long table, facing Case at the head. The hall door of the dining-room was just at my right hand.

One evening in early December I was so seated at the foot of the table. The weather had been barely coolish for some days, the skies had been clear and everything was dry. That night was particularly mild. We had sat down rather early and it was not yet seven o'clock when Pompey began to pass the cigars. No one had yet lit up. Someone had asked Case a question and the table was still listening for his answer. I, like the rest, was looking at him. Then it all happened in a tenth, in a hundredth of the time necessary to tell it; so quickly that, except Case, no one had time to move a muscle.

Case's eyes were on his questioner. I did not see the door open, but I saw his gaze shift to the door, saw his habitual glance of startled uncertainty. But instead of the lightning query of his eyes softening into relief and indifference, it hardened instantaneously into decision. I saw his hand go to his holster, saw the revolver leap out, saw the aim, saw his face change, heard his explosive exclamation:

"Good God, it is!" saw the muzzle kick up as the report crushed our ear drums and through the smoke saw him push back his chair and spring up.

The rest of us were all too dazed to try to stand. Like me they all looked toward the door.

There stood Mary Kenton, all in pink, a pink silk opera cloak half off her white shoulders, a single strand of pale coral round her slender throat, a pink pompom in her glossy hair. She was standing as calmly as if nothing had happened, her arms hidden in the cloak, her right hand holding it together in front. Her rings sparkled on her fingers as her breast-pin sparkled on her low corsage.

"Cousin Cassius," she said, "you have a theatrical way of receiving unexpected visitors."

"Good God, Mary," he said. "It is really you. I saw it was really you just in time."

"Of course it is really I," she retorted. "Whom or what did you think it really was?"

"Not you," he answered thickly. "Not you."

His voice died away.

"Now you know it is really I," she said crisply, "you might at least offer me a chair."

At that the spell of our amazement left us and we all sprang to our feet.

She seated herself placidly to the right of the fireplace.

"I hear your port is excellent," she said laughingly.

Before Case could hand her the glass she wavered a little in the chair, but a mere swallow revived her.

"I had not anticipated," she said, "so startling a reception."

We stood about in awkward silence.

"Pray as your guests to be seated, Cousin Cassius," she begged. "I did not mean to disturb your gaiety."

We took our chairs, but those on her side of the table were turned outward toward the fireplace, where Case stood facing her.

"I owe you an explanation," she said easily. "Milly Wilberforce is staying with me and she bet me a box of Maillard's that I would not pay you a call. As I never take a dare, as the weather is fine, and as we have all your guests for chaperons, I thought a brief call between cousins could do no harm."

"It has not," said Case fervently; "but it very nearly did. And now will you let me escort you home? The Judge will be anxious about you."

"Papa doesn't know I am here, of course," she said. "When he finds out, I'll quiet him. If you won't come to see me, at least I have once come to see you."

Case held the door wide for her, shut it behind him, and left us staring at the bullet hole in the door frame.

※ ※ ※

One morning of the following spring Case was driving me townward from Shelby Manor, when, not a hundred feet in front of us, Mary Kenton's buggy entered the pike from a cross-road. As it turned, mare, vehicle and all went over sideways with a terrific crash. Mary must have fallen clear, for the next instant she was at the mare's head.

Case did succeed in holding his fiery colts and in pulling them to a stand-still alongside the wreck, but it was all he could do. I jumped out, meaning to take the colts' bits and let Case help Mary. But she greeted me imperiously.

"Cousin Jack, please come sit on Bonnie's head."

I took charge of Bonnie in my own fashion and she stood up entirely unhurt.

"How on earth did you come to do it, Mary?" Colonel Case wondered, for she was a perfect horsewoman.

"Accidents will happen," she answered lightly, "and I am glad of this one. You have really spoken to me, and that is worth a hundred smashes."

"But I wrote to you," he protested. "I wrote to you and explained."

"One letter," she sniffed contemptuously. "You should have kept on, you silly man, I might have answered the fifth or sixth or even the second."

He stared at her and no wonder, for she was fascinatingly coquettish.

"I don't mind Jack a bit, you know," she went on. "Jack is my loyal knight and unfailing partisan. He keeps my secrets and does everything I ask of him. For instance, he will not demur an atom now when I ask him to throw Bonnie's harness into the buggy and ride her to town for me.

"You see," she smiled at him dazzlingly, "another advantage of my upset is that the buggy is so smashed that you cannot decently refuse to drive me home."

"But Mary," he protested, "I explained fully to you."

"You didn't really expect me to believe all that fol-de-rol?" she cried. "Suppose I did, I don't see any dwergs around, and if all Malebolge were in plain sight I'd make you take me anyhow."

Inevitably he did, but that afternoon their daily ceremony of hand-wave from the portico and hat-wave from horseback was resumed and was continued as their sole intercourse.

VI

It was full midsummer when a circus came to Brexington. Case and I started for a ride together on the afternoon of its arrival, passed the tents already raised and met the procession on its way through town from the freight yard of the railroad. We pulled our horses to one side of the street and sat watching the show.

There were Cossacks and cowboys, Mexican vaqueros and Indians on mustangs. There were two elephants, a giraffe, and then some camels which set our mounts snorting and swerving about. Then came the cages, one of monkeys, another of parrots, cockatoos and macaws, others with wolves, bears, hyenas, a lion, a lioness, a tiger, and a beautiful leopard.

Case made a movement and I heard a click. I looked round and beheld him with his revolver cocked and pointed at the leopard's cage. He did not fire but kept the pistol aimed at the cage until it was out of range. Then he thrust it back into its holster and watched the fag-end of the procession go by. All he said was:

"You will have to excuse me, Radford, I have urgent business at home."

Towards dusk Cato came to me in great agitation.

"Mahs'r Cash done gone off'n he haid," he declared. "He shuah done loss he sainsus." I told him to return home and I would stroll up there casually.

I found Case in the woodshed, uncle Rastus with him. Hung by the hind legs like new-slaughtered hogs were a dozen of the biggest dogs of which Rastus had had charge. Their throats were cut and each dripped into a tin pail. Rastus, his ebony face paled to a sort of mud-gray, held a large tin pail and a new white-washer's brush.

Case greeted me as usual, as if my presence there were a matter of course and he were engaged upon nothing out of the common.

"Uncle," he said, "I judge those are about dripped out. Pour it all into the big pail."

He took the brush from Rastus, who followed him to the gate.

There Case dipped the brush into the blood and painted a broad band across the gravel of the drive and the flagstones of the footpath. He proceeded as if he were using lime white-wash to mark off a lawn-tennis court in the early days of the game, when wet markers were not yet invented and dry markers were still undreamed of. He continued the stripe of blood all round his place, just inside the hedge. He made it about three inches wide and took great pains to make it plain and heavy.

When he had come round to the entrance again he went over the stripe on the path and drive a second time. Then he straightened up and handed the brush to Rastus.

"Just enough," he remarked. "I calculated nicely."

I had so far held my tongue. But his air of self-approval, as if in some feat of logic, led me to blurt out:

"What is it for?"

"The Chinese," said Case, "esteem dogs' blood a defense against sorcery. I doubt its efficacy, but I know of no better fortification."

No reply seemed expected and I made none.

That evening I was at Case's, with some six or seven others. We sat indoors, for the cloudy day had led up to a rainy evening. Nothing unusual occurred.

Next day the town was plastered with posters of the circus company offering five hundred dollars reward for the capture of an escaped leopard.

Cato came to my office just as I was going out to lunch.

"Mahs'r Cash done gone conjuhin' agin," he announced.

I found out that a second batch of dogs had been brought in by uncle Rastus in his covered wagon behind his unfailing mules, had been butchered like the former convoy and the band of blood gone over a second time. Case had not gone outside that line since he first made it, no drive to Shelby Manor that morning.

The day was perfect after the rain of the day before, and the bright sunlight dried everything. The evening was clear and windless with a nearly full moon intensely bright and very high. Practically the whole population went to the circus.

Beverly and I dined at Case's. He had no other guests, but such was his skill as a host that our dinner was delightfully genial. After dinner the three of us sat on the veranda.

The brilliance of the moonlight on and through the unstirred trees made a glorious spectacle and the mild, cool atmosphere put us in just the humor to enjoy it and each other. Case talked quietly, mostly of art galleries in Europe, and his talk was quite as charming and entertaining as usual. He seemed a man entirely sane and altogether at his ease.

We had been on the veranda about half an hour and in that time neither team nor pedestrian had passed. Then we saw the figure of a woman approaching down the middle of the roadway from the direction of the country. Beverly and I caught sight of her at about the same instant and I saw him watching her as I did, for she had the carriage and bearing of a lady and it seemed strange that she should be walking, stranger that she should be alone, and strangest that she should choose the road instead of the footpath which was broad and good for half a mile.

Case, who had been describing a carved set of ivory chessmen he had seen in Egypt, stopped speaking and stared as we did. I began to feel as if I ought to recognize the advancing figure, it seemed unfamiliar and yet familiar too in outline and carriage, when Beverly exclaimed:

"By Jove, that is Mary Kenton."

"No," said Colonel Case in a combative, resonant tone like the slow boom of a big bell. "No, it is not Mary Kenton."

I was astonished at the animus of his contradiction and we intensified our scrutiny. The nearing girl really suggested Mary Kenton and yet, I felt sure, was not she. Her bearing made me certain that she was young, and she had that indefinable something about her which leads a man to expect that a woman will turn out to be good looking. She walked with a sort of insolent, high-stepping swing.

When she was nearly opposite us Case exclaimed in a sort of chopped-off, guttural bark:

"Nay, not even in that shape, foul fiend, not even in that."

The tall, shapely young woman turned just in front of the gateway and walked towards us.

"I think," said Beverly, "the lady is coming in."

"No," said Colonel Case, again with that deep, baying reverberation behind his voice. "No, not coming in."

The young woman laid her hand on the pathway gate and pushed it open. She stepped inside and then stopped, stopped suddenly, abruptly, with an awkward half-stride, as if she had run into an obstacle in the path, a low obstruction like a wheelbarrow. She stood an instant, looked irresolutely right and left, and then stepped back and shut the gate. She turned and started across the street, fairly striding in a sort of incensed, wrathful haste.

My eyes, like Beverly's, were on the figure in the road. It was only with a sort of sidelong vision that I felt rather than saw Case whip a rifle from the door jamb to his shoulder and fire. Almost before the explosion rent my ear drums I saw the figure in the roadway crumple and collapse vertically. Petrified with amazement I was frozen with my stare upon the huddle on the macadam. Beverly had not moved and was as dazed as I. My gaze still fixed as Case threw up a second cartridge from the magazine and fired again, I saw the wretched heap on the piking leap under the impact of the bullet with the yielding quiver of totally dead flesh and bone. A third time he fired and we saw the like. Then the spell of our horror broke and we leapt up, roaring at the murderer.

With a single incredibly rapid movement the madman disembarrassed himself of his rifle and held us off, a revolver at each of our heads.

"Do you know what you have done?" we yelled together.

"I am quite sure of what I have done," Case replied in a big calm voice, the barrels of his pistols steady as the pillars on the veranda. "But I am not quite so clear whether I have earned five hundred dollars reward. Will you gentlemen be kind enough to step out into the street and examine that carcass?"

Woodenly, at the muzzles of those unwavering revolvers, we went down the flagged walk side by side, moving in a nightmare dream.

I had never seen a woman killed before and this woman was presumably a lady, young and handsome. I felt the piking of the roadway under my feet, and looked everywhere, except downward in front of me.

I heard Beverly give a coughing exclamation:

"The leopard!"

Then I looked, and I too shouted:

"The leopard!"

She lay tangible, unquestionable, in plain sight under the silver moonrays with the clear black shadows of the maple leaves sharp on her sleek hide.

Gabbling our excited astonishment we pulled at her and turned her over. She had six wounds, three where the bullets entered and three where they came out, one through spine and breast-bone and two through the ribs.

We dropped the carcass and stood up.

"But I thought . . ." I exclaimed.

"But I saw . . ." Beverly cried.

"You gentlemen," thundered Colonel Case, "had best not say what you saw or what you thought you saw."

We stood mute, looking at him, at each other, and up and down the street. No one was in sight. Apparently the circus had so completely drained the neighborhood that no one had heard the shots.

Case addressed me in his natural voice:

"If you will be so good, Radford, would you oblige me by stepping into my house and telling Jeff to fetch the wheelbarrow. I must keep watch over this carrion."

There I left him, the two crooked revolvers pointed at the dead animal.

Jeff, and Cato with him, brought the wheelbarrow. Upon it the two negroes loaded the warm, inert mass of spotted hide and what it contained. Then Jeff lifted the handles and taking turns they wheeled their burden all the way to uncle Rastus', Case walking on one side of the barrow with his cocked revolvers, we on the other, quite as a matter of course.

Jeff trundled the barrow out to the hay barrack on the knoll. He and Cato and uncle Rastus carried out cord-wood until they had an enormous pile well out in the field. Then they dug up a barrel of kerosene from near one corner of the barrack. When the leopard had been placed on the top of the firewood they broached the barrel and poured its contents over the carcass and its pyre. When it was set on fire Case gave an order to Jeff, who went off. We stood and watched the pyre burn down to red coals. By that time Jeff had returned from Shelby Manor with a double team.

Case let down the hammers of his revolvers, holstered them, unbuckled his belt and threw it into the dayton.

Never had we suspected he could sing a note. Now he started "Dixie" in a fine, deep baritone and we sang that and other rousing songs all the way home. When we got out of the dayton he walked loungingly up the veranda steps, his belt hanging over his arm. He took the rifles from the door jamb.

"I have no further use for these trusty friends," he said. "If you like, you may each have one as a souvenir of the occasion. My defunct pistols and otiose belt I'll even keep myself."

Next morning as I was about to pass Judge Kenton's house I heard heavy footsteps rapidly overtaking me. Turning I saw Case, not in his habitual gray clothes and broad-rimmed semi-sombrero, but wearing a soft brown felt hat, a blue serge suit, set off by a red necktie and tan shoes. He was conspicuously beltless.

"You might as well come with me, Radford," he said. "You will probably be best man later anyhow."

We found Judge Kenton on his porch, and Mary, all in pink, with a pink rose in her hair, seated between her father and her pretty step-mother.

"I sent Jeff with a note," Case explained as we approached the steps, "to make sure of finding them."

After the greetings were over Case said:

"Judge, I am a man of few words. I love your daughter and I ask your permission to win her if I can."

"You have my permission, Suh," the Judge answered.

Case rose.

"Mary," he said, "would you walk with me in the garden, say to the grape arbor?"

When they returned Mary wore a big ruby ring set round with diamonds. Her color was no bad match for the ruby. And, beyond a doubt, Case's cheeks showed a trace of color too.

"Father," Mary said as she seated herself, "I am going to marry Cousin Cassius."

"You have my blessing, my dear," the Judge responded. "I am glad of it."

"Everybody will be glad, I believe," said Mary. "Cassius is glad, of course, and he is glad of two other things. One is that he feels free to dine with us tonight, he has just told me so.

"The other" (a roguish light sparkled in her eyes) "he has not confessed. But I just know that, next to marrying me, the one thing in all this world that makes him gladdest is that now at last he feels at liberty to see a horse race and go to the races every chance he gets."

In fact, when they returned from their six-months' wedding tour, they were conspicuous at every race meeting. Case's eyes had lost their restlessness and his cheeks showed as healthy a coloring as I ever saw on any human being.

It might be suggested that there should be an explanation to this tale. But I myself decline to expound my own theory. Mary never told what she knew, and her husband, in whose after life there has been nothing remarkable as far as I know, has never uttered a syllable.

The Song of the Sirens

I FIRST caught sight of him as he sat on the wharf. He was seated on a rather large seaman's chest, painted green and very much battered. He wore gray, his shirt was navy-blue flannel, his necktie a flaring red bandana handkerchief knotted loosely under the ill-fitting lop-sided collar, his hat was soft, gray felt and he held it in his hands on his knees. His hair was fine, straight and lightish, his eyes china-blue, his nose straight, his skin tanned. His features were those of an intelligent face, but there was in it no expression of intelligence, in fact no expression at all. It was this absence of expression that caught my eye. His face was blank, not with the blankness of vacuity, but with the insensibility of abstraction. He sat there amid the voluble negro loafers, the hurrying stevedores, the shouting wharf-hands, the clattering tackles, the creaking shears and all the hurry and bustle of unloading or loading four vessels, as imperturbable as a bronze statue of Buddha in meditation. His gaze was fixed unvaryingly straight before him and he seemed to notice and observe more distant objects; the larger panorama of moving craft in the harbor, the fussy haste of the scuttling tugboats tugging nothing, the sullen reluctance of the urged scows, the outgoing and incoming pungies and schooners, the interwoven pattern they all formed together, the break in it now and again from the dignified passage of a towed bark or ship or from the stately progress of a big steamer. Of all this he seemed aware, but of what went on about him he seemed not only unaware but unconscious, with an impassivity not as if intentionally aloof nor absorbingly preoccupied but as if utterly unconscious or totally insensible to it all. During my long, fidgety wait that first morning I watched him at intervals a good part of the time. Once a pimply, bloated boarding-master, patrolling the wharf, stopped full in front of him, caught his eye and exchanged a few words with him, otherwise no one seemed to notice him, and he scarcely moved, bare-headed all the while in the June sunlight. When I was at last notified that the *Medorus* would not sail that day, went over her side, and left the pier, I saw him sitting as when I first caught sight of him.

Next morning I found him in almost the same spot, in precisely the same attitude, and with the same demeanor. He might have been there all night.

Soon after I reached the *Medorus* the second morning the bloated boarding-master came on board with that rarity, a native American seaman. I was sitting on the cabin-deck by the saloon-skylight, Griswold on one side of me and Mr. Collins on the other. Captain Benson, puffy, pasty-faced and shifty-eyed, was sitting on the booby-hatch, whistling in an exasperatingly monotonous, tuneless and meaningless fashion. As soon as the Yankee came up the companion-ladder he halted, turned to the boarding master who was following him and blurted out.

"What! Beast Benson! Me ship with Beast Benson!" And back he went down the ladder and off up the pier.

Benson said never a word, but recommenced his whistling. It was part of his undignified shiftlessness that he aired his shame on deck. Almost any captain, fool or knave or both, would have kept his cabin or sat by his saloon table. Benson advertised his helplessness to crew, loafers and passers by alike.

The boarding master walked up to Mr. Collins and said:

"You see, Sir. I can't do anything. You're lucky enough to be only two hands short for a crew and luckier to have gotten a second mate to sign. Wilson's the best I can do for first mate. He's willing and he's the only man I can get. Not another boarding-master will so much as try for you."

Mr. Collins kept his irritating set smile, his mean little eyes peering out of his narrow face, his stubby scrubbing-brush pepper-and-salt mustache bristling against his nose. He made no reply to the boarding-master but turned to Griswold.

"You're a doctor, aren't you?" he queried.

"Not yet," Griswold replied.

"Well," said Mr. Collins impatiently, "you know pretty much what doctors know?"

"Pretty much, I trust," Griswold answered cheerfully.

"Can you tell whether a man is deaf or not?" Mr. Collins pursued.

"I fancy I could," Griswold declared, gaily.

"Would you mind testing that man over there for me?" Mr. Collins jerked his thumb toward the impassive figure on the seaman's chest.

Griswold stared.

"He looks deaf enough from here," he asserted.

"Try him nearer," Mr. Collins insisted.

Griswold swung off the cabin deck, lounged over to the companion ladder, went down it leisurely and sauntered toward the seated mariner. Griswold had a taking way with him, a jaunty manner, an agreeable smile, a charming demeanor and plenty of self-confidence. He usually got on immediately with strangers. So now you could see him win at once the confidence of the man. He looked up at him with a sentient and interested personal glance. They talked some little time and then Griswold sauntered back. He did not speak but seated himself by me as before, lit a fresh cigarette and smoked reflectively.

"Is he deaf?" Mr. Collins inquired.

"Deaf is no word for it," Griswold declared, "an adder is nothing to him. I'll bet he has neither tympanum, malleus, incus nor stapes in either ear, and that both cochleas are totally ossified; that the middle ear is annihilated and the inner ear obliterated on both sides of his head. His hearing is not defective, it is abolished, non-existent. I never saw or heard of a man who impressed me as being so totally deaf."

"What did I tell you?" broke in Captain Benson from the booby-hatch.

"Benson, shut up," said Mr. Collins. Benson took it without any change of expression or attitude.

"You seemed to talk to him," Mr. Collins said to Griswold.

"He can read lips cleverly," Griswold replied. "Only once did I have to repeat anything."

"Did you ask him if he was deaf?" Mr. Collins inquired.

"I did," said Griswold, "and he told the truth instanter."

"Impressed you as truthful, did he?" Mr. Collins queried.

"Notably," said Griswold. "There is a gentlemanly something about him. He is the kind of man you respect from the first, and truthful as possible."

"You hear that, Benson?" Mr. Collins asked.

"What's truthfulness of a pitch-dark night in a gale of wind!" Benson snorted. "The man's stone deaf."

Mr. Collins flared up.

"You may take your choice of three ways," he said, "the *Medorus* tows out at noon. If you can find a first-mate to suit you by then, or if you take Wilson as first-mate, you take her out. If not, I'll find another master for her and you can find another ship."

Benson lumbered off the booby-hatch and disappeared down the cabin companion-way. The cabin-boy came up whistling, went briskly over the side, and scampered some little distance up the pier to where three boarding-masters stood chatting. One of them came back with him, three or four half sober sailors tagging after him. These he left by the deaf man's sea-chest. Its owner came aboard with him and together they went down into the cabin.

"Look here, Mr. Collins," I said, "I've half a mind to back out of this and stay ashore!"

"Why?" he queried, his little gray eyes like slits in his face.

"I hear this captain called Beast Benson, I see he has difficulty in getting a crew and before me you force him to take a deaf mute. An unwilling crew, a defective officer and an unpopular captain seem to me to make a risky combination."

"All combinations are risky at sea, as far as that goes," said Mr. Collins easily. "Most crews are unwilling and few captains popular. Benson is not half a bad captain. He always has bother getting a crew because he is economical of food with them. But you'll find good eating in the cabin. He has never had any trouble with a crew, once at sea. He is cautious, takes better care of his sails, rigging and tackle than any man I know, is a natural genius at seamanship, humoring his ship, coaxing the wind and all that. And he is a precious sharp hand to sell flour and buy coffee, I can tell you. You'll be safe with him. I should feel perfectly safe with him. I'm sorry I can't go, I can tell you."

"But the deaf mute," I persisted.

"He has good discharges," said Mr. Collins, "and is well spoken of. He's all right."

At that moment the boarding-master came out of the cabin and went over the side. Two of the sailors picked up the first-mate's chest and it was soon aboard. The two men went down into the cabin to sign articles. As they went down and as they came up I had a good look at them. One was a Mecklenburger, a lout of a hulking boy, with an ugly face made uglier by loathsome swellings under his chin. The other was a big, stout Irishman, his curly hair tousled, his fat face flushed, his eyes wild and rolling with the after-effects of a shore debauch. His eyes were notable, one bright enamel-blue, the other skinned-over with an opaque, white film. He lurched against the companion-hatch, as he came up, and half-rolled, half-stumbled forward. He was still three-quarters drunk.

The *Medorus* towed out at noon. Mr. Collins and Griswold stayed aboard till the tug cast loose, about dusk. After that we worked down the bay under our own sail. Even in the bay I was seasick and for some days I took little interest in anything. I had made some attempt to eat, but beyond calling the first-mate Mr. Wilson and the second mate Mr. Olsen, my brief stays at table had profited me little. I had brought a steamer-chair with me and lolled in it most of the daylight, too limp to notice much of anything.

I couldn't help noticing Captain Benson's undignified behavior. A merchant captain, beyond taking the sun each morning and noon and being waked at midnight by the mate just off watch to hear his report, plotting his course on his chart and keeping his log, concerns himself not at all with the management of his ship, except when he takes the wheel at the critical moment of tacking, or of box-hauling, if the wind changes suddenly, or when a dangerous storm makes it incumbent upon him to take charge continually. Otherwise he leaves all routine matters to the mate on watch. Benson transgressed sea-etiquette continually in this respect. He was forever nosing about and interfering with one or the other mate in respect to matters too small for a self-respecting captain's notice. His mates' contempt for him was plain enough, but was discreetly veiled behind silent lips, expressionless faces and far-off eyes. The men were more open and exchanged sneering glances. The captain would sit on the edge of the cabin-deck, his feet dangling over the poop-deck, and continually nag the steersman, keeping it up for hours.

"Keep her up to the wind," he would say, "keep that royal lifting."

"Aye, aye, Sir," would come from the man at the wheel.

Next moment the captain would call out:

"Let her go off, you damn fool. You'll have her aback!"

"Let her go off, Sir," the victim would reply.

Presently again Benson would snarl:

"Where are you lettin' her go to? Keep her up to the wind."

"Keep her up to the wind, Sir," would come the reply and so on in maddening reiteration.

A day or two after we cleared the capes the big one-eyed Irishman had the wheel. His name, I found afterwards, was Terence Burke and he was from Five Rivers, Canada. He had been a mariner all his life; knew most of the seas and ports of the world. He was especially proud of having been in the United States Navy and of his Civil War record. He had been one of the seamen on the *Congress* or the *Cumberland,* I forget which, and graphic were his descriptions of his sensations while the *Merrimac's* shells were tearing through the helpless ship, the men lying flat in rows on the farther side of the decks, and the six-foot live-oak splinters, deadly as the bits of shell themselves, flying murderously about as each shell burst; of how they took to their boats after dark, and reached the shore, expecting to be captured every moment; of how they saw the Ericsson's lights (Burke always called the *Monitor* the *Ericsson*) coming in from the sea, and took heart. Burke was justly proud that he had been one of the men detailed, as biggest and strongest, to work the Ericsson's guns, and that he had helped fight her big turret guns in her famous first battle.

All this about Burke I did not learn till many days later. But it was plain to be seen, even by a sea-sick land-lubber, that he was an able seaman, seasoned, competent and self-respecting. All that was manifest all over him as he stood at the wheel. Likewise it was plain that he had brought liquor aboard with him, for he was still half-drunk, and quarrelsome drunk. Even I could see that in his attitude, in his florid face, in his boiled eye. But Captain Benson did not see it when presently he came on deck and seated himself on the edge of the cabin-deck. He cocked his eye up the main-mast and presently growled.

"Let her go off."

Burke shifted the wheel a quarter of a spoke, his jaws clenched, his lips tight shut.

Benson chewed on his big quid and kept his eye aloft. Again he growled:

"Keep her up to the wind."

Burke shifted the wheel back a quarter of a spoke, again without a word.

"I'll learn ye sea-manners," Benson snarled, "I'll learn ye to repeat after me what I say. Do ye hear me?"

"Aye, aye, Sor," Burke replied, smartly enough.

Shortly Benson came at him again.

"Let her go off, you damn fool."

"Let her go off, you damn fool, Sor," Burke sang out in a rasping Celtic roar which carried to the jibboom.

It was Olsen's watch and the big Norseman was standing by the weather-rigging, his hand on one of the main shrouds. He grinned broadly, full in Captain Benson's face, and then looked away to windward. Burke was clutching the spokes as if he were ready to tear them out of the wheel. He looked fighting mad all over. Captain Benson looked aft at him, looked forward, looked aloft, and then rose and went below without a word. Henceforward he worried the steersman no more, unless it were Dutch Charlie, the big loutish boy with the ulcerated chin, or Pomeranian Emil, a timid Baltic waif. Burke and the other full-grown men he let alone.

Next day Burke looked drunker and more belligerent than ever. I noted it, even in my half-daze of flabby nauseated weakness, which subdued me so totally that not even a beautiful and novel spectacle revived me. It was just before noon. The captain and the first-mate had come on deck with their sextants to determine our latitude. The day was fine with a gentle steady breeze, a clear sky and unclouded sunlight, over all the white-capped blue waters. Smoke sighted a little before turned out to be that of a British man-of-war. Just as the captain told the man at the wheel to make it eight-bells, the man-of-war crossed our bows, all white paint and gilding, her ensign spread, flags everywhere, her band playing and her crew manning the yards. The cabin-boy said it was an English bank-holiday, and that she was bound for Bermuda. I was too flaccid to ask further or to care. I made no attempt to go below for the noon meal. I lay at length in my chair. While the captain and mates were at their dinner I could hear loud voices from the forecastle, or perhaps round the galley door. Presently the first-mate came on deck. He walked to starboard, which was to windward, and stood staring after the far off smoke of the vanished man-of-war. He was a tall, clean-built square-shouldered man, English in every detail of movement, attitude and demeanor. He interested me, for in spite of his expressionless face he looked far too intelligent for his calling. I was watching him when I was aware of Burke puffing and snorting aft along the main deck. He puffed and snorted up the port companion-ladder to the poop-deck. His face was redder than ever and his eyes redder than his face. He carried a pan of scouse or biscuit-hash or some such mess. He approached the first-mate from behind and hailed him.

"Luke at thot, Sor," he said, "uz thot fit fude fur min?"

The mate, unaware of his presence, did not move or speak.

"Luke at thot Oi say," Burke roared, "uz thot fit to fade min on?"

The mate remained immobile.

Burke gave a sort of snarling howl, hurled at the mate the pannikin, which hit him on the back of the head, its contents going all over his neck and down his collar. As he threw it Burke leaped at the officer. He whirled round before he was seized and met the attack with a short, right-hand jab on Burke's jaw. There was not enough swing in the blow to down the sailor. He clutched both lapels of the mate's open pea-jacket and pulled him forward. The force the mate had put into the blow, and the impetus it had imparted to Burke, besides his sideways wrench, took the mate half off his feet. He got in a second jab, this time with his left hand, but again too short to be effective. Both men lurched toward the booby-hatch and the inside breast-pockets of the mate's jolted jacket cascaded a shower of letters upon the deck, which blew hither and thither to port. My chair was on the cabin-deck just above the port companion-ladder. The booky man's instinct to save written paper shook me out of my lethargy. In an instant I was out of my chair, down the ladder and picking up the scattered envelopes. Not one, I think, went over-board. I saved three by the port rail and a half a dozen more further inboard. As I scrambled about from one to the other I glanced again and again at the men struggling on the other side of the booby-hatch. His short-arm jabs had pushed Burke back till he lost hold of the pea-jacket. The Irishman gathered himself for a rush, the mate squared off, in perfect form, met the rush with a left-hand upper cut on the seaman's chin, calculated his swing and planted a terribly accurate right-hand drive full in Burke's face. He went backward over the starboard companion-ladder down into the main deck.

Paying no more attention to him the mate turned to pick up his letters. He found several on the deck against the booby-hatch, and one by the break of the cabin. Then he looked about for more. I stepped unsteadily toward him and handed him those I had gathered up. In gathering them it had been impossible for me to help noting the address, and the stamps and the postmarks, which on several were English, on two or three French, on two Italian, on one German, on one Egyptian and on one Australian. The address, the same on all, was:

GEOFFREY CECIL, ESQ.
   c.o. ALEXANDER BROWN & SON
     Baltimore, Maryland,
     U. S. A.

Instinctively I turned the packet face down as I handed it to him. He took it gracefully and in his totally toneless voice said:
"Thank you very much."

As he said the words Captain Benson appeared in the cabin companion-way, his revolver in his hands. The mate in the act of stowing with his left hand the letters in his inner breast-pocket, pointed his extended index finger at the pistol.

"Put that thing away!" he commanded.

The voice was as toneless as before, but far otherwise than the blurred British evenness of his acknowledgment to me, these words rang hard and sharp. Benson took the rebuke as if he had been the mate and the other his captain, turned and shuffled fumblingly back down the companion-way. As he passed the pantry door the cabin-boy whipped out of it and popped up the companion-way to see, and the big Norse mate emerged deliberately behind him.

By this time the fat negro steward and most of the crew had come aft and gathered about the prostrate Burke.

The first-mate cleared the scouse from his neck and collar, took some tarred marline from an outside pocket of his pea-jacket, and in a leisurely way went down into the waist. He had the men turn Burke over and tie his hands behind him and his ankles together. Then he had buckets of sea-water dashed over him. Burke soon regained consciousness.

"Carry him forward and put him in his bunk," the mate commanded. "When he says he will behave cut him loose."

Captain Benson had come on deck and was standing by the booby-hatch.

"That man ought to be put in irons," he said as the mate turned.

The mate's eyes were on his face as he said it.

"He needs no irons," he retorted crisply. "Why make a mountain out of a mole-hill."

I had been hoping that I was getting used to the sea, for I was only passively uncomfortable and mildly wretched. But sometime that night it came on to blow fresh and I waked acutely sea-sick and suffering violently from horrible surging qualms in every joint. I clambered out of my bunk, struggled into some clothes and crawled across the cabin and up the after companion-way to the wheel-deck. There I collapsed at full length into four inches of warm rain water against the lee-rail. At first the baffling breeze was comforting after the stuffy cabin, smelling of stale coffee, damp sea-biscuit, prunes, oilskins and what not. But I was soon too cold, for I was vestless and coatless, and before long my teeth were chattering and I had a general chill to add to my misery. It was the first-mate's watch and coming aft on his eternal round he found me there. He at once went below and brought me not only vest and jacket but my mackintosh also. I was wet to the skin all over, but the mackintosh was gratefully warm. Forgetting that he could not hear I thanked him inarticulately, and relapsed into my shifting pond, where I slipped into oblivion, my head on the outer timber, the tearing dawn-wind across my face.

Sometime before noon I was again in my chair, as on the day before, and it was again the first-mate's watch. Again I saw Burke come aft. He was not puffing and snorting this time, but very silent. His florid face was a sort of gray-brown. His head was tied up and the bandage tilted sideways over his bad eye. He came up to port companion ladder half way from the waist of the poop-deck. There he stood holding on to the top of the rail, looking very humble and abashed. It was some time before the first-mate noticed him or deigned to notice him. In that interval Burke said a score of times:

"Mr. Wilson, Sor."

Each time he realized that he was ignored he waited meekly for a chance to try again. Finally the mate saw him speak and said:

"What is it, Burke?"

Burke began to pour out a torrent of speech.

"Come here," said the mate.

When Burke was close to him he said:

"Speak slow."

"Shure, Sor," he said, "ye wudn't go fur to call ut mut'ny whan a man's droonk an' makes a fule of himsilf?"

"Perhaps not," the mate replied, his steady eyes on Burke's face.

"Ye wudn't, I know," Burke went on confidently. "Ye see, Sor, Oi was half droonk whan Oi cum aboord. An' Oi had licker tu, more fule Oi. Mr. Olsen, he cum forrard in the dog-watch afther ye'd taat me me place, and he routed ut out an' hove ut overboord. Oi'm sobered now, Sor, with the facer ye giv me an' the cowld wather an' the slape, Oi'm sobered, an' Oi'm sobered for the voyage, Sor. Ye'll foind me quoite and rispectful, Sor. Oi was droonk, Sor, an' the scouse misloiked me, an' Oi made a fule ov mesilf. Ye'll foind me quoite and rispectful, Sor, indade ye wull. Ye wudn't go for to log me for mut'ny for makin' a fule ov mesilf, Sor, wud ye now, Sor?"

"No, Burke," said the mate. "I shall not log you. Go forward." Burke went.

Some days later I was forward on the forecastle deck, ensconced against the big canvas-covered anchor, leaning over the side and watching the foam about the cut-water and the upspurted coveys of sudden flying fish, darting out of the waves, at the edge of the bark's shadows and veering erratically in their unpredictable flights. Burke, barefoot and chewing a large quid, was going about with a tar-bucket, swabbing mats and other such devices. He approached me.

"Mr. Ferris, Sor," he said, "ye wudn't have a bit of washin' a man cud du for ye? Ye'll be strange loike aboord ship, an' this yer foorst voyge, an' ye the only passenger, an' this a sailin' ship, tu. Ye'll be thinkin' ov a hotel, Mr. Ferris, Sor. An' there's no wan to du washin' here fur ye, Sor. The naygur cuke is no manner ov use tu ye. Ye giv me anny bits ye want washed an Oi'll wash 'em nate fur ye. A man-o-war's man knows a dale ov washin' an' ye'll pay me wut ye loike. Thin I'll not be set ashore in Rio wudout a cint, Sor."

"You'll have your wages," I hazarded.

"Not with Beast Benson," he replied, "little duh ye know Beast Benson. Oi know um. Wut didn't go into me advances ull go into the shlop-chest. Oi may have a millrace or maybe tu at Rio, divil a cint moor."

This was the beginning of many chats with Burke. He told me of Five Rivers, of his life on men-of-war, of his participation in the battle between the *Merrimac* and the *Ericsson*, as he called the *Monitor*, of unholy adventures in a hundred ports, of countless officers he had served under.

"An' niver wan uz foine a gintlemin uz Mr. Willson," he would wind up. "Niver wan ov them all. Shure, he's no Willson. He ships as John Willson, Liverpool. Now all the seas knows John Willson ov Liverpool. There's thousands ov him. He's afloat all over the wurruld. He's always the same, short and curly-headed, black-haired and dark-faced, ivery John Willson is loike ivery other wan. Ivery Liverpool Portugee uz John Willson whin he cooms to soign articles. But Mr. Willson's no Dago, no Liverpool man at all. He's a gintlemin, British all over, an' a midlander at thot an' no seaman be naature at all. But he's the gintlemin. Ye saa him down me. He's the foine gintlemin. Not a midshipman or liftenant did iver Oi see a foiner gintlemin than him, and how sensible he uz. Haff the officers Oi've served under wuz lunies, sinsible on this or thot, but half luny on most things and luny all over on this or thot. But luke at Mr. Willson. Sinsible all over he uz, sinsible all thru. Luke at the discipline he huz. An' no wunder. Luke at huz oi! He cudn't du a mane thing av he wanted tu, he cudn't tell a loi av he throid, thrust me, Sor, Oi know, the min knows. It's loike byes at skule wid a tacher, or min in the army wid their orficers. You can't fule thim, they knows, an' wull they knows a man whin they say wan. Oi'd thrust Mr. Willson annywhere and annyhow. So wud anny other sailor man or anny man. Deef he uz, deef as an anchor fouled on a rock bottom. But he hears wid huz eyes, wid huz fingers, wid the hull skin av him. He's all sinse an' trewth an' koindness."

Not any other of the sailors besides Burke did I find sociable or communicative or capable, apparently, of intelligent discourse. Of the captain I saw and heard enough, and more than enough, at meal times. He deserved his nickname and I avoided him with detestation.

The second mate, a big Norwegian named Olaf Olsen, was a kindly soul, but dull and uncommunicative. He had a companionable eye, but felt neither any need of converse nor any promptings toward it. Speech he never volunteered, questions he answered monosyllabically. One Sunday indeed he so far unbent as to ask if he might borrow one of my books. I told him I doubted if any would please him. He looked them over disappointedly.

"Have you any books of Doomuses?" I queried.

"Doomus?" I repeated after him reflectively.

"You're a scholar, aren't you?" he demanded.

"I aim to be," I said.

"How do you pronounce, D-u-m-a-s?" he inquired.

"I am no Frenchman," I told him, "but Dumás is pretty close to it."

"That's what I said," he shouted, "and they all laughed at me and said 'Doomus, ye damn fool.' Have you any of his books?"

"No," I confessed and he ceased to regard me as worth borrowing from.

Not so Mr. Wilson. Before we ran into the doldrums I had found my sea-legs and exhausted the diversion of learning the name of every bit of rope, metal and wood on the bark, and also the amusement of climbing the rigging. I settled down to luxurious days of reading. The first Sunday afterwards Mr. Wilson asked for a book. I took him into my cabin and showed him my stock, one-volume poets mostly, the *Iliad*, the *Odyssey*, the *Greek Anthology*, Dante, Carducci, Goethe, Heine, Shakespeare, Milton, Shelley, Keats, Tennyson, Browning, Swinburne and Rossetti, and a dozen volumes of Hugo's lyrics. I watched him as he conned them over and thought I saw his eyes light over the Greek volumes, thought I saw in them both desire and resignation. He took Milton to begin on and afterwards borrowed my English books in series. I believe he read each entire, certainly he read much during his watches below.

At first I felt equal only to the English myself. But after we entered the glorious south-east trades, I read first Faust, then the *Divina Commedia*, then the *Iliad*, and, as our voyage neared its end gave myself up to the delights of the *Odyssey*.

Meanwhile I had come to feel very well acquainted with the deaf mate. Generally we had spent part of each fair Sunday in conversation. He read lips so instantly and accurately that if I faced the sun and he was close to me we talked almost as easily as if he had heard perfectly. The conversations were all of his making. He was not a man whom one would question, whereas he questioned me freely after he had made sure, but very delicately managed tentative beginnings, that I did not at all object to being questioned. He was a little stiff at first, half timid, half wary. When he found in me no disposition to intrude upon his reserve, and felt my manner untinged by either condescension, which I did not feel, or curiosity, which I sedulously repressed, he surrendered himself somewhat to the pleasure of exchanging ideas as an equal with a man of his own kind. We came to an unspoken understanding and talked openly on a level footing as two men of education, as two aspirants after culture. He relaxed his caution sufficiently to discard any concealment of his attainments and we discussed freely not only my books which he had borrowed but also whatever I had in hand. He never let slip anything which could tell me whether his spiritual background had been Oxford or Cambridge, yet I knew that only at one or the other could he have developed the mind he revealed.

Toward the end of the voyage our day-time chats usually began with his asking what I was reading. Even in the midst of the steady routine of his unremitting seamanly diligence he often paused by my chair on a week-day and delighted me with a brief talk which I enjoyed as much as he. Our Sunday talks came to take up much of his deck-watches. But what most delighted me was to listen to his monologues at night. Monologues they were, for I could neither interrupt nor reply. He would begin his watch by a double turn round the bark, twice speaking to the steersman, twice to the lookout. Then he would pace the poop-deck, just aft of the break, from rail to rail. As he turned by the lee rail he would throw a comprehensive glance over the whole spread of the bark's canvas, so he turned by the weather rail he would stoop down, peer out under the mainsail and sweep his eyes along the horizon on our lee bow. In the early part of our voyage I had watched him night after night keep this up for an entire watch, evenly as an automaton, breaking it only by three rounds of the vessel made precisely on the hours. After we grew to know each other he would patrol the deck only at intervals, spending most of his watch seated on the cabin-deck at the break, on the rail or on the booby-hatch, according to the position of my chair. He mostly began.

"Have you read——?" Or,

"Did you ever read——?"

Sometimes I had read the book, oftener I had not. In either case I was fascinated by his sane, cool judgment, equally trenchant and subtle, and by the even flow of his well-chosen words.

Our voyage neared its end sooner than I had anticipated. The south-east trades had been almost head winds for us and we had tacked through them close-hauled, a long leg on the port tack and a short leg on the starboard. Then the proximity of the land blurred the unalterable perpetuity of the trade winds and on a Sunday morning the wind came fair. It was my first experience of running before the wind and it intoxicated me with elation. We were out of sight of land, even of its loom, yet no longer in blue water, but over that enormous sixty-fathom shelf which juts out more than a hundred miles into the Atlantic between Bahia and Rio de Janeiro, or to be more precise, between Cannavieiras and Itapemirim. The day was bright and the sky sufficiently diversified with clouds to vary pleasingly its insistent blue, the sea a pale, golden green all torn by racing white-caps and dappled with the scurrying shadows of the clouds. The bark leapt joyously, the combers overtaking her charged in smothers of foam past each counter, the delight of merely living in such a glorious day infected even the crew.

I had my chair amidships by the break of the deck, just abaft the booby-hatch. There I was reading the *Odyssey*. The mate came and sat down by me on the booby-hatch.

"What are you reading?" he asked as usual.

"About the Sirens," I answered.

The strangest alteration came over his expression.

"Did you ever notice," he asked, "how little Homer really tells about them?"

"I was meditating on just that," I replied. "He tells only that there were two of them and that they sang. I was wondering where the popular notions of their appearance came from."

"What is your idea of the popular notions of their appearance?" he demanded.

"I have a very vague idea," I confessed. "They are generally supposed to have had bird's feet. It seems to me I have seen figures of them as so depicted on Greek tombs and coins. And there is Boecklin's picture."

"Boecklin?" he ruminated. "The Munich man? The morbid man?"

"If you choose to call him so," I assented. "I shouldn't call him morbid."

"His ugly idea is a mere personal conception," he said.

"I grant you that," I agreed, "as far as the age and the ugliness go. But the bird's feet of some kind are in the general conception."

"The general conception is wrong," he asserted, with something more like an approach to heat than anything I had seen in him.

"You seem to feel very sure," I replied.

"I do not feel," he answered, "I know."

"How do you know?" I inquired.

"I have seen them," he asserted.

"Seen them?" I puzzled.

"Yes, seen them," he asseverated. "Seen the twain Sirens under the golden sun, under the silver moon, under the countless stars; watched them singing as they are singing now!"

"What?" I exclaimed.

My face must have painted my amazement, my tone must have betrayed my startled bewilderment.

His face went scarlet and then pale. He sprang up and strode off to the weather rail. There he stood for a long time. Presently he wheeled, crossed the deck, the booby-hatch between us, and plunged down the cabin companion-way without looking at me.

He did not once meet my eye during the remaining days of the voyage, let alone approach me. He was again the impassive, inscrutable figure I had first seen him on the wharf at Baltimore.

We drew near Rio harbor, late of a perfect tropic September day, just too late to enter before sunset. In the brief tropic dusk we anchored under the black beetling shoulder of Itaipu inside the little islands of Mai and Pai. There we lay wobbling at anchor, there I watched the cloudless sky fill with the infinite multitudes of tropic stars, and gazed at the lights of the city, plainly visible through the harbor mouth between Morro de San Joao and the Sugar Loaf, twinkling brighter than the stars, not three miles away.

It must have been somewhere toward midnight when he approached me. My chair was by the rail on which he half sat, leaning down to me. So placed he began such a monologue as I had often heard from him, a monologue I could neither question nor modify, which I must listen to entire or break off completely.

"You were astonished," he said, "when I told you I had seen the Sirens, but I have. It was about six years ago, in 1879. I was in New York and I had my usual difficulty getting a ship on account of my deafness. My boarding-master tried a Captain George Andrews of the *Joyous Castle*. Andrews looked me over and said he liked me. Then he talked to me alone.

"'We are bound on an adventure,' he said, 'and I want a man who will obey orders and keep his mouth shut.'

"I told him I was his man for whatever risk. With a light mixed cargo, hardly more than half a cargo, hardly more than ballast, we cleared for Guam and a market. I was second mate. The first mate was a big Swede named Gustave Obrink. The very first meal I ever sat down to with him he made an impression on me as one of the greediest men I had ever seen. He not only ate enormously, but he seemed more than half unsatisfied after he had stuffed himself with an amazing quantity of food. He seemed to possess an unbluntable zest in the act of swallowing, an ever fresh gusto for any and every food flavor. I never saw a man relish his food so. He was an equally inordinate drinker, the quantity of coffee he could swill at one meal was amazing. Between meals he was always thirsty and drank incredible quantities of water. He was forever going to the butt by the galley door and drinking from it. And he would smack his lips over it and enjoy it as a connoisseur would a rare wine.

"When we came to choose watches Captain Andrews told us to choose a bo'sun for each watch. Obrink wanted to know why.

"The captain told him it was none of his business to ask questions. The Swede assented and backed down. We chose each an Irishman. Obrink, a tall, loose-jointed man named Pat Ryan and I, a compact stocky fellow named Mike Leary. Next day the captain had the boatswains shift their dunnage and bunk and mess aft. They were nearly as great gluttons as Obrink. They fed like animals and the subject of food and drink was the backbone of their conversation.

"The crew were hearty eaters as well and Captain Andrews catered to their likings. The *Joyous Castle* was amazingly well found, the cabin fare very abundant and varied, the forecastle food plenty and good.

"Soon after Captain Andrews was sure that the crew had entirely sobered up from their shore-drinking he called them aft one noon and announced that the steward was to serve grog daily until further notice. Naturally they cheered. After that we had a good, cheap wine daily in the cabin. When Captain Andrews had made up his mind that both mates and both boatswains were sober men he had a bottle of whisky placed on the rack over the table and kept filled. It was a curiosity to watch Obrink, Ryan and Leary patronize that bottle. Not one of the three but was cautious, not one of the three but could have drunk three times as much as he did. But the way they savored every drop they took, the affectionate satisfaction they exhibited over each nip, their eager anticipation of the next made a spectacle.

"Captain Andrews kept good discipline, we crossed the line and rounded the Cape of Good Hope without any event.

"When we were off Madagascar, Obrink, going below to get his sextant, missed it from its place. The ship was searched and Captain Andrews held an inquisition. But the sextant was never found, nor any light thrown on how it had disappeared. After that the captain alone took the observations.

"Then began a series of erratic changes of our course. We kept on dodging about for six weeks, until the crew talked of nothing else and openly said the captain was trying to lose us; certainly not one of us except the captain could have designated our position. We knew we were south of the line, not ten degrees south of it, and between 50 and 110 east longitude, but within those limits we might be almost anywhere.

"We had had nothing that could be called a storm since we left New York. When a storm struck us it was a storm indeed. When it blew over it left us making water fast. After a day and a night at the pumps, we took to our boats. Captain Andrews had the cook and the cabin boy in his boat, gave each boatswain a dory and two men, and directed us to steer north by east. When Obrink and I asked for our latitude and longitude he said that was his business. He had had the boats provisioned while we pumped and they were well supplied. We left the ship under a clear sky, the wind light after the storm, the ground-swell running heavy and slow. We lowered near sunset.

"Next morning the captain's boat had vanished, and there we were, two whale boats, two dories, twenty men in all and no idea of our position.

"The third day we sighted land. It was a low atoll, not much more than a mile across, nearly circular as far as we could make out, with the usual cocoa palms all along its ring, the surf breaking on interrupted reefs off shore, and, as we drew nearer, a channel into the lagoon facing us; as we threaded it we saw about the center of the lagoon a steep, narrow, pinkish crag, maybe fifty feet high, with a bit of flat island showing behind it. Otherwise the lagoon was unbroken. We made a landing on the atoll near the channel where we had entered, found good water, cocoanuts in abundance and hogs running wild all about, but no traces of human beings. I shot a hog and the men roasted it at once. As they ate they talked of nothing but the short rations they had had in the boats. They were all docile enough and good natured, but I believe every man of them said a dozen times how much he missed his grog, and Obrink, who had kept himself and his boat-load well in hand, said a score of times how much he would like to serve out grog, but must take care of his small supply. They talked a great deal of their hunger in the boats and of their relish for the pork; they ate an astonishing number of cocoanuts. It seemed to me that they were as greedy a set of men as could be met with.

"We cut down five palm-trees, and on supports made of the others set one horizontally as a ridge pole. Over this we stretched the sails of the whale-boats. So we camped on the sand-beach of the lagoon. I slept utterly. But when I waked I understood the men one and all to complain of light and broken sleep, of dreams, of dreaming they heard a queer noise like music, of seeming to continue to hear it after they woke. They breakfasted on another hog and on more cocoanuts.

"Then Obrink told me to take charge of the camp. I agreed. He had everything removed from his whale-boat and into it piled all the men, except a little Frenchman who went by no name save 'Frenchy,' a New Englander named Peddicord, a short red-headed Irishman named Mullen, Ryan, my boatswain and myself. Those of my watch who wanted to go I let go. They rowed off, across the lagoon toward the pink crag.

"After Obrink and the men were gone I meant to take stock of our stores. I sent Ryan with Frenchy around the atoll in one direction and Peddicord, who had sense for a foremast hand, with Mullen in the other direction. I then went over the stores. Fairly promising for twenty men they were, even a random boat-voyage in the Indian Ocean. With unlimited cocoanuts and abundant hogs they were a handsome provision, and need only be safeguarded from the omnipresent rats.

"Very shortly my four men returned, the two parties nearly at the same time. It was nearly noon, and no sign of Obrink or the boat. I had followed the whale-boat with my glass till it rounded the pink crag, a short half mile away, and had disappeared. Ryan asked my permission to take one dory and go join the rest on the crag. I readily agreed, for I had not yet cached the spirits. They rowed off as the others had.

"I made use of their welcome absence to conceal the liquor in four different places, carefully writing, in my note-book, the marks by which I was to find the caches again. I did the like with most of the ammunition. I had no idea of trying to get the upper hand of Obrink. I meant to tell him of my proceedings and expected him to approve.

"I expected the men back about two hours before sunset. No sign of them appeared. No sign of them near sunset, nor at sunset. Of course I had waited inactive till it was too late for me to venture alone on the unknown lagoon at night, and there would have been no sense in one man going to look for nineteen anyhow. Moreover I must protect our stores from hogs and rats. I turned over in my mind a thousand conjectures and slept little.

"Next morning I slung what I could of our stores from our jury-ridge-pole, out of the reach of hogs and rats, made sure that the remaining whale-boat would not get adrift, prepared the remaining dory with cocoanuts, biscuits, a keg of water, liquor, some miscellaneous stores, medicine, ammunition, repeating rifle, my glass and my compass. I carried two revolvers. I knew by this time something was wrong and I rowed warily across the placid lagoon toward the pink crag.

"As I approached it I could not but remark the peacefulness and beauty of my surroundings. The sky was deep tropic blue, the sun not an hour high, the wind a mild breeze, hardly more than rippling the lagoon, my horizon was all the tops of palms on the atoll except the one glimpse of white surf on the reef beyond the channel where we had entered.

"I rowed slowly, for the dory was heavy, and kept looking over my shoulder.

"The crag rose sheer out of deep water. It might have been granite, but I could not tell what sort of stone it was. It was very pink and nothing grew on it, not anything whatever. It was just sheer naked rock. As I rounded it I could see the flattish island beyond. There was not a tree on it and I could see nothing but the even beach of it rising some six or eight feet above high-water mark. Nothing was visible beyond the crest of the beach.

I knew our men had meant to land on it and I stopped and considered. Then I rowed round the base of the crag. Facing the flat islet was a sort of a shelf of the pink rock, half submerged, half out of the water, sloping very gently and just the place to make a landing. I rowed the dory carefully till its bottom grated on the flat top of this shelf, the bow in say a foot of water, the stern over water maybe sixty fathom deep, for I could see no bottom to its limpid blue. I stepped out and drew the dory well up on the shelf. Then I essayed to climb the crag. I succeeded at once, but it was none too easy and I had no leisure to look behind me till I reached the top. Once on the fairly flat top, which might have been thirty feet across, I turned and looked over the islet.

"Then I sat down heavily and took out my flask. I took a big drink, shut my eyes, said a prayer, I think, and looked again. I saw just what I had seen before.

"There was about a ship's-length of water between the crag and the islet, which might have been four ships'-lengths across and was nearly circular. All round it was a white beach of clean coral-sand sloping evenly and rising perhaps ten feet at most above the high-water mark. The rest of the island was a meadow, nearly level but cupping ever so little from the crest of the beach. It was covered with short, soft-looking grass, of a bright pale green, a green like that of an English lawn in Spring. In the center of the island and of the meadow was an oval slab of pinkish stone, the same stone, apparently, as made up the crag on which I sat. On it were two shapes of living creatures, but shapes which I rubbed my eyes to look at. Midway between the slab and the crest of the beach a long windrow heap of something white swept in a circle round the slab, maybe ten fathom from it. I did not surely make out what the windrow was composed of until I took my glasses to it.

"But it needed no glass to see our men, all nineteen of them, all sitting, some just inside the white windrow, some just outside of it, some on it or in it. Their faces were turned to the slab.

"I took my glass out of my pocket, trembling so I could hardly adjust it. With it I saw clearly, the windrow as I had guessed, the shapes on the slab as I had seemed to see them with my unaided eyes.

"The windrow was all of human bones. I could see them clearly through the glass.

"The two creatures on the slab were shaped like full-bodied young women. Except their faces nothing of their flesh was visible. They were clad in something close-fitting, and pearly gray, which clung to every part of them, and revealed every curve of their forms; as if it were a tight-fitting envelopment of fine moleskin or chinchilla. But it shimmered in the sunlight more like eider-down.

"And their hair! I rubbed my eyes. I took out my handkerchief and rubbed the lenses of my glasses. I looked again. I saw as before. Their hair was abundant, and fell in curly waves to their hips. But it seemed a deep dark blue, or a dull intense shot-green or both at once or both together. I could not see it any other way.

"And their faces!

"Their faces were those of white women, of European women, of young handsome gentlewomen.

"One of them lay on the slab half on her side, her knees a little drawn up, her head on one bent arm, her face toward me, as if asleep. The other sat, supporting herself by one straight arm. Her mouth was open, her lips moved, her face was the face of a woman singing. I dared not look any more. It was so real and so incredible.

"I scanned our men through my glass. I could see their shoulders heave as they breathed, otherwise not one moved a muscle, while I looked him.

"I shut my glass and put it in my pocket. I shouted. Not a man turned. I fixed my gaze so as to observe the whole group at once. I shouted again. Not a man moved. I took my revolver from its holster and fired in the air. Not a man turned.

"Then I started to clamber down the crag. I had to turn my back on the islet, regard the far horizon, fix my gaze on the camp, discernible by the white patch, where the white sails were stretched over the palm trunk and try to realize the reality of things before I could gather myself together to climb down.

"I made it, but I nearly lost my hold a dozen times.

"I pushed off the dory, rowed to the islet, and beached the dory between the other and the whale-boat. Both were half adrift and I hauled them up as well as I could.

"Then I went up the beach. When I came to its crest and saw the backs of our men I shouted again. Not a man turned his head. I approached them, their faces were set immovably towards the rock and the two appearances on it.

"Peddicord was nearest to me, the windrow of bones in front of him was not wide nor high. He stared across it. I caught him by the shoulders and shook him, then he did turn his head and look up at me, just a glance, the glance of a peevish, protesting child disturbed at some absorbing play, an unintelligent vacuous glance, unrecognizing and uncomprehending.

"The glance startled me enough, for Peddicord had been a hard-headed, sensible Yankee. But the change in his face, since yesterday, startled me more. Of a sudden I realized that Peddicord, Ryan, Mullen and Frenchy had been without food or water since I last saw them, that they had been just where I found them since soon after they left me, had been exposed the day before to a tropical sun for some six hours, had sat all night also without moving, or sleeping. At the same instant I realized that the rest had been in the same state for some hours longer, some hours of a burning, morning tropical sun. The realization of it lost my head completely. I ran from man to man, I yelled, I pulled them, I struck them.

"Not one struck back, or answered, or looked at me twice. Each shook me off impatiently and relapsed into his intent posture, even Obrink.

"Obrink, it is true, partially opened his mouth, as if to speak.

"I saw his tongue!

"I ran to the boat, took a handful of ship-biscuit and a pan of water, with these I returned to the men.

"Not one would notice the biscuit, not one showed any interest in the water, not one looked at it as if he saw it when I held it before his face, not one tried to drink, not one would drink when I tried to force it on him.

"I emptied my flask into the water, with that I went from man to man. Not even the smell of the whisky roused them. Each pushed the pan from before his face, each resisted me, each shoved me away.

"I went back to the boat, filled a tin cup with raw whisky and went the round with that. Not one would regard it, much less swallow it.

"Then I myself turned to the slab of stone.

"There sat the sirens. Well I recognized now what they were. Both were awake now and both singing. What I had seen through the glass was visible more clearly, more intelligibly. They were indeed shaped like young, healthy women; like well-matured Caucasian women. They were covered all over with close, soft plumage, like the breast of a dove, colored like the breast of a dove, a pale, delicate, iridescent, pinkish gray. As a woman's long hair might trail to her hips, there trailed from their heads a mass of long, dark strands. Imagine single strands of ostrich feathers, a yard long or more, curling spirally on at random, colored the deep, shot, blue-green of the eye of a peacock feather, or of a gamecock's shackles. That was what grew from their heads, as I seemed to see it.

"I stepped over the windrow of bones. Some were mere dust; some leached gray by sun, wind and rain; some white. Skulls were there, five or six I saw in as many yards of the windrow near me and more beyond. In some places the windrow was ten feet wide and three feet deep in the middle. It was made up of the skeletons of hundreds of thousands of victims.

"I took out my other revolver, spun the cylinder, and strode toward the slab.

"Forty feet from it I stopped. I was determined to abolish the superhuman monsters. I was resolute. I was not afraid. But I stopped. Again and again I strove to go nearer, I braced my resolutions. I tried to go nearer. I could not.

"Then I tried to go sideways. I was able to step. I made the circuit of the slab, some forty feet from it. Nearer I could not go. It was as if a glass wall were between me and the sirens.

"Standing at my distance, once I found I could go no nearer, I essayed to aim my revolver at them. My muscles, my nerves refused to obey me. I tried in various ways. I might have been paralyzed. I tried other movements, I was capable of any other movement. But aim at them I could not.

"I regarded them. Especially their faces, their wonderful faces.

"Their investiture of opalescent plumelets covered their throats. Between it and the deep, dark chevelure above, their faces showed ivory-smooth, delicately tinted. I could see their ears too, shell-like ears, entirely human in form, peeping from under the glossy shade of their miraculous tresses.

"They were as like each other as any twin sisters.

"Their faces were oval, their features small, clean-cut, regular and shapely, their foreheads were wide and low, their brows were separate, arched, penciled and definite, not of hair, but of tiny feathers, of gold-shot, black, blue-green, like the color of their ringlets, but far darker. I took out my binoculars and conned their brows. Their eyes were dark blue-gray, bright and young, their noses were small and straight, low between the eyes, neither wide nor narrow, and with molded nostrils, rolled and fine. Their upper lips were short, both lips crimson red and curved about their small mouths, their teeth were very white, their chins round and babyish. They were beautiful and the act of singing did not mar their beauty. Their mouths did not strain open, but their lips parted easily into an opening. Their throats seemed to ripple like the throat of a trilling canary-bird. They sang with zest and the zest made them all the more beautiful. But it was not so much their beauty that impressed me, it was the nobility of their faces.

"Some years before I had been an officer on the private steam-yacht of a very wealthy nobleman. He was of a family fanatically devoted to the church of Rome and all its interests. Some Austrian nuns, of an order made up exclusively of noble-women, were about to go to Rome for an audience with the Pope. My employer placed his yacht at their disposal and we took them on at Trieste. They several times sat on deck during the voyage and the return. I watched them as much as I could, for I never had seen such human faces, and I had seen many sorts. Their faces seemed to tell of a long lineage of men all brave and honorable, women gentle and pure. There was not a trace on their faces of any sort of evil in themselves or in anything that had ever really influenced them. They were really saintly faces, the faces of ideal nuns.

"Well, the sirens' faces were like that, only more ineffably perfect. There was no guile or cruelty in them, no delight in the exercise of their power, no consciousness of it, no consciousness of my proximity, or of the spell-bound men, or of the uncountable skeletons of their myriad victims. Their faces expressed but one emotion: utter absorption in the ecstasy of singing, the infinite preoccupation of artists in their art.

"I walked all round them, gazing now with all my eyes, now through my short-focused glass. Their coat of feathers was as if very short and close like seal-skin fur and covered them entirely from the throat down, to the ends of their fingers and the soles of their feet. They did not move except to sit up to sing or lie down to sleep. Sometimes both sang together, sometimes alternately, but if one slept the other sang on and on without ceasing.

"I of course could not hear their music, but the mere sight of them fascinated me so that I forgot my weariness from anxiety and loss of sleep, forgot the vertical sun, forgot food and drink, forgot my shipmates, forgot everything.

"But as I could not hear this state was transitory. I began to look elsewhere than at the sirens. My gaze turned again upon the men. Again I made futile efforts to reach the sirens, to shoot at them, to aim at them. I could not.

"I returned to my dory and drank a great deal of water. I ate a ship-biscuit or two. I then made the round of the men, and tried on each food, water and spirits. They were oblivious to everything except the longing to listen, to listen, to listen.

"I walked round the windrow of bones. With the skulls and collapsing rib-arches I found leather boots, guns of various patterns, pistols, watches, gold and jeweled finger rings and coins, many coins, copper, silver and gold. The grass was short, not three inches deep, and the earth under it smooth as a rolled lawn.

"The bones were of various ages, but all old, except two skeletons, entire, side by side, just beyond the windrow at the portion opposite where the men sat. There was long fine golden hair on one skull. Women too!

"I went back to the dory, rowed to the camp, shot a hog, roasted it, wrapped the steaming meat in fresh leaves and rowed back to the islet. It was not far from sunset.

"Not a man heeded the savory meat, still warm. They just sat and gazed and listened.

"I was free of the spell. I could do them no good by staying. I rowed back to camp before sunset and slept, yes I slept all night long.

"The sun woke me. I shot and cooked another hog, took every bit of rope or marline I could find and rowed back to the islet.

"You are to understand that the men had by then been more than forty hours, all of them, without moving or swallowing anything. If I was to save any it must be done quickly.

"I found them as they had been, but with an appalling change in themselves. The day before they had been uncannily unaware of their sufferings, today they were hideously conscious of them.

"Once I had a pet terrier, a neat, trim, intelligent little beast. He ran under a moving train and had both his hind legs cut off. He dragged himself to me, and the appealing gaze of his eyes expressed at once his inability to comprehend what had happened to him, his bewilderment at pain, the first really excruciating pain he had ever known in all his little life, and his dumb wonder that I could not help him, that it could be possible he could be with me and his trouble continue.

"Once I had the misfortune to see a lovely child, a beautiful little girl, not six years old, frightfully burned. Her look haunted me with the like incomprehension of what had befallen her, the like incredulity at the violence of her suffering, the like amazement at our failure to relieve her.

"Well, out of the staring, blood-shot eyes of those bewitched men I saw the same look of helpless wonderment and mute appeal.

"Strange, but I never thought of knocking them senseless. I had an idea of tying them one by one, carrying or dragging them to the dory and ferrying my captives to camp.

"I began on Frenchy, he was nearest the boat and smallest.

"He fought like a demon. After all that sleeplessness and fasting he was stronger than I. Our tussle wore me out, but moved him not at all.

"I tried them with the warm, juicy, savory pork. They paid no heed to it and pushed me away. I tried them with biscuit, water and liquor. Not one heeded. I tried Obrink particularly. Again he opened his lips. His tongue was black, hard, and swelled till it filled his mouth.

"Then I lost count of time, of what I did, of what happened. I do not know whether it was on that day or the next that the first man died. He was Jack Register, a New York wharf-rat. The next died a few hours later, a Philadelphia seaman he was, named Tom Smith.

"They putrefied with a rapidity surpassing anything I ever saw, even in a horse dropped dead of over-driving.

"The rest sat there by the carrion of their comrades, rocking with weakness, crazed by sleeplessness, racked by tortures inexpressible, the gray of death deepening on their faces, listening, listening, listening.

"As I said, I had lost consciousness of time. I do not know how many days Obrink lived, and he was the last to die. I do not know how long it was after his death before I came to myself.

"I made one last effort to put an end to the enchantresses. The same spell possessed me. I could not aim, much less pull trigger; I could not approach nearer than before.

"When I was myself I made haste to leave the accursed isle. I made ready the second whale-boat with all the best stores she could carry and spare sails. I stepped the mast and steered across the lagoon, for the wind was southerly and there was a wider channel at the north of the atoll.

"As I passed the islet, I could see nothing but the white sand beach that ringed it. For all my horror I could not resist landing once more for one last look.

"Under the afternoon sun I saw the green meadow, the white curve of bones, the rotting corpses, the pink slab, the feathered sirens, their sweet serene faces uplifted, singing on in a rapt trance.

"I took but one look. I fled. The whale-boat passed the outlet of the lagoon. North by east I steered.

"Parts of the Indian Ocean are almost free of storms. The atoll was apparently in one of those parts. I soon passed out of it. Three storms blew me about, I lost my dead-reckoning, I lost count of the days. Between the storms I lashed the tiller amidships, double-reefed the sail and slept as I needed sleep. Through the storms I bailed furiously, the whale-boat riding at a sea-anchor of oars and sails. I had been at sea alone for all of twenty-one days when I was rescued, not three hundred miles from Ceylon, by a tramp steamer out of Colombo bound for Adelaide."

Here he broke off, stood up and for the rest of the watch maintained his sentry-go by the break of the poop.

Next day we towed into the harbor of Rio de Janeiro, then still the capital of an Empire, and mildly enthusiastic for Dom Pedro. I hastened to go ashore. When my boat was ready the deaf mate was forward, superintending the sealing of the hatches.

After some days of discomfort at the Hotel des Etrangers and of worse at Young's Hotel I found a harborage with five jolly bachelors housekeeping in a delightful villa up on Rua dos Jonquillos on Santa Theresa. The *Nipsic* was in the harbor and I thought I knew a lieutenant on her and went off one day to visit her. After my visit my boatman landed me at the Red Steps. As I trod up the steps a man came down. He was English all over, irreproachably shod, trousered, coated, gloved, hatted and monocled. Behind him two porters carried big, new portmanteaux. I recognized the man whom I had known as John Wilson of Liverpool, second mate of the *Medorus*, the man who had seen the Sirens.

Not only did I recognize him, but he recognized me. He gave me no far off British stare. His eyes lit, even the monocled eye. He held out his hand.

"I am going home," he said, nodding toward a steamer at anchor. "I am glad we met. I enjoyed our talks. Perhaps we may meet again."

He shook hands without any more words. I stood at the top of the steps and watched his boat put off, watched it as it receded. As I watched a bit of paper on a lower step caught my eye. I went down and picked it up. It was an empty envelope, with an English stamp and postmark, addressed:

GEOFFREY CECIL, ESQ.,
  c.o. SWANWICK & CO.,
    54 Rua de Alfandega,
      Rio de Janeiro, Brazil.

I looked after the distant boat, I could barely make him out as he sat in the stern. I never saw him again.

Naturally I asked every Englishman I ever met if he had ever heard of a deaf man named Geoffrey Cecil. For more than ten years I elicited no response. Then at lunch, in the Hotel Victoria at Interlaken, I happened to be seated opposite a stout, elderly Briton. He perceived that I was an American and became affable and agreeable. I never saw him after that lunch and never learned his name. But through our brief meal together we conversed freely.

At a suitable opportunity I put my usual query.

"Geoffrey Cecil?" he said. "Deaf Geoffrey Cecil? Of course I know of him. Knew him too. He was or is Earl of Aldersmere."

"Was or is?" I queried.

"It was this way," my interlocutor explained. "The ninth Earl of Aldersmere had three sons. All predeceased him and each left one son. Geoffrey was the heir. He had wanted to go into the Navy, but his deafness cut him off from that. When he quarreled with his father he naturally ran away to sea. Track of him was lost. He was supposed dead. That was years before his father's death. When his father died nothing had been heard of him for ten years. But when his grandfather died and his cousin Roger supposed himself Earl, some firm of solicitors interposed, claiming that Geoffrey was alive. That was in 1885. It was a full six months before Geoffrey turned up. Roger was no end disappointed. Geoffrey paid no attention to anything but buying or chartering a steam-yacht. She sailed as soon as possible, passed the canal, touched at Aden, and has never been heard of since. That was nine years ago."

"Is Roger Cecil alive?" I asked.

"Very much alive," affirmed my informant.

"You may tell him from me," I declared, "that he is now the Eleventh Earl of Aldersmere."

The Picture Puzzle

I

OF COURSE the instinct of the police and detectives was to run down their game. That was natural. They seemed astonished and contemptuous when I urged that all I wanted was my baby; whether the kidnappers were ever caught or not made no difference to me. They kept arguing that unless precautions were taken the criminals would escape and I kept arguing that if they became suspicious of a trap they would keep away and my only chance to recover our little girl would be gone forever. They finally agreed and I believe they kept their promise to me. Helen always felt the other way and maintained that their watchers frightened off whoever was to meet me. Anyhow I waited in vain, waited for hours, waited again the next day and the next and the next. We put advertisements in countless papers, offering rewards and immunity, but never heard anything more.

I pulled myself together in a sort of a way and tried to do my work. My partner and clerks were very kind. I don't believe I ever did anything properly in those days, but no one ever brought any blunder to my attention. If they came across any they set it right for me. And at the office it was not so bad. Trying to work was good for me. It was worse at home and worse at night. I slept hardly at all.

Helen, if possible, slept less than I. And she had terrible spasms of sobs that shook the bed. She would try to choke them down, thinking I was asleep and she might wake me. But she never went through a night without at least one frightful paroxysm of tears.

In the daylight she controlled herself better, made a heartbreaking and yet heart-warming effort at her normal cheeriness over the breakfast things, and greeted me beautifully when I came home. But the moment we were alone for the evening she would break down.

I don't know how many days that sort of thing kept up. I sympathized in silence. It was Helen herself who suggested that we must force ourselves to be diverted, somehow. The theater was out of the question. Not merely the sight of a four-year-old girl with yellow locks threw Helen into a passion of uncontrollable sobbing, but all sorts of unexpected trifles reminded her of Amy and affected her almost as much. Confined to our home we tried cards, chess and everything else we could think of. They helped her as little as they helped me.

Then one afternoon Helen did not come to greet me. Instead as I came in I heard her call, quite in her natural voice.

"Oh, I'm so glad that is you. Come and help me."

I found her seated at the library table, her back to the door. She had on a pink wrapper and her shoulders had no despondent droop, but a girlish alertness. She barely turned her head as I entered, but her profile showed no signs of recent weeping. Her face was its natural color.

"Come and help me," she repeated. "I can't find the other piece of the boat."

She was absorbed, positively absorbed in a picture puzzle.

In forty seconds I was absorbed too. It must have been six minutes before we identified the last piece of the boat. And then we went on with the sky and were still at it when the butler announced dinner.

"Where did you get it?" I asked, over the soup, which Helen really ate.

"Mrs. Allstone brought it," Helen replied, "just before lunch."

I blessed Mrs. Allstone.

Really it seems absurd, but those idiotic jig-saw puzzles were our salvation. They actually took our minds off everything else. At first I dreaded finishing one. No sooner was the last piece in place than I felt a sudden revulsion, a booming of blood in my ears, and the sense of loss and misery rushed over me like a wave of scalding water. And I knew it was worse for Helen.

But after some days each seemed not merely a respite from pain, but a sedative as well. After a two hours' struggle with a fascinating tangle of shapes and colors, we seemed numb to our bereavement and the bitterness of the smart seemed blunted.

We grew fastidious as to manufacture and finish; learned to avoid crude and clumsy products as bores; developed a pronounced taste for pictures neither too soft nor too plain in color-masses; and became connoisseurs as to cutting, utterly above the obvious and entirely disenchanted with the painfully difficult. We evolved into adepts, quick to recoil from fragments barren of any clue of shape or markings and equally prompt to reject those whose meaning was too definite and insistent. We trod delicately the middle way among segments not one of which was without some clue of outline or tint, and not one of which imparted its message without interrogation, inference and reflection.

Helen used to time herself and try the same puzzle over and over on successive days until she could do it in less than half an hour. She declared that a really good puzzle was interesting the fourth or fifth time and that an especially fine puzzle was diverting if turned face down and put together from the shapes merely, after it had been well learned the other way. I did not enter into the craze to that extent, but sometimes tried her methods for variety.

We really slept, and Helen, though worn and thin, was not abject, not agonized. Her nights passed, if not wholly without tears, yet with only those soft and silent tears, which are more a relief than suffering. With me she was nearly her old self and very brave and patient. She greeted me naturally and we seemed able to go on living.

Then one day she was not at the door to welcome me. I had hardly shut it before I heard her sobbing. I found her again at the library table and over a puzzle. But this time she had just finished it and was bowed over it on the table, shaken all over by her grief.

She lifted her head from her crossed arms, pointed and buried her face in her hands. I understood. The picture I remembered from a magazine of the year before: a Christmas tree with a bevy of children about it and one (we had remarked it at the time) a perfect likeness of our Amy.

As she rocked back and forth, her hands over her eyes, I swept the pieces into their box and put on the lid.

Presently Helen dried her eyes and looked at the table.

"Oh! why did you touch it," she wailed. "It was such a comfort to me."

"You did not seem comforted," I retorted. "I thought the contrast: . . ." I stopped.

"You mean the contrast between the Christmas we expected and the Christmas we are going to have?" she queried. "You mean you thought that was too much for me?"

I nodded.

"It wasn't that at all," she averred. "I was crying for joy. That picture was a sign."

"A sign?" I repeated.

"Yes," she declared, "a sign that we shall get her back in time for Christmas. I'm going to start and get ready right away."

At first I was glad of the diversion. Helen had the nursery put in order as if she expected Amy the next day, hauled over all the child's clothes and was in a bustling state of happy expectancy. She went vigorously about her preparation for a Christmas celebration, planned a Christmas Eve dinner for our brothers and sisters and their husbands and wives, and a children's party afterwards with a big tree and a profusion of goodies and gifts.

"You see," she explained, "everyone will want their own Christmas at home. So shall we, for we'll just want to gloat over Amy all day. We won't want them on Christmas any more than they'll want us. But this way we can all be together and celebrate and rejoice over our good luck."

She was as elated and convinced as if it was a certainty. For a while her occupation with preparations was good for her, but she was so forehanded that she was ready a week ahead of time and had not a detail left to arrange. I dreaded a reaction, but her artificial exaltation continued unabated. All the more I feared the inevitable disappointment and was genuinely concerned for her reason. The fixed idea that that accidental coincidence was a prophecy and a guarantee dominated her totally. I was really afraid that the shock of the reality might kill her. I did not want to dissipate her happy delusion, but I could not but try to prepare her for the certain blow. I talked cautiously in wide circles around what I wanted and I did not want to say.

II

On December 22nd, I came home early, just after lunch, in fact. Helen met me, at the door, with such a demeanor of suppressed high spirits, happy secrecy and tingling anticipation that for one moment I was certain Amy had been found and was then in the house.

"I've something wonderful to show you," Helen declared, and led me to the library.

There on the table was a picture-puzzle fitted together.

She stood and pointed to it with the air of exhibiting a marvel.

I looked at it but could not conjecture the cause of her excitement. The pieces seemed too large, too clumsy and too uniform in outline. It looked a crude and clumsy picture, beneath her notice.

"Why did you buy it?" I asked.

"I met a peddler on the street," she answered, "and he was so wretched-looking, I was sorry for him. He was young and thin and looked haggard and consumptive. I looked at him and I suppose I showed my feelings. He said:

"'Lady, buy a puzzle. It will help you to your heart's desire.'

"His words were so odd I bought it, and now just look at what it is."

I was groping for some foothold upon which to rally my thoughts.

"Let me see the box in which it came," I asked.

She produced it and I read on the top:

"GUGGENHEIM'S DOUBLE PICTURE
PUZZLE.
TWO IN ONE.
MOST FOR THE MONEY.
ASK FOR GUGGENHEIM'S"

And on the end—

"ASTRAY.
A BREATH OF AIR.
50 CENTS."

"It's queer," Helen remarked. "But it is not a double puzzle at all, though the pieces have the same paper on both sides. One side is blank. I suppose this is ASTRAY. Don't you think so?"

"Astray?" I queried, puzzled.

"Oh," she cried, in a disappointed, disheartened, almost querulous tone. "I thought you would be so much struck with the resemblance. You don't seem to notice it at all. Why, even the dress is identical!"

"The dress?" I repeated. "How many times have you done this?"

"Only this once," she said. "I had just finished it when I heard your key in the lock."

"I should have thought," I commented, "that it would have been more interesting to do it face up first."

"Face up!" she cried. "It is face up."

Her air of scornful superiority completely shook me out of my sedulous consideration of a moment before.

"Nonsense," I said, "that's the back of the puzzle. There are no colors there. It's all pink."

"Pink!" she exclaimed, pointing. "Do you call that pink?"

"Certainly it's pink," I asserted.

"Don't you see there the white of the old man's beard," she queried, pointing again. "And there the black of his boots? And there the red of the little girl's dress?"

"No," I declared. "I don't see anything of the kind. It's all pink. There isn't any picture there at all."

"No picture!" she cried. "Don't you see the old man leading the child by the hand?"

"No," I said harshly, "I don't see any picture and you know I don't. There isn't any picture there. I can't make out what you are driving at. It seems a senseless joke."

"Joke! I joke!" Helen half whispered. The tears came into her eyes.

"You are cruel," she said, "and I thought you would be struck by the resemblance."

I was overwhelmed by a pang of self-reproach, solicitude and terror.

"Resemblance to what?" I asked gently.

"Can't you see it?" she insisted.

"Tell me," I pleaded. "Show me just what you want me to notice most."

"The child," she said, pointing, "is just exactly Amy and the dress is the very red suit she had on when—"

"Dear," I said, "try to collect yourself. Indeed you only imagine what you tell me. There is no picture on this side of the sections. The whole thing is pink. That is the back of the puzzle."

"I don't see how you can say such a thing," she raged at me. "I can't make out why you should. What sort of a test are you putting me through? What does it all mean?"

"Will you let me prove to you that this is the back of the puzzle?" I asked.

"If you can," she said shortly.

I turned the pieces of the puzzle over, keeping them together as much as possible. I succeeded pretty well with the outer pieces and soon had the rectangle in place. The inner pieces were a good deal mixed up, but even before I had fitted them I exclaimed:

"There, look at that!"

"Well," she asked. "What do you expect me to see?"

"What do you see?" I asked in turn.

"I see the back of a puzzle," she answered.

"Don't you see those front steps?" I demanded, pointing.

"I don't see anything," she asserted, "except green."

"Do you call that green?" I queried, pointing.

"I do," she declared.

"Don't you see the brickwork front of the house?" I insisted, "and the lower part of a window and part of a door. Yes, and those front steps in the corner?"

"I don't see anything of the kind," she asseverated. "Any more than you do. What I see is just what you see. It's the back of the puzzle, all pale green."

I had been feverishly putting together the last pieces as she spoke. I could not believe my eyes and, as the last piece fitted in, was struck with amazement.

The picture showed an old red-brick house, with brown blinds, all open. The top of the front steps was included in the lower right hand corner, most of the front door above them, all of one window on its level, and the side of another. Above appeared all of one of the second floor windows, and parts of those to right and left of it. The other windows were closed, but the sash of the middle one was raised and from it leaned a little girl, a child with frowzy hair, a dirty face and wearing a blue and white check frock. The child was a perfect likeness of our lost Amy, supposing she had been starved and neglected. I was so affected that I was afraid I should faint. I was positively husky when I asked:

"Don't you see that?"

"I see Nile green," she maintained. "The same as you see."

I swept the pieces into the box.

"We are neither of us well," I said.

"I should think you must be deranged to behave so," she snapped, "and it is no wonder I am not well the way you treat me."

"How could I know what you wanted me to see?" I began.

"Wanted you to see!" she cried. "You keep it up? You pretend you didn't see it, after all? Oh! I have no patience with you."

She burst into tears, fled upstairs and I heard her slam and lock our bedroom door.

I put that puzzle together again and the likeness of that hungry, filthy child in the picture to our Amy made my heart ache.

I found a stout box, cut two pieces of straw-board just the shape of the puzzle and a trifle larger, laid one on top of it and slid the other under it. Then I tied it together with string and wrapped it in paper and tied the whole.

I put the box in my overcoat pocket and went out carrying the flat parcel.

I walked round to MacIntyre's.

I told him the whole story and showed him the puzzle.

"Do you want the truth?" he asked.

"Just that," I said.

"Well," he reported. "You are as overstrung as she is and the same way. There is absolutely no picture on either side of this. One side is solid green and the other solid pink."

"How about the coincidence of the names on the box?" I interjected. "One suited what I saw, one what she said she saw."

"Let's look at the box," he suggested.

He looked at it on all sides.

"There's not a letter on it," he announced. "Except 'picture puzzle' on top and '50 cents' on the end."

"I don't feel insane," I declared.

"You aren't," he reassured me. "Nor in any danger of being insane. Let me look you over."

He felt my pulse, looked at my tongue, examined both eyes with his ophthalmoscope, and took a drop of my blood.

"I'll report further," he said, "in confirmation tomorrow. You're all right, or nearly so, and you'll soon be really all right. All you need is a little rest. Don't worry about this idea of your wife's, humor her. There won't be any terrible consequences. After Christmas go to Florida or somewhere for a week or so. And exert yourself from now till after that change."

When I reached home, I went down into the cellar, threw that puzzle and its box into the furnace and stood and watched it burn to ashes.

III

When I came upstairs from the furnace Helen met me as if nothing had happened. By one of her sudden revulsions of mood she was even more gracious than usual, and was at dinner altogether charming. She did not refer to our quarrel or to the puzzle.

The next morning over our breakfast we were both opening our mail. I had told her that I should not go to the office until after Christmas and that I wanted her to arrange for a little tour that would please her. I had phoned to the office not to expect me until after New Year's.

My mail contained nothing of moment.

Helen looked up from hers with an expression curiously mingled of disappointment, concern and a pleased smile.

"It is so fortunate you have nothing to do," she said. "I spent four whole days choosing toys and favors and found most of those I selected at Bleich's. They were to have been delivered day before yesterday but they did not come. I telephoned yesterday and they said they would try to trace them. Here is a letter saying that the whole lot was missent out to Roundwood. You noticed that Roundwood station burned Monday night.

They were all burnt up. Now I'll have to go and find more like them. You can go with me."

I went.

The two days were a strange mixture of sensations and emotions.

Helen had picked over Bleich's stock pretty carefully and could duplicate from it few of the burned articles, could find acceptable substitutes for fewer. There followed an exhausting pursuit of the unattainable through a bewildering series of toyshops and department-stores. We spent most of our time at counters and much of the remainder in a taxicab.

In a way it was very trying. I did not mind the smells and bad air and other mere physical discomforts. But the mental strain continually intensified. Helen's confidence that Amy would be restored to us was steadily waning and her outward exhibition of it was becoming more and more artificial, and consciously sustained, and more and more of an effort. She was coming to foresee, in spite of herself, that our Christmas celebration would be a most terrible mockery of our bereavement. She was forcing herself not to confess it to herself and not to show it to me. The strain told on her. It told on me to watch it, to see the inevitable crash coming nearer and nearer and to try to put away from myself the pictures of her collapse, of her probable loss of reason, of her possible death, which my imagination kept thrusting before me.

On the other hand Helen was to all appearance, if one had no prevision by which to read her, her most charming self. Her manner to shop-girls and other sales-people was a delight to watch. Her little speeches to me were full of her girlish whimsicality and unexpectedness. Her good will towards all the world, her resolution that everything must come right and would come right haloed her in a sort of aureole of romance. Our lunches were ideal hours, full of the atmosphere of courtship, of love-making, of exquisite companionship. In spite of my forebodings, I caught the contagion of the Christmas shopping crowds; in spite of her self-deception Helen revelled in it. The purpose to make as many people as possible as happy as might be irradiated Helen with the light of fairyland; her resolve to be happy herself in spite of everything made her a sort of fairy queen. I found myself less and less anxious and more and more almost expectant. I knew Helen was looking for Amy every instant. I found myself in the same state of mind.

Our lunch on Christmas Eve was a strange blend of artificiality and genuine exhilaration. After it we had but one purchase to make.

"We are in no hurry," Helen said. "Let's take a horse-hansom for old time's sake."

In it we were like boy and girl together until the jeweler's was reached.

There gloom, in spite of us, settled down over our hopes and feelings. Helen walked to the hansom like a gray ghost. Like the whisper of some far-off stranger I heard myself order the driver to take us home.

In the hansom we sat silent, looking straight in front of us at nothing. I stole a glance at Helen and saw a tear in the corner of her eye. I sat choking.

All at once she seized my hand.

"Look!" she exclaimed, "look!"

I looked where she pointed, but discerned nothing to account for her excitement.

"What is it?" I queried.

"The old man!" she exclaimed.

"What old man?" I asked, bewildered.

"The old man on the puzzle," she told me. "The old man who was leading Amy."

Then I was sure she was demented. To humor her I asked:

"The old man with the brown coat?"

"Yes," she said eagerly. "The old man with the long gray hair over his collar."

"With the walking stick?" I inquired.

"Yes," she answered. "With the crooked walking stick."

I saw him too! This was no figment of Helen's imagination.

It was absurd of course, but my eagerness caught fire from hers. I credited the absurdity. In what sort of vision it mattered not she had seen an old man like this leading our lost Amy.

I spoke to the driver, pointed out to him the old man, told him to follow him without attracting his attention and offered him anything he asked to keep him in sight.

Helen became possessed with the idea that we should lose sight of the old man in the crowds. Nothing would do but we must get out and follow him on foot. I remonstrated that we were much more likely to lose sight of him that way, and still more likely to attract his notice, which would be worse than losing him. She insisted and I told the man to keep us in view.

A weary walk we had, though most of it was mere strolling after a tottering figure or loitering about shops he entered.

It was near dusk and full time for us to be at home when he began to walk fast. So fast he drew away from us in spite of us. He turned a corner a half a square ahead of us. When we turned into that street he was nowhere to be seen.

Helen was ready to faint with disappointment. With no hope of helping her, but some instinctive idea of postponing the evil moment I urged her to walk on, saying that perhaps we might see him. About the middle of the square I suddenly stood still.

"What is the matter?" Helen asked.

"The house!" I said.

"What house?" she queried.

"The house in the puzzle picture," I explained. "The house where I saw Amy at the window."

Of course she had not seen any house on the puzzle, but she caught at the last straw of hope.

It was a poor neighborhood of crowded tenements, not quite a slum, yet dirty and unkempt and full of poor folks.

The house door was shut. I could find no sign of any bell. I knocked. No one answered. I tried the door. It was not fastened and we entered a dirty hallway, cold and damp and smelling repulsively. A fat woman stuck her head out of a door and jabbered at us in an unknown tongue. A man with a fez on his greasy black hair came from the back of the hallway and was equally unintelligible.

"Does nobody here speak English?" I asked.

The answer was as incomprehensible as before.

I made to go up the stairs.

The man, and the woman, who was now standing before her door, both chattered at once, but neither made any attempt to stop me. They waved vaguely explanatory, deprecating hands towards the blackness of the stairway. We went up.

On the second floor landing we saw just the old man we had been following.
He stared at us when I spoke to him.
"Son-in-law," he said, "son-in-law."
He called and a door opened. An oldish woman answered him in apparently the same jargon. Behind was a young woman holding a baby.
"What is it?" she asked with a great deal of accent but intelligibly.
Three or four children held on by her skirts.
Behind her I saw a little girl in a blue-check dress.
Helen screamed.

IV

The people turned out to be refugees from the settlement about the sacked German Mission at Dehkhargan near Tabriz, Christianized Persians, such stupid villagers that they had never thought or had been incapable of reporting their find to the police, so ignorant that they knew nothing of rewards or advertisements, such simple-hearted folk that they had shared their narrow quarters and scanty fare with the unknown waif their grandmother had found wandering alone, after dark, months before.

Amy, when we had leisure to ask questions and hear her experiences, declared they had treated her as they treated their own children. She could give no description of her kidnappers except that the woman had on a hat with roses in it and the man had a little yellow mustache. She could not tell how long they had kept her nor why they had left her to wander in the streets at night.

It needed no common language, far less any legal proof, to convince Amy's hosts that she belonged to us. I had a pocket full of Christmas money, new five and ten dollar gold pieces and bright silver quarters for the servants and children. I filled the old grandfather's hands and plainly overwhelmed him. They all jabbered at us, blessings, if I judged the tone right. I tried to tell the young woman we should see them again in a day or two and I gave her a card to make sure.

I told the cabman to stop the first taxicab he should see empty. In the hansom we hugged Amy alternately and hugged each other.

Once in the taxicab we were home in half an hour; more, much more than half an hour late. Helen whisked Amy in by the servants' door and flew upstairs with her by the back way. I faced a perturbed and anxious parlorful of interrogative relatives and in-laws.

"You'll know before many minutes," I said, "why we were both out and are in late. Helen will want to surprise you and I'll say nothing to spoil the effect."

Nothing I could have said would have spoiled the effect because they would not have believed me. As it was Helen came in sooner than I could have thought possible, looking her best and accurately playing the formal hostess with a feeble attempt at a surprise in store.

The dinner was a great success, with much laughter and high spirits, everybody carried away by Helen's sallies and everybody amazed that she could be so gay.

"I cannot understand," Paul's wife whispered to me, "how she can ever get through the party. It would kill me in her place."

"It won't kill her," I said confidently. "You may be sure of that."

The children had arrived to the number of more than thirty and only the inevitably late Amstelhuysens had not come. Helen announced that she would not wait for them.

"The tree is lighted," she said. "We'll have the doors thrown open and go in."

We were all gathered in the front parlor. The twins panted in at the last instant. The grown-ups were pulling motto-crackers and the children were throwing confetti. The doors opened, the tree filled all the back of the room. The candles blazed and twinkled. And in front of it, in a simple little white dress, with a fairy's wand in her hand, tipped with a silver star, healthy-looking and full of spirits was Amy, the fairy of the hour.

The Snout

I

I WAS not so much conning the specimens in the Zoölogical Garden as idly basking in the agreeable morning sunshine and relishing at leisure the perfect weather. So I saw him the instant he turned the corner of the building. At first, I thought I recognized him, then I hesitated. At first he seemed to know me and to be just about to greet me; then he saw past me into the cage. His eyes bulged; his mouth opened into a long egg-shaped oval, till you might almost have said that his jaw dropped; he made an inarticulate sound, partly a grunt, partly the ghost of a howl, and collapsed in a limp heap on the gravel. I had not seen a human being since I passed the gate, some distance away. No one came when I called. So I dragged him to the grass by a bench, untied his faded, shiny cravat, took off his frayed collar and unbuttoned his soiled neckband. Then I peeled his coat off him, rolled it up, and put it under his knees as he lay on his back. I tried to find some water, but could see none. So I sat down on the bench near him. There he lay, his legs and body on the grass, his head in the dry gutter, his arms on the pebbles of the path. I was sure I knew him, but I could not recall when or where we had encountered each other before. Presently he answered to my rough and ready treatment and opened his eyes, blinking at me heavily. He drew up his arms to his shoulders and sighed.

"Queer," he muttered, "I come here because of you and I meet you."

Still I could not remember him and he had revived enough to read my face. He sat up.

"Don't try to stand up!" I warned him.

He did not need the admonition, but clung to the end of the bench, his head bowed wagglingly over his arms.

"Don't you remember," he asked thickly. "You said I had a pretty good smattering of an education on everything except Natural History and Ancient History. I'm hoping for a job in a few days, and I thought I'd put in the time and keep out of mischief brushing up. So I started on Natural History first and—"

He broke off and glared up at me. I remembered him now. I should have recognized him the moment I saw him, for he was daily in my mind. But his luxuriant hair, his tanned skin and above all his changed expression, a sort of look of acquired cosmopolitanism, had baffled me.

"Natural History!" he repeated, in a hoarse whisper. His fingers digging in the slats of the bench he wrenched himself round to face the cage.

"Hell!" he screamed. "There it is yet!"

He held on by the end iron-arm of the bench, shaking, almost sobbing.

"What's wrong with you?" I queried. "What do you think you see in that cage?"

"Do you see anything in that cage?" he demanded in reply.

"Certainly," I told him.

"Then for God's sake," he pleaded, "what do you see?"

I told him briefly.

"Good Lord," he ejaculated. "Are we both crazy?"

"Nothing crazy about either of us," I assured him. "What we see in the cage is what is in the cage."

"Is there such a critter as that, honest?" he pressed me.

I gave him a pretty full account of the animal, its habits and relationships.

"Well," he said, weakly, "I suppose you're telling the truth. If there is such a critter let's get where I can't see it."

I helped him to his feet and assisted him to a bench altogether out of sight of that building. He put on his collar and knotted his cravat. While I had held it I had noticed that, through its greasy condition, it showed plainly having been a very expensive cravat. His clothes I remarked were seedy, but had been of the very best when new.

"Let's find a drinking fountain," he suggested. "I can walk now."

We found one not far away and at no great distance from it a shaded bench facing an agreeable view. I offered him a cigarette and we smoked. I meant to let him do most of the talking.

"Do you know," he said presently, "things you said to me run in my head more than anything anybody ever said to me. I suppose it's because you're a sort of philosopher and student of human nature and what you say is true. For instance, you said that criminals would get off clear three times out of four, if they just kept their mouths shut, but they have to confide in someone, even against all reason. That's just the way with me now."

"You aren't a criminal," I interrupted him. "You lost your temper and made a fool of yourself just once. If you'd been a criminal and had done what you did, you'd have likely enough got off, because you'd have calculated how to do it. As it was you put yourself in a position where everything was against you and you had no chance. We were all sorry for you."

"You most of all," he amplified. "You treated me bully."

"But we were all sorry for you," I repeated, "and all the jury too, and the judge. You're no criminal."

"How do you know," he demanded defiantly, "what I have done since I got out?"

"You've grown a pretty good head of hair," I commented.

"I've had time," he said. "I've been all over the world and blown in ten thousand dollars."

"And never seen—" I began.

He interrupted me at the third word.

"Don't say it," he shuddered. "I never had, nor heard of one. But I wasn't after caged animals while I had any money left. I didn't remember your advice and your other talk till I was broke. Now, it's just as you said, I've just got to tell you. That's the criminal in me, I suppose."

"You're no criminal," I repeated soothingly.

"Hell," he snarled, "a year in the pen makes a man a criminal, if he never was before."

"Not necessarily," I encouraged him.

"It's pretty sure to," he sighed. "They treated me mighty well and put me to bookkeeping, and I got my full good-conduct allowance. But I met professionals, and they never forget a man.

"Now it don't make any difference what I did when I got out, nor what I tried to do nor how I met Rivvin, nor how he put Thwaite after me. No, nor how Thwaite got hold of me, nor what he said to me, nor anything, right up to the very night, till after we had started."

He looked me in the eye. His attitude became alert. I could see him warming to his narrative. In fact, when after very little rumination he began it, his early self dropped from him with his boyhood dialect and the jargon of his late associates. He was all the easy cosmopolitan telling his tale with conscious zest.

II

As if it had been broad day Thwaite drove the car at a terrific pace for nearly an hour. Then he stopped it while Rivvin put out every lamp. We had not met or overtaken anything, but when we started again through the moist, starless blackness it was too much for my nerves. Thwaite was as cool as if he could see. I could not so much as guess at him in front of me, but I could feel his self-confidence in every quiver of the car. It was one of those super-expensive makes which are, on any gear, at any speed, on any grade, as noiseless as a puma. Thwaite never hesitated in the gloom; he kept straight or swerved, crept or darted, whizzed or crawled for nearly an hour more. Then he turned sharp to the left and uphill. I could feel and smell the soaked, hanging boughs close above and about me, the wet foliage on them, and the deep sodden earth mold that squelched under the tires. We climbed steeply, came to a level and then backed and went forward a length or so a half dozen times, turning. Then we stopped dead. Thwaite moved things that clicked or thumped and presently said:

"Now I'll demonstrate how a man can fill his gasoline tank in the pitch dark if he knows the touch system."

After some more time he said:

"Rivvin, go bury this."

Rivvin swore, but went. Thwaite climbed in beside me. When Rivvin returned he climbed in on the other side of me. He lit his pipe, Thwaite lit a cigar and looked at his watch. After I had lit too, Thwaite said:

"We've plenty of time to talk here and all you have to do is to listen. I'll begin at the beginning. When old Hiram Eversleigh died—"

"You don't mean—" I interrupted him.

"Shut up!" he snapped, "and keep your mouth shut. You'll have your say when I've done."

I shut up.

"When old man Eversleigh died," he resumed, "the income of the fortune was divided equally among his sons. You know what the others did with their shares: palaces in New York and London and Paris, chateaux on the Breton Coast, deer and grouse moors in Scotland, steam yachts and all the rest of it, the same as they have kept it up ever since. At first Vortigern Eversleigh went in for all that sort of thing harder than any one of his brothers. But when his wife died, more than forty years ago, he stopped all that at once. He sold everything else, bought this place, put the wall round it and built that infinity of structures inside. You've seen the pinnacles and roofs of them, and that's all anybody I ever talked to has ever seen of them since they were finished about five years after his wife's death. You've seen the two gate-houses and you know each is big even for a millionaire's mansion. You can judge of the size and extent of the complication of buildings that make up the castle or mansion-house or whatever you choose to call it. There Vortigern Eversleigh lived. Not once did he ever leave it that I can learn of. There he died. Since his death, full twenty years ago, his share of the Eversleigh income has been paid to his heir. No one has ever seen that heir. From what I'll tell you presently you'll see as I have that the heir is probably not a woman. But nobody knows anything about him, he has never been outside these miles of wall. Yet not one of the greedy, selfish Eversleigh grandsons and granddaughters, and sons-in-law and daughters-in-law, has ever objected to the payment to that heir of the full entire portion of Vortigern Eversleigh, and that portion has been two hundred thousand dollars a month, paid in gold on the first banking day of each month. I found that out for sure, for there have been disputes about the division of Wulfstan Eversleigh's share and of Cedric Eversleigh's share and I made certain from the papers in the suits. All that money, or the value of it, has been either reinvested or spent inside that park wall. Not much has been reinvested. I got on the track of the heir's purchases. He buys musical instruments any quantity and at any price. Those were the first things I made sure of. And artists' materials, paints, brushes, canvas, tools, woods, clay, marble, tons of clay and great blocks of superfine-grained marble. He's no magpie collecting expensive trash for a whim; he knows what he wants and why; he has taste. He buys horses and saddlery and carriages, furniture and carpets and tapestries, pictures, all landscapes, never any figure pictures, he buys photographs of pictures by the ten thousand, and he buys fine porcelains, rare vases, table silver, ornaments of Venetian glass, silver and gold filigree, jewelry, watches, chains, gems, pearls, rubies, emeralds and—diamonds; diamonds!"

Thwaite's voice shook with excitement, though he kept it soft and even.

"Oh, I did two years investigating," he went on, "I know. People blabbed. But not any of the servants or grooms or gardeners. Not a word could I get, at first or second or third hand, from them or any of their relatives or friends. They keep dumb. They know which side their bread is buttered on. But some of the discharged tradesmen's assistants told all I wanted to know and I got it straight, though not direct. No one from outside ever gets into that place beyond the big paved courtyards of the gatehouses. Every bit of supplies for all that regiment of servants goes into the brown-stone gate-house. The outer gates open and the wagon or whatever it is drives under the archway. There it halts. The outer gates shut and the inner gates open. It drives into the courtyard. Then the Major-domo (I suppose that wouldn't be too big a name for him) makes his selections. The inner gates of the other gateway open and the wagon drives under the archway and halts. The inner gates close fast and the outer gates open. That's the way with every wagon and only one enters at a time. Everything is carried through the gate-house to the smaller inner courtyard and loaded on the wagons of the estate to be driven up to the mansion.

"Everything like furniture, for instance, comes into the courtyard of the green-stone gate-house. There a sort of auditor verifies the inventory and receipts for the goods before two witnesses from the dealers and two for the estate. The consignment may be kept a day or a month; it may be returned intact or kept entire; any difference is settled for at once upon return of what is rejected. So with jewelry. I had luck. I found out for certain that more than a million dollars' worth of diamonds alone have gone into this place in the last ten years and stayed there."

Thwaite paused dramatically. I never said a word and we sat there in the rear seat of that stationary auto, the leather creaking as we breathed, Rivvin sucking at his pipe, and the leaves dripping above us; not another sound.

"It's all in there," Thwaite began again. "The biggest stack of loot in North America. And this is going to be the biggest and most successful burglary ever perpetrated on this continent. And no one will ever be convicted for it or so much as suspected of it. Mark my words."

"I do," I broke in, "and I don't feel a bit better than when we started. You promised to explain and you said I'd be as eager and confident as you and Rivvin. I acknowledge the bait, admitting all you say is true, and it doesn't seem likely. But do you suppose any recluse millionaire eccentric is going to live unguarded? If he is careless himself his household are the reverse. By what you tell of the gate-houses there are precautions enough. Diamonds are tempting if you like, but so is the bullion in the mint. By your account all this accumulation of treasure you imagine is as safe where it is as the gold reserve in the United States Treasury. You scare me, you don't reassure me."

"Keep your head," Thwaite interrupted. "I'm no fool. I've spent years on this scheme. After I was sure of the prize I made sure of the means. There are precautions a-many, but not enough. How simple to put a watchman's cottage every hundred yards on the other side of the road across from the wall? They haven't done it. How simple to light the road and the outside of the wall? They haven't done that. Nor have they thought of any one of the twenty other simple outside precautions. The park's big enough to be lonely. And outside the wall is all dark, lonely road and unfenced, empty woods like this. They're overconfident. They think their wall and their gate-houses are enough. And they are not. They think their outside precautions are perfect. They are not. I know. I've been over that wall ten times, twenty times, fifty times. I've risked it and I have risked mantraps and spring guns and alarm wires. There aren't any. There isn't any night patrol, nor any regular day patrol, only casual gardeners and such. I know. I made sure of it by crawling all over the place on my belly like an Iroquois Indian in one of Cooper's novels. They are so confident of the potency of their wall that they haven't so much as a watch dog, nor any dog of any kind."

I was certainly startled.

"No dog!" I exclaimed. "Are you sure?"

"Dead sure!" Thwaite returned, triumphantly. "And sure there never has been a dog on the place."

"How could you be sure of that?" I cavilled.

"I'm coming to that," Thwaite went on. "I could not get anybody that ever belonged to the place to talk, but I managed to arrange to overhear two of them talking to each other; and more than once, too. Most of what they said was no use to me, but I overheard scraps I could piece together. There's a cross-wall that divides the park. In the smaller division, into which the lodge gates lead, are the homes of all the caretakers and servants, of the overseers and manager and of the estate doctor; for there is an estate doctor. He has two assistants, young men, frequently changed. He is married like most of the retinue. There is a sort of village of them inside the outer wall, outside the inner cross-wall. When they get too old they are pensioned off and sent away, somewhere; far off, for I could not get a clue to any pensioner.

"The valets or keepers, whichever they are, and there are many of them, to relieve each other, are all unmarried except two or three of the most trusted. The rest are all brought over from England and shipped back usually after four or five years of service. The men I overheard were two of these, an old hand soon to finish his enlistment, as he called it, and go home, and the lad he was training to take his place. All these specials have plenty of time off to spend outside. They'd sit over their beer for two or three hours at a time, chatting on, Appleshaw giving points to Kitworth or Kitworth asking questions. I learned from them about the cross-wall.

"'Never's been a woman t' other side of it since it was built,' Appleshaw said.

"'I shouldn't have thought it,' Kitworth ruminated.

"'Can you imagine a woman,' Appleshaw asked, 'standin' him?'

"'No,' Kitworth admitted, 'I hardly can. But some women 'll stand more'n a man.'

"'Anyhow,' Appleshaw added, 'he can't abide the sight of a woman.'

"'Odd,' said Kitworth, 'I've heard his kind are all the other way.'

"'They are, as we know,' Appleshaw replied, 'havin' watched 'em; but he ain't. He can't endure 'em.'

"'I suppose it's the same way about dogs,' Kitworth reflected.

"'No dog'd ever get used to him,' Appleshaw agreed, 'and he's that afraid of dogs, they're not allowed inside the place anywhere. Never's been one here since he was born, I'm told. No, nor any cat, either, not even one.'

"Another time I heard Appleshaw say:

"'He built the museums, and the pavilion and the towers, the rest was built before he grew up.'

"Generally I could not hear much of Kitworth's utterances, he talked so low. I once heard Appleshaw reply:

"'Sometimes nights and nights he'll be quiet as anybody, lights out early and sleep sound for all we know. Again he'll be up all night, every window blazin', or up late, till after midnight. Whoever's on duty sees the night out, nobody else's business, unless they send an alarm for help, and that ain't often; not twice a year. Mostly he's as quiet as you or me, as long as he's obeyed.

"'His temper's short though. Now he'll fly into a rage if he's not answered quick; again he'll storm if the watchers come near him uncalled.'

"Of long inaudible whispers I caught fragments.

"Once:

"'Oh, then he'll have no one near. You can hear him sobbing like a child. When he's worst you'll hear him, still nights, howlin' and screamin' like a lost soul.'

"Again:

"'Clean-fleshed as a child and no more hairy than you or me.'

"Again:

"'Fiddle? No violinist can beat him. I've listened hours. It makes you think of your sins. An' then it'll change an' you remember your first sweetheart, an' spring rains and flowers, an' when you was a child on your mother's knee. It tears your heart out.'

"The two phrases that seemed to mean most were:
"'He won't stan' any interference.'
"And:
"'Never a lock touched till daylight after he's once locked in.'
"Now what do you think?" Thwaite asked me.

"It sounds," I said, "as if the place were a one-patient asylum for a lunatic with long lucid intervals."

"Something like that," Thwaite answered, "but there seems to be more in it than that. I can't make all the things I hear fit. Appleshaw said one thing that runs in my head:
"'Seein' him in the suds give me a turn.'
"And Kitworth said once:
"'It was the bright colors alongside of it that made my blood run cold.'
"And Appleshaw said more than once, in varying words, but always with the same meaning tone:
"'You'll never get over bein' afraid of him. But you'll respect him more and more, you'll almost love him. You won't fear him for his looks, but for his awful wisdom. He's that wise, no man is more so.'
"Once Kitworth answered:
"'I don't envy Sturry locked in there with him.'
"'Sturry nor none of us that's his most trusted man for the time bein' is not to be envied,' Appleshaw agreed. 'But you'll come to it, as I have, if you're the man I take you for.'

"That's about all I got from listening," Thwaite went on, "the rest I got from watching and scouting. I made sure of the building they call the Pavilion, that's his usual home. But sometimes he spends his nights in one or the other of the towers, they stand all by themselves. Sometimes the lights are all out after ten o'clock or even nine; then again they're on till after midnight. Sometimes they come on late, two o'clock or three. I have heard music too, violin music, as Appleshaw described it, and organ music, too; but no howling. He is certainly a lunatic, judging by the statuary."

"Statuary?" I queried.

"Yes," Thwaite said, "statuary. Big figures and groups, all crazy men with heads like elephants or American eagles, perfectly crazy statuary. But all well-done. They stand all about the park. The little, square building between the Pavilion and the green tower is his sculpture studio."

"You seem to know the place mighty well," I said.

"I do," Thwaite assented, "I've gotten to know it well. At first I tried nights like this. Then I dared starlight. Then I dared even moonlight. I've never had a scare. I've sat on the front steps of the Pavilion at one o'clock of starlight night and never been challenged. I even tried staying in all day, hiding in some bushes, hoping to see him."

"Ever see him?" I inquired.

"Never," Thwaite answered, "I've heard him though. He rides horseback after dark. I've watched the horse being led up and down in front of the Pavilion, till it got too dark to see it from where I was hid. I've heard it pass me in the dark. But I could never get the horse against the sky to see what was on it. Hiding and getting downhill on a road, close to it, don't go together."

"You didn't see him the day you spent there?" I insisted.

"No," Thwaite said, "I didn't. I was disappointed too. For a big auto purred up to the Pavilion entrance and stood under the porte cochère. But when it spun round the park there was nobody in it, only the chauffeur in front and a pet monkey on the back seat."

"A pet monkey!" I exclaimed.

"Yes," he said. "You know how a dog, a Newfoundland, or a terrier, will sit up in an auto and look grand and superior and enjoy himself? Well, that monkey sat there just like that turning his head one way and the other taking in the view."

"What was he like?" I asked.

"Sort of dog-faced ape," Thwaite told me, "more like a mastiff."

Rivvin grunted.

"This isn't business," Thwaite went on, "we've got to get down to business. The point is the wall is their only guard, there's no dog, perhaps because of the pet monkey as much as anything else. They lock Mr. Eversleigh up every night with only one valet to take care of him. They never interfere whatever noise they hear or light they see, unless the alarm is sent out and I have located the alarm wires you are to cut. That's all. Do you go?"

Rivvin was sitting close to me, half on me. I could feel his great muscles and the butt of his pistol against my hip.

"I come with you," I said.

"Of your own accord?" Thwaite insisted.

The butt of that pistol moved as Rivvin breathed.

"I come of my own accord," I said.

III

Afoot Thwaite led as confidently as he had driven the car. It was the stillest, pitchiest night I ever experienced, without light, air, sound or smell to guide anyone: through that fog Thwaite sped like a man moving about his own bedroom, never for a second at a loss.

"Here's the place," he said at the wall, and guided my hand to feel the ring-bolt in the grass at its foot. Rivvin made a back for him and I scrambled up on the two. Tip-toe on Thwaite's shoulders I could just finger the coping.

"Stand on my head, you fool!" he whispered.

I clutched the coping. Once astraddle of it I let down one end of the silk ladder.

"Fast!" breathed Thwaite from below.

I drew it taut and went down. The first sweep of my fingers in the grass found the other ring-bolt. I made the ladder fast and gave it the signal twitches. Rivvin came over first, then Thwaite. Through the park he led evenly. When he halted he caught me by the elbow and asked:

"Can you see any lights?"

"Not a light," I told him.

"Same here," he said, "there are no lights. Every window is dark. We're in luck."

He led again for a while. Stopping he said only:

"Here's where you shin up. Cut every wire, but don't waste time cutting any twice."

The details of his directions were exact. I found every handhold and foothold as he had schooled me. But I needed all my nerve. I realized that no heavyweight like Rivvin or Thwaite could have won it. When I came down I was limp and tottery.

"Just one swallow!" Thwaite said, putting a flask to my lips. Then we went on. The night was so black and the fog so thick that I saw no loom of the building till we were against its wall.

"Here's where you go in," Thwaite directed.

Doubly I understood why I was with them. Neither could have squeezed through that aperture in the stone. I barely managed it. Inside, instead of the sliding crash I had dreaded, I landed with a mere crunch, the coal in that bin was not anthracite. Likewise the bin under the window was for soft-coal. I blessed my luck and felt encouraged. The window I got open without too much work. Rivvin and Thwaite slid in. We crunched downhill four or five steps and stood on a firm floor. Rivvin flashed his electric candle boldly around. We were between a suite of trim coal-bins and a battery of serried furnaces. There was no door at either end of the open space in which we stood. I had a momentary vision of the alternative windows and coal-chutes above the bins, of two big panels of shiny, colored tiling, of clear brick-work, fresh-painted, jetty iron and dazzling-white brass-ringed asbestos, of a black vacancy between two furnaces. Toward that I half heard, half felt Rivvin turn. During the rest of our adventure he led, Thwaite followed and I mostly tagged or groped after Thwaite, often judging of their position or movement by that combination of senses which is neither hearing nor touch, though partly both.

Rivvin's torch flashed again. We were in a cement-floored, brick-walled passage, with a door at each end and on the side facing us doors in a bewildering row. In the darkness that came after the flash I followed the others to the right. Well through the doorway we stood still, breathing and listening. When Rivvin illuminated our environment we saw about us thousands of bottles, all set aslant, neck down, in tiers of racks that reached to the ceiling. Edging between them we made the circuit of the cellar, but found no sign of any door save that by which we had entered. A whispered growl from Rivvin, a nudge from Thwaite and we went back the full length of the passage. Again we found ourselves in a wine vault, the duplicate of that we had left, and with the same peculiarity.

Our curiosity overcame any prudence. Rivvin, instead of flashing his torch at intervals, kept the light steady, and we scrutinized, examined and whispered our astonishment. As in its fellow there was not in all this vault any spare space, the aisles were narrow, the racks reached the girders supporting the flat arches, every rack was so full that a holder empty of its bottle was scarcely findable. And there was not in all that great cellar, there was not among all those tens of thousands of bottles a magnum, or a quart or even a pint. They were all splits. We handled a number and all had the same label. I know now what the device was, from seeing it so often and so much larger afterwards, but there it seemed a picture of a skirt-dancer leading an alligator by a dog chain. There was no name of any wine or liquor on any bottle, but each label had a red number, 17, or 45 or 328, above the picture, and under it:

"Bottled for Hengist Eversleigh."

"We know his name now," Thwaite whispered.

Back in the passage Rivvin took the first door to the left. It brought us to an easy stone stair between walls, which turned twice to the left at broad landings.

When we trod a softer footing we stood a long time breathing cautiously and listening.

Presently Rivvin flashed his light. It showed to our left a carpeted stair, the dull red carpet bulging up over thick pads and held down by brass stair-rods; the polished quartered oak of the molded door-jamb or end of wainscot beyond it; the floor-covering of brownish-yellow or yellowish brown linoleum or something similar, made to look like inlaid wood; and the feet, legs and thighs of a big stocky man. The light shone but the fraction of a second, yet it showed plain his knee-breeches, tight stockings on his big calves, and bright buckles at his knees and on his low shoes.

There was no loud sound, but the blurred brushy noise of a mute struggle. I backed against a window-sill and could back no further. All I could hear was the shuffling, rasping sounds of the fight, and panting that became a sort of gurgle.

Again the light flashed and stayed full bright. I saw that it was Thwaite struggling with the man, and that one of his big hands was on Thwaite's throat. Thwaite had him round the neck and his face was against Thwaite's chest. His hair was brownish. Rivvin's slung-shot crunched horribly on his skull. Instantly the light went out.

Thwaite, radiating heat like a stove, stood gasping close by me. I heard no other noise after the body thudded on the floor except that on the carpeted stair I seemed to hear light treads, as it were of a big dog or of a frightened child, padding away upward.

"Did you hear anything?" I whispered.

Rivvin punched me.

After Thwaite was breathing naturally, he turned on his torch and Rivvin did the same.

The dead man was oldish, over fifty I should judge, tall, large in all his dimensions, and spare, though heavy. His clothing was a gold-laced livery of green velvet, with green velvet knee breeches, green silk stockings and green leather pumps. The four buckles were gold.

Thwaite startled me by speaking out loud.

"I take it, Rivvin," he said, "this is the trusted valet. He would have yelled if there had been anybody to call. Either we have this building to ourselves or we have no one to deal with except Mr. Hengist Eversleigh."

Rivvin grunted.

"If he is here," Thwaite went on, "he's trying to send the alarm over the cut wires, or he's frightened and hiding. Let's find him and finish him, if he's here, and then find his diamonds. Anyway let's find those diamonds."

Rivvin grunted.

Swiftly they led from room to room and floor to floor. Not a door resisted. We had been curious and astonished in the wine-vaults; above we were electrified and numb. We were in a palace of wonders, among such a profusion of valuables that even Rivvin, after the second or third opportunity, ceased any attempt to pocket or bag anything. We came upon nothing living, found no door locked and apparently made the tour of the entire building.

When they halted, I halted. We were delirious with amazement, frantic with inquisitiveness, frenzied with curiosity, incredulous, hysterical, dazed and quivering.

Thwaite spoke in the dark.

"I'm going to see this place plain, all over it, if I die for it."

They flashed their torches. We were right beside the body of the murdered footman. Rivvin and Thwaite did not seem to mind the corpse. They waved their torches until one fell on an electric-light button.

"Hope those wires are underground," Thwaite remarked. He pushed the button and the electric lights came on full and strong. We were apparently at the foot of the back stairs, in a sort of lobby, an expanded passage-way out of which opened several doors.

We all three regarded the knobs of those doors. As we had half seen by flash-light on every door everywhere each door had two knobs, one like any door-knob, the other about half way between it and the floor. Rivvin opened one which proved to lead into a broom closet. He tried the knobs, Thwaite and I watching too. The lock and latch were at the upper knob, but controlled by either knob indifferently. They tried another door, but my eyes would roam to the dead body.

Rivvin and Thwaite paid no more attention to it than if it had not been there. I had never seen but one killed man before and neither wanted to be reminded of that one nor relished the sight of this one. I stared down the blackness of the stone stair up which we had come or glanced into the dimness of the padded stairway.

Then Rivvin, feeling inside the open door, found the button and turned on the lights. It was a biggish dining-room, the four corners cut off by inset glass-framed shelved closets, full of china and glassware. The furniture was oak.

"Servants' dining-room," Thwaite commented.

Turning on the lights in each we went through a series of rooms; a sort of sitting-room, with card-tables and checker-boards; a library walled with bookcases and open book-shelves, its two stout oak tables littered with magazines and newspapers; a billiard room with three tables, a billiard-table, a pool-table and one for bagatelle; a sort of lounging room, all leather-covered sofas and deep armchairs; an entry with hat-hooks and umbrella-stands, the outer door dark oak with a great deal of stained glass set in and around it.

"All servants' rooms," Thwaite commented. "Every bit of the furniture is natural man-size. Let's go on."

Back we went along a passage and into a big kitchen beyond the dining-room.

"Never mind the pantries till we come down again," Thwaite commanded. "Let's go upstairs. We'll do the banqueting-hall after those bedrooms, and the writing rooms and study last. I want a real sight of those pictures."

They passed the dead flunkey as if he had not been there at all.

On the floor above Thwaite touched Rivvin's elbow.

"I forgot these," he said.

We inspected a medium-sized sitting-room with a round center-table, an armchair drawn up by it, and in the armchair a magazine and a sort of wadded smoking-jacket. Next this room was a bedroom and a bathroom.

"Mr. Footman's quarters," Thwaite remarked, staring unconcernedly at a photograph of a dumpy young woman and two small children, set on the bureau. "All man-size furniture here, too."

Rivvin nodded.

Up the second flight of that back-stair we went again. It ended in a squarish hallway or lobby or room with nothing in it but two settees. It had two doors.

Rivvin pushed one open, felt up and down for the electric button and found it.

We all three gasped; we almost shouted. We had had glimpses of this gallery before, but the flood of light from a thousand bulbs under inverted trough-reflectors dazzled us; the pictures fairly petrified us.

The glare terrified me.

"Surely we are crazy," I objected, "to make all this illumination. It's certain to give the alarm."

"Alarm nothing," Thwaite snapped. "Haven't I watched these buildings night after night? I told you he is never disturbed at any hour, lights or no lights."

My feeble protest thus brushed away I became absorbed, like the others, in those incredible paintings. Rivvin was merely stupidly dazed in uncomprehending wonder, Thwaite keenly speculative, questing for a clue to the origin of their peculiarities, I totally bewildered at the perfection of their execution, shivering at their uncanniness.

The gallery was all of ninety feet long, nearly thirty wide and high. Apparently it had a glass roof above the rectangle of reflectors. The pictures covered all four walls, except the little door at either end. None was very small and several were very large. A few were landscapes, but all had figures in them, most were crowded with figures.

Those figures!

They were human figures, but not one had a human head. The heads were invariably those of birds, animals or fishes, generally of animals, some of common animals, many of creatures I had seen pictures of or had heard of, some of imaginary creatures like dragons or griffons, more than half of the heads either of animals I knew nothing of or which had been invented by the painter.

Close to me when the lights blazed out was a sea picture, blurred grayish foggy weather and a heavy ground-swell; a strange other-world open boat with fish heaped in the bottom of it and standing among them four human figures in shining boots like rubber boots and wet, shiny, loose coats like oilskins, only the boots and skins were red as claret, and the four figures had hyenas' heads. One was steering and the others were hauling at a net. Caught in the net was a sort of merman, but different from the pictures of mermaids. His shape was all human except the head and hands and feet; every bit of him was covered with fish-scales all rainbowy. He had flat broad fins in place of hands and feet and his head was that of a fat hog. He was thrashing about in the net in an agony of impotent effort. Queer as the picture was it had a compelling impression of reality, as if the scene were actually happening before our eyes.

Next to it was a picnic in a little meadow by a pond between woods with mountains behind it higher up. Every one of the picnickers about the white tablecloth spread on the grass had the head of a different animal, one of a sheep, one of a camel, and the rest of animals like deer, not one of them known to me.

Then next to that was a fight of two compound creatures shaped like centaurs, only they had bulls' bodies, with human torsos growing out of them, where the necks ought to be, the arms scaly snakes with open-mouthed, biting heads in place of hands; and instead of human heads roosters' heads, bills open and pecking. Under the creatures in place of bulls' hoofs were yellow roosters' legs, stouter than chickens' legs and with short thick toes, and long sharp spurs like game roosters'. Yet these fantastic chimeras appeared altogether alive and their movements looked natural, yes that's the word, natural.

Every picture was as complete a staggerer as these first three. Every one was signed in the lower left hand corner in neat smallish letters of bright gold paint:

> "Hengist Eversleigh"

and a date.

"Mr. Hengist Eversleigh is a lunatic, that's certain," Thwaite commented, "but he unquestionably knows how to paint."

There must have been more than fifty pictures in that gallery, maybe as many as seventy-five, and every one a nightmare.

Beyond was a shorter gallery of the same width, end on to the side of the first, and beyond that the duplicate of the first; the three taking up three sides of the building. The fourth side was a studio, the size of the second gallery; it had a great skylight of glass tilted sideways all along over one whole wall. It was whitewashed, very plain and empty-looking, with two easels, a big one and a little one.

On the little one was a picture of some vegetables and five or six little fairies, as it were, with children's bodies and mice's heads, nibbling at a carrot.

On the big one was a canvas mostly blank. One side of it had a palm-tree in splashy, thick slaps of paint and under it three big crabs with cocoanuts in their claws. A man's feet and legs showed beside them and the rest was unfinished.

The three galleries had fully three hundred paintings, for the smaller gallery contained only small canvases. Besides being impressed with the grotesqueness of the subjects and the perfection of the drawing and coloring, two things struck me as to the pictures collectively.

First, there was not represented in any one of all those paintings any figure of a woman or any female shape of any kind. The beast-headed figures were all, whether clothed or nude, figures of men. The animals, as far as I could see, were all males.

Secondly, nearly half of the pictures were modifications or parallels or emulations (I could hardly say travesties or imitations) of well-known pictures by great artists, paintings I had seen in public galleries or knew from engravings or photographs or reproductions in books or magazines.

There was a picture like Washington crossing the Delaware and another like Washington saying farewell to his generals. There was a batch of Napoleon pictures; after the paintings of Napoleon at Austerlitz, at Friedland, giving the eagles to his regiments, on the morning of Waterloo, coming down the steps at Fontainebleau, and on the deck of the ship going to St. Helena. There were dozens of other pictures of generals or kings or emperors reviewing victorious armies; two or three of Lincoln. One that hit me hardest, obviously after some picture I had never seen or heard of, of the ghost of Lincoln, far larger than a life-size man, towering above the surviving notabilities of his time on the grandstand reviewing the homecoming Federal army marching through Washington.

In every one of these pictures, the dominant figure, whether it stood for Lincoln, Napoleon, Washington, or some other general or ruler; whatever uniform or regalia clothed its human shape, had the same head. The heads of the fighting men in all these pictures were those of dogs, all alike in any one picture, but differing from one to another; terriers or wolf-hounds or mastiffs or what not. The heads of any men not soldiers were those of oxen or sheep or horses or some other mild sort of animal. The head of the dominant figure I then took to be invented, legendary, fabulous—oh, that's not the word I want.

"Mythological?" I suggested, the only interruption I interjected into his entire narrative.

Yes, mythological, he returned. I thought it was a mythological creature. The long-jawed head, like a hound's; the little pointed yellow beard under the chin; the black, naked ears, like a hairless dog's ears and yet not doggy, either; the ridge of hair on top of the skull; the triangular shape of the whole head; the close-set, small, beady, terribly knowing eyes; the brilliant patches of color on either side of the muzzle; all these made a piercing impression of individuality and yet seemed not so much actual as mythological.

It takes a great deal longer to tell what we saw on that third floor than it took to see it. All round the galleries under the pictures were cases of drawers, solidly built in one length like a counter and about as high. Thwaite went down one side of the gallery and Rivvin down the other, pulling them out and slamming them shut again. All I saw held photographs of pictures. But Rivvin and Thwaite were taking no chances and looked into every drawer. I had plenty of time to gaze about me and circulated at a sort of cantering trot around the green-velvet miniature sofas and settees placed back to back down the middle of the floor-space. It seemed to me that Mr. Hengist Eversleigh was a great master of figure and landscape drawing, color, light and perspective.

As we went down the duplicate staircase at the other corner from where we came up Thwaite said:

"Now for those bedrooms."

By the stair we found another valet's or footman's apartment, sitting-room, bedroom and bathroom, just like the one by the other stair. And there were four more between them, under the studio and over the lounging-rooms.

On the east and west sides of the building were "the" bedrooms, twelve apartments, six on each side; each of the twelve made up of a bedroom, a dressing-room and a bathroom.

The beds were about three feet long, and proportionately narrow and low. The furniture, bureaus, tables, chairs, chests-of-drawers and the rest, harmonized with the dimensions of the beds, except the cheval-glasses and wall-mirrors which reached the ceilings. The bathtubs were almost pools, about nine feet by six and all of three feet deep, each a single block of porcelain.

The shapes and sizes and styles of the furniture were duplicated all through, but the colors varied, so that the twelve suites were in twelve colors; black, white, gray and brown, and light and dark yellow, red, green and blue; wall coverings, hangings, carpets and rugs all to match in each suite. The panels of the walls had the same picture, however, repeated over and over, two, four or six times to a room and in every suite alike.

This picture was the design I had failed to make out on the labels of the bottles. It was set as a medallion in each panel of the blue or red walls, or whatever other color they were. The background of the picture was a vague sort of palish sky and blurred, hazy clouds above tropical-looking foliage. The chief figure was an angel, in flowing white robes, floating on silvery-plumed wings widespread. The angel's face was a human face, the only human face in any picture in that palace, the face of a grave, gentle, rather girlish young man.

The creature the angel was leading was a huge, bulky crocodile, with a gold collar about its neck, and a gold chain from that, not to the angel's hand, but to a gold fetter about his wrist.

Under each picture was a verse of four lines, always the same.

> "Let not your baser nature drag you down.
> Utter no whimper, not one sigh or moan,
> Hopeless of respite, solace, palm or crown
> Live out your life unflinching and alone."

I saw it so often I shall never forget it.

The bathrooms were luxurious in the extreme, a needle-bath, a shower-bath, two basins of different sizes in each, besides the sunk pool-tub. The dressing-rooms had each a variety of wardrobes. One or two we opened, finding in each several suits of little clothes, as if for a boy under six years old. One closet had shelf above shelf of small shoes, not much over four inches long.

"Evidently," Thwaite remarked, "Hengist Eversleigh is a dwarf, whatever else he is."

Rivvin left the wardrobes and closets alone after the first few.

Each bedroom had in it nothing but the bed and on each side of it a sort of wine-cooler, like a pail with a lid, but bigger, set on three short legs so that its top was level with the bed. We opened most of them; every one we opened was filled with ice, bedded in which were several half-pint bottles. Every one of the twelve beds had the covers carefully turned down. Not one showed any sign of having been occupied. The wine-coolers were solid silver but we left them where they were. As Thwaite remarked, it could have taken two full-sized freight cars to contain the silver we had seen.

In the dressing-rooms the articles like brushes and combs on the bureaus were all of gold, and most set with jewels. Rivvin began to fill a bag with those entirely of metal, but even he made no attempt to tear the backs off the brushes or to waste energy on any other breakage. By the time we had scanned the twelve suites Rivvin could barely carry his bag.

The front room on the south side of the building was a library full of small, showily-bound books in glass-fronted cases all the way to the ceiling, covering every wall except where the two doors and six windows opened. There were small, narrow tables, the height of those in the dressing-rooms. There were magazines on them and papers. Thwaite opened a bookcase and I another and we looked at three or four books. Each had in it a book-plate with the device of the angel and the crocodile.

Rivvin did not find the electric button in the main hallway and we went down the great broad, curving stair by our electric candles. Rivvin turned to the left and we found ourselves in the banquet hall as Thwaite had called it, a room all of forty by thirty and gorgeous beyond any description.

The diminutive table, not three feet square, was a slab of crystal-white glass set on silver-covered legs. The tiny armchair, the only chair in the big room, was solid silver, with a crimson cushion loose in it.

The sideboards and glass-fronted closets paralyzed us. One had fine china and cut glass; wonderful china and glass. But four held a table service of gold, all of pure gold; forks, knives, spoons, plates, bowls, platters, cups, everything; all miniature, but a profusion of everything. We hefted the pieces. They were gold. All the pieces were normal in shape except that instead of wine-glasses, goblets and tumblers were things like broad gravy-boats on stems or short feet, all lopsided, with one projecting edge like the mouth of a pitcher, only broader and flatter. There were dozens of these. Rivvin filled two bags with what two bags would hold. The three bags were all we three could carry, must have been over a hundred and fifty pounds apiece.

"We'll have to make two trips to the wall," Thwaite said. "You brought six bags, didn't you, Rivvin?"

Rivvin grunted.

At the foot of the grand staircase Rivvin found the electric button and flooded the magnificent stairway with light.

The stair itself was all white marble, the rails yellow marble, and the paneling of the dado malachite. But the main feature was the painting above the landing. This was the most amazing of all the paintings we had come upon.

I remembered something like it, an advertisement of a root-beer or talcum powder, or some other proprietary article, representing all the nations of the earth and their rulers in the foreground congratulating the orator.

This picture was about twenty feet wide and higher than its width. There was a throne, a carved and jeweled throne, set on an eminence. There was a wide view on either side of the throne, and all filled with human figures with animal heads, an infinite throng, all facing the throne. Nearest it were figures that seemed meant for all the presidents and kings and queens and emperors of the world. I recognized the robes or uniforms of some of them. Some had heads taken from their national coat of arms, like the heads of the Austrian and Russian eagles. All these figures were paying homage to the figure that stood before the throne; the same monster we had seen in place of Lincoln or Washington or Napoleon in the paintings upstairs.

He stood proudly with one foot on a massive crocodile. He was dressed in a sort of revolutionary uniform, low shoes, with gold buckles, white stockings and knee-breeches, a red waistcoat, and a bright blue coat. His head was the same beast-head of the other pictures, triangular and strange, which I then thought mythological.

Above and behind the throne floated on outspread silver wings the white-robed angel with the Sir Galahad face.

Rivvin shut off the lights almost instantly, but even in the few breaths while I looked I saw it all.

The three sacks of swag we put down by the front door.

The room opposite the banquet-hall was a music room, with an organ and a piano, both with keys and keyboards far smaller than usual; great cases of music books; an array of brass instruments and cellos and more than a hundred violin cases. Thwaite opened one or two.

"These'd be enough to make our fortune," he said. "If we could get away with them."

Beyond the music room was the study. It had in it four desks, miniature in size and the old-fashioned model with drawers below, a lid to turn down and form a writing surface, and a sort of bookcase above with a peaked top. All were carved and on the lids in the carving we read:

JOURNAL
MUSIC
CRITICISM
BUSINESS

Thwaite opened the desk marked BUSINESS and pulled open the drawers.

In pigeon-holes of the desk were bundles of new, clean greenbacks and treasury notes of higher denominations; five each of fives, tens, twenties, fifties and hundreds. Thwaite tossed one bundle of each to me and Rivvin and pocketed the rest.

He bulged.

One drawer had a division down the middle. One half was full of ten-dollar gold pieces, the other half of twenties.

"I've heard of misers," said Thwaite, "but this beats hell. Think of that crazy dwarf, a prisoner in this palace, running his hands through this and gloating over the cash he can never use."

Rivvin loaded a bag with the coin and when he had them all he could barely lift the bag. Leaving it where it lay before the desk he strode the length of the room and tried the door at the end.

It was fast.

Instantly Rivvin and Thwaite were like two terriers after a rat.

"This is where the diamonds are," Thwaite declared, "and Mr. Hengist Eversleigh is in there with them."

He and Rivvin conferred a while together.

"You kneel low," Thwaite whispered. "Duck when you open it. He'll fire over you. Then you've got him. See?"

Rivvin tip-toed to the door, knelt and tried key after key in the lock.

There were at least twenty bulbs in the chandelier of that room and the light beat down on him. His red neck dew-lapped over the low collar of his lavenderish shirt, his great broad back showed vast and powerful.

On the other side of the doorway Thwaite stood, his finger at the electric button.

Each had his slung-shot in his left hand. They had spun the cylinders of their revolvers and stuck them in their belts in front before Rivvin began work on the lock.

I heard a click.

Rivvin put up his hand.

The lights went out.

In the black dark we stood, stood until I could almost see the outlines of the windows; less black against the intenser blackness.

Soon I heard another click, and the grate of an opened door.

Then a kind of snarl, a thump like a blow, a sort of strangling gasp, and the cushiony sounds of a struggle.

Thwaite turned on the lights.

Rivvin was in the act of staggering up from his knees. I saw a pair of small, pink hands, the fingers intertwined, locked behind Rivvin's neck. They slipped apart as I caught sight of them.

I had a vision of small feet in little patent leather silver-buckled low-shoes, of green socks, of diminutive legs in white trousers flashing right and left in front of Rivvin, as if he held by the throat a struggling child.

Next I saw that his arms were thrown up, wide apart.

He collapsed and fell back his full length with a dull crash.

Then I saw the snout!

Saw the wolf-jaws on his throat!

Saw the blood welling round the dazzling white fangs, and recognized the reality of the sinister head I had seen over and over in his pictures.

Rivvin made the fish-out-of-water contortions of a man being killed.

Thwaite brought his slung-shot down on the beast-head skull.

The blow was enough to crush in a steel cylinder.

The beast wrinkled its snout and shook its head from side to side, worrying like a bull-dog at Rivvin's throat.

Again Thwaite struck and again and again. At each blow the portentous head oscillated viciously. The awful thing about it to me was the two blue bosses on each side of the muzzle, like enamel, shiny and hard looking; and the hideous welt of red, like fresh sealing-wax, down between them and along the snout.

Rivvin's struggles grew weaker as the great teeth tore at his throat. He was dead before Thwaite's repeated blows drove in the splintered skull and the clenched jaws relaxed, the snout crinkling and contracting as the dog-teeth slid from their hold.

Thwaite gave the monster two or three more blows, touched Rivvin and fairly dashed out of the room, shouting:

"You stay here!"

I heard the sound of prying and sawing. There alone I looked but once at the dead cracksman.

The thing that had killed him was the size of a four to six year old child, but more stockily built, looked entirely human up to the neck, and was dressed in a coat of bright dark blue, a vest of crimson velvet, and white duck trousers. As I looked the muzzle wriggled for the last time, the jaws fell apart and the carcass rolled sideways. It was the very duplicate in miniature of the figure in the big picture on the staircase landing.

Thwaite came dashing back. Without any sign of any qualm he searched Rivvin and tossed me two or three bundles of greenbacks.

He stood up.

He laughed.

"Curiosity," he said, "will be the death of me."

Then he stripped the clothing from the dead monster, kneeling by it.

The beast-hair stopped at the shirt collar. Below that the skin was human, as was the shape, the shape of a forty-year-old man, strong and vigorous and well-made, only dwarfed to the smallness of a child.

Across the hairy breast was tattooed in blue,

"HENGIST EVERSLEIGH."

"Hell," said Thwaite.

He stood up and went to the fatal door. Inside he found the electric button.

The room was small and lined with cases of little drawers, tier on tier, rows of brass knobs on mahogany.

Thwaite opened one.

It was velvet lined and grooved like a jeweler's tray and contained rings, the settings apparently emeralds.

Thwaite dumped them into one of the empty bags he had taken from Rivvin's corpse.

The next case was of similar drawers of rings set with rubies. The first of these Thwaite dumped in with the emeralds.

But then he flew round the room pulling out drawers and slamming them shut, until he came upon trays of unset diamonds. These he emptied into his sack to the last of them, then diamond rings on them, other jewelry set with diamonds, then rubies and emeralds till the sack was full.

He tied its neck, had me open a second sack and was dumping drawer after drawer into that when suddenly he stopped.

His nose worked, worked horridly like that of the dead monster.

I thought he was going crazy and was beginning to laugh nervously, was on the verge of hysterics when he said:

"Smell! Try what you smell."

I sniffed.

"I smell smoke," I said.

"So do I," he agreed. "This place is afire."

"And we locked in!" I exclaimed.

"Locked in?" he sneered. "Bosh. I broke open the front door the instant I was sure they were dead. Come! Drop that empty bag. This is no time for haggling."

We had to step between the two corpses. Rivvin was horridly dead. The colors had all faded from the snout. The muzzle was all mouse-color.

When we had hold of the bag of coin, Thwaite turned off the electric lights and we struggled out with that and the bag of jewels, and went out into the hallway full of smoke.

"We can carry only these," Thwaite warned me. "We'll have to leave the rest."

I shouldered the bag of coin, and followed him down the steps, across a gravel road, and, oh the relief of treading turf and feeling the fog all about me.

At the wall Thwaite turned and looked back.

"No chance to try for those other bags," he said.

In fact the red glow was visible at that distance and was fast becoming a glare.

I heard shouts.

We got the bags over the wall and reached the car. Thwaite cranked up at once and we were off.

How we went I could not guess, nor in what directions, nor even how long. Ours was the only vehicle on the roads we darted along.

When the dawn light was near enough for me to see Thwaite stopped the car.

He turned on me.

"Get out!" he said.

"What?" I asked.

He shoved his pistol muzzle in my face.

"You've fifty thousand dollars in bank bills in your pockets," he said. "It's a half a mile down that road to a railway station. Do you understand English? Get out!"

I got out.

The car shot forward into the morning fog and was gone.

IV

He was silent a long time.

"What did you do then?" I asked.

"Headed for New York," he said, "and got on a drunk. When I came round I had barely eleven thousand dollars. I headed for Cook's office and bargained for a ten thousand dollar tour of the world, the most places and the longest time they'd give for the money; the whole cost on them. I not to need a cent after I started."

"What date was that?" I asked.

He meditated and gave me some approximate indications rather rambling and roundabout.

"What did you do after you left Cook's?" I asked.

"I put a hundred dollars in a savings bank," he said. "Bought a lot of clothes and things and started.

"I kept pretty sober all round the world because the only way to get full was by being treated and I had no cash to treat back with.

"When I landed in New York I thought I was all right for life. But no sooner did I have my hundred and odd dollars in my pockets than I got full again. I don't seem able to keep sober."

"Are you sober now?" I asked.

"Sure," he asserted.

He seemed to shed his cosmopolitan vocabulary the moment he came back to everyday matters.

"Let's see you write what I tell you on this," I suggested, handing him a fountain-pen and a torn envelope, turned inside out.

Word by word after my dictation he wrote.

"Until you hear from me again
   Yours truly,
      No Name."

I took the paper from him and studied the handwriting.

"How long were you on that spree?" I asked.

"Which?" he twinkled.

"Before you came to and had but eleven thousand dollars left," I explained.

"I don't know," he said, "I didn't know anything I had been doing."

"I can tell you one thing you did," I said.

"What?" he queried.

"You put four packets, each of one hundred hundred-dollar bills, in a thin manila clasp-envelope, directed it to a New York lawyer and mailed the envelope to him with no letter in it, only a half sheet of dirty paper with nothing on it except: 'Keep this for me until I ask for it,' and the signature you have just written."

"Honest?" he enunciated incredulously.

"Fact!" I said.

"Then you believe what I've told you," he exclaimed joyfully.

"Not a bit I don't," I asseverated.

"How's that?" he asked.

"If you were drunk enough," I explained, "to risk forty thousand dollars in that crazy way, you were drunk enough to dream all the complicated nightmare you have spun out to me."

"If I did," he argued, "how did I get the fifty thousand odd dollars?"

"I'm willing to suppose you got it with no more dishonesty on your part," I told him, "than if you had come by it as you described."

"It makes me mad you won't believe me," he said.

"I don't," I finished.

He gloomed in silence.

Presently he said:

"I can stand looking at him now," and led the way to the cage where the big blue-nosed mandrill chattered his inarticulate bestialities and scratched himself intermittently.

He stared at the brute.

"And you don't believe me?" he regretted.

"Couldn't there be a mongrel, a hybrid?" he suggested.

"Put that out of your head," I told him, "the whole thing's incredible."

"Suppose she'd seen a critter like this," he persisted, "just at the wrong time?"

"Bosh!" I said. "Old wives' tales! Superstition! Impossibility!"

"His head," he declared, "was just like that." He shuddered.

"Somebody put drops in some of your drink," I suggested. "Anyhow, let's talk about something else. Come and have lunch with me."

Over the lunch I asked him:

"What city did you like best of all you saw?"

"Paris for mine," he grinned, "Paris forever."

"I tell you what I advise you to do," I said.

"What's that?" he asked, his eyes bright on mine.

"Let me buy you an annuity with your forty thousand," I explained, "an annuity payable in Paris. There's enough interest already to pay your way to Paris and leave you some cash till the first quarterly payment comes due."

"You wouldn't feel yourself defrauding the Eversleighs?" he questioned.

"If I'm defrauding any people," I said, "I don't know who they are."

"How about the fire?" he insisted. "I'll bet you heard of it. Don't the dates agree?"

"The dates agree," I admitted. "And the servants were all dismissed, the remaining buildings and walls torn down and the place cut up and sold in portions just about as it would have been if your story were true."

"There now!" he ejaculated. "You do believe me!"

"I do not!" I insisted. "And the proof is that I'm ready to carry out my annuity plan for you."

"I agree," he said, and stood up from the lunch table.

"Where are we going now?" he inquired as we left the restaurant.

"Just you come with me," I told him, "and ask no questions."

I piloted him to the Museum of Archæology and led him circuitously to what I meant for an experiment on him. I dwelt on other subjects nearby and waited for him to see it himself.

He saw.

He grabbed me by the arm.

"That's him!" he whispered. "Not the size, but his very expression, in all his pictures."

He pointed to that magnificent, enigmatical black-diorite twelfth-dynasty statue which represents neither Anubis nor Seth, but some nameless cynocephalous god.

"That's him," he repeated. "Look at the awful wisdom of him."

I said nothing.

"And you brought me here!" he cried. "You meant me to see this! You do believe!"

"No," I maintained. "I do not believe."

V

After I waved a farewell to him from the pier I never saw him again.

We had an extensive correspondence six months later when he wanted his annuity exchanged for a joint-life annuity for himself and his bride. I arranged it for him with less difficulty than I had anticipated. His letter of thanks, explaining that a French wife was so great an economy that the shrinkage in his income was more than made up for, was the last I heard from him.

As he died more than a year ago and his widow is already married, this story can do him no harm. If the Eversleighs were defrauded they will never feel it and my conscience, at least, gives me no twinges.

Sorcery Island

WHEN I regained consciousness I was on my feet, standing erect, near enough to my burning aeroplane to feel the warmth radiated by the crackling flames with which every part of it was ablaze; far enough from it to be, despite the strong breeze, much more aware of the fierce heat of the late forenoon sunrays beating down on me from almost overhead out of the cloudless sky. My shadow, much shorter than I, was sharply outlined before me on the intensely white sand of the beach; which dazzling expanse, but a few paces to my right, ended abruptly in an almost straight line, at a little bank of about eight inches of exposed blackish loam, beyond which was dense tropical vegetation gleaming in the brilliant sunshine. Not much farther away on my left were great patches, almost heaps, fathoms long, yards wide and one or even two or three feet high, of unwholesome looking grayish white slimy foam, like persistent dirty soap-bubbles, strung along the margin of the sparkling dry sand, between it and the swishes of hissing froth that lashed lazily up from the sluggish breakers in which ended the long, broad-backed, sleepy swells of the endlessly recurrent ocean surges. As there was no cloud in the dark blue firmament, so there was no sail, no funnel-smoke in sight on the deep blue sea. Overhead, against the intense blue sky, whirled uncountable flocks of garishly pink flamingoes, some higher, some lower, crossing and recrossing each other, grotesque, flashing, and amazing in their myriads.

To my scrutinizing gaze, as to my first glance, it was manifest that there was no indication of wreckage, breakage or injury to any part of my aeroplane visible through the flames now fast consuming it. No bone of me was broken, no ligament strained. I had not a bruise on me, not a scratch. I did not feel shaken or jarred, my garments were untorn and not even rumpled or mussed. I conjectured at once, what is my settled opinion after long reflection, that I, in my stupor or trance or daze or whatever it was, had made some sort of a landing, had unstrapped myself, had clambered out of the fuselage, had staggered away from it, and had fainted; and that, while I was unconscious, someone had set fire to my aeroplane.

As I stood there on the beach I was flogging my memory to make it bridge over my interval of unconsciousness and I recollected vividly what had preceded my lapse and every detail of my sensations. I had been flying my aeroplane between the wide blue sky, unvaried by any cloud, and the wide blue sea, unbroken by any sign of sail, steamer or island. Then I descried a difference of appearance at one point of the horizon forward and on my right and steered towards it. Soon I made sure of a low island ahead of me.

Up to that instant I had never, in all my life, had anything resembling a delusion or even any thoughts that could be called queer. But, just as I made certain that I was approaching an island, there popped into my head, for no assignable reason, the recollection of the flock of white geese on my grandmother's farm and of how I, when seven years old or so, or maybe only six or perhaps even younger, used to make a pet of an unusually large and most uncommonly docile and friendly white gander, used to fondle him, and, in particular, used to straddle him and fairly ride about on him, he flapping his wings and squawking.

While I was wondering what in the world had made me think of that gander, all of a sudden, as I neared the island and would soon be over it, I had an indubitable delusion. Instead of seeing before me and about me the familiar parts of my aeroplane, I seemed to see nothing but sky and sea and myself astraddle of an enormous white gander, longer than a canoe, and bigger than a dray-horse; I seemed to see his immense, dazzlingly white wings, ten yards or more in spread, rhythmically beating the air on either side of me; I seemed to see, straight out in front of me, his long white neck, the flattened, rounded top of his big head, and the tip of his great yellow bill against the sky; what was more, instead of seeing my knees clad in khaki, my calves swathed in puttees and my feet in brown boots, I seemed to see my knees in blue corduroy knickerbockers, my legs in blue ribbed woolen stockings, against the white feathers of that gigantic dream-gander's back, and my feet sticking out on either side of him encased in low, square-toed shoes of black leather, of the cut one sees in pictures of Continental soldiers or of Benjamin Franklin as a lad, their big silver buckles plain to me against the blueness of the ocean far below me.

After being swallowed up in this astounding hallucination, which I vividly recalled, I remembered nothing until I came to myself, standing on the beach by what was left of my blazing aeroplane.

While struggling to recollect what I could remember and trying to surmise what had happened during my unconsciousness, I had been surveying my surroundings. On one hand I saw only the limitless and unvaried ocean from which came the cool seabreeze that fanned my left cheek and stirred my hair under the visor of my cap; on the other opened a wide, flat-floored valley, bounded by low hills, the highest, at the head of the valley, not over ninety feet above sea-level, crowned by a huge palatial building of pinkish stone, its two lofty stories topped by an ornate carved balustrade above which no roof showed, so that I inferred that the roof was flat. The hills shutting in my view on either side, lower and lower towards the sea, were rounded and covered with a dense growth of scrubby trees, not quite tall enough to be called forest. Close to the beach and hills, on each side of the valley, was what looked like a sort of model garden village. That on my right, as I faced inland, was of closely-set one-story cottages, bowered in flowering vines, under a grove of handsome, exotic-looking trees. The other, which I saw beyond the slackening flames above the embers of my aeroplane, was of roomy, broad-verandahed, two-story villas, generously spaced, beneath magnificent young shade-trees, mostly loaded with brilliant flowers.

As I was looking at the valley, the villages, the palace on the hill-top and from one to the other, with now and then a glance overhead at the hosts of wheeling flamingoes, I thought I had a second hallucination. I seemed to see, along a path through the riotous greenery, a human figure approaching me, but, when it drew near and I seemed to see it more clearly, I felt that it must be a figment of my imagination.

It was that of a tall, perfectly formed and gracefully moving young man. But, under the scorching rays of that caustic sunshine he was bare-headed and his shock of abundant, wavy and brilliantly yellow golden hair was bobbed off short below his ears like the hair of Italian page-boys in early Florentine and Venetian paintings. His eyes were very bright and a very light blue, his cheeks rosy, his bare neck pinkish. He was clad only in a tight-fitting stockinet garment of green silk, something like the patent underwear shown in advertising pictures. It looked very new, very silky and very green, and as unsuitable as possible for the climate, for its long, clinging sleeves reached to his wrists and the tight legs of it sheathed him to his ankles. His feet were encased in high laced shoes of a very bright, and apparently very soft, yellow leather, with (I was sure he was an hallucination) *every one of the five toes of each formed separately.*

Just as I was about to rub my eyes to banish this disconcerting apparition, I recognized him and saw him recognize me.

It was Pembroke!

His face, as he recognized me, did not express pleasure; what mine expressed, besides amazement, I could not conjecture. All in a flash my mind ran over what I knew of him and had heard. We had first met as freshmen and had seen little of each other during our life as classmates. Pembroke, at college, had been noted as the handsomest student of his day; as the youngest student of his class; as surrounding himself with the most luxurious furnishings, the most beautiful and costly pictures, bronzes, porcelains and art objects ever known in the quarters of any student at our college; as very self-indulgent, yet so brilliantly gifted that he stood fifth or sixth in a large class with an unusual proportion of bright students; as daft about languages, music and birds, and, frequently descanting on the wickedness and folly of allowing wild bird-life to be all-but exterminated; as so capricious and erratic that most of his acquaintances thought him odd and his enemies said he was cracked.

I had not seen him since our class dispersed after its graduation and the attendant ceremonies and festivities. I had heard that, besides having a very rich father, he had inherited, on his twenty-first birthday, an income of over four hundred thousand dollars a year and a huge accumulation of ready cash; that he had at once interested himself in the creation of refuges for migratory, rare and picturesque birds; that his fantastic whimsicalities and eccentricities had intensified so as to cause a series of quarrels and a complete estrangement between himself and his father; that he had bought an island somewhere and had absorbed himself in the fostering of wild bird-life and in the companionship of very questionable associates.

He held out his hand and we shook hands.

"You don't seem injured or hurt at all, Denbigh," he said. "How did you manage to get out of that blazing thing alive, let alone without any sign of scratch or scorch?"

"I must have gotten out of it before it caught fire," I replied. "I must have gone daffy or lost my wits as I drew over your island. I have no idea how I landed or why. The whole thing is a blank to me."

"You are lucky," he said, matter-of-factly, "to have landed at all. If your mind wandered, it is a miracle you did not smash on the coral rocks on the other side of the island or on one of the outlying keys, or fall into the ocean and drown.

"However, all's well that ends well. Nothing can be salvaged from the wreckage of your conveyance, that is clear. What you need is a bracer, food, rest, a bath, sleep, fresh clothes and whatever else will soothe you. Come along. I'll do all I can for you."

I followed him past the remnants of my aeroplane, along the beach, to the group of villas. Close to them and to the beach was a sort of park or open garden, with fountains playing and carved marble seats set here and there along concrete walks between beds of flowers, shrubberies, and trim lawns, all canopied by astonishingly vigorous and well-grown ornamental trees.

As we approached the nearest villa I saw a family group on its veranda, obviously parents and children; also I heard someone whistling "Annie Laurie" so exquisitely as to evidence superlative artistry. As we passed the entrance to the villa I was amazed to recognize Radnor, another classmate. But, as he ran down the steps to greet me, I reflected that there was nothing really astonishing in a man as opulent as Pembroke having as dependable a physician as he could engage resident on his island nor anything unnatural in his choosing an acquaintance.

"Denbigh," said Pembroke, "has dropped on us out of the wide blue sky. His aeroplane has been demolished, so he'll sojourn with us a while."

"You don't seem to need me," Radnor commented, conning me. "I see no blood and no indications of any broken bones. Can I patch you up, anywhere?"

"Not a bruise on me, as far as I know," I replied.

"Then," he laughed, "my prescription is two hours abed. Get undressed and horizontal and stay so till you really feel like getting up. And not more than one nip of Pembroke's guest-brandy, either. Get flat with no unnecessary delay and sleep if you can."

As we went on I noted that neither Radnor close by nor Mrs. Radnor on the veranda seemed aware of anything remarkable in Pembroke's attire; they must be habituated by him to it or to similar or even more fantastic raiment.

We appeared to walk the length or width of the village, to the villa farthest from the beach. As we entered I had a glimpse on one hand of a parlor with an ample round center-table, inviting armchairs and walls lined with bookcases, through whose doors I espied some handsome bindings; on the other hand of a cozy dining-room with a polished table and beyond it a sideboard loaded with silverware and decorated porcelain.

By the newel-post of the broad, easy stair stood a paragon of a Chinese butler.

"Wu," said Pembroke, "Mr. Denbigh is to occupy this house. Show him to his bedroom and call Fong. Mr. Denbigh needs him at once. And tell Fong that Mr. Denbigh has lost all his baggage and needs a change of clothes promptly."

Without any sudden movement or appearance of haste, without a word, he turned and was out of the villa and away before I could speak.

I found myself domiciled in an abode delightfully situated, each outlook a charming picture, and inside admirably designed and lavishly provided with every imaginable comfort and luxury. The servants were all Chinese. One took care of the lawn, flowers and shrubberies, another swept the rooms; there was an unsurpassable Chinese cook, whom I never saw, and something I heard made me infer that he had a helper. I had at my beck a

Chinese valet, a Chinese errand-boy and the deferential butler, who managed the house and anticipated my every want.

Except for frequent baths I think I slept most of the ensuing forty-eight hours. What I swallowed I took in bed. My second breakfast on the island I ate in the dainty, exquisitely appointed dining-room. After that I had energy enough to loll in one of the rattan lounging-chairs on the veranda, comfortably clad in neat, cool, well-cut, well-fitting garments chosen from the amazing abundance which Fong had ready for me, how so exactly suitable for me I could not conjecture. I had not been long on the veranda when Radnor strolled by, whistling "The Carnival of Venice." He came up and joined me. Early in our chat he said:

"Probably you will be unable to refrain from asking questions; but I fancy that I shall feel at liberty to answer very few of your queries. Nearly everything I know about this island and about happenings on it I have learned not as a mere man or as a mere dweller here, but as Pembroke's resident physician; it is all confidential. Most of what you learn here you'll have to absorb by observation and inference. And I don't mind telling you that the less you learn the better will Pembroke be pleased, and I likewise."

He did tell me that the villas were tenanted chiefly by the members of Pembroke's private orchestra and band, mostly Hungarians, Bohemians, Poles and Italians, with such other satellites as a sculptor, an architect, an engineer, a machinist, a head carpenter, a tailor and an accountant. The other village was populated entirely by Asiatics, Chinese, Japanese, Hindoos, and others; who performed all the labor of the island.

The next morning, about the same time, as I was similarly lounging on my veranda, Pembroke appeared, in the same bizarre attire, or lack of attire, in which I had previously seen him. He sat with me a half hour or so, asked courteously after my health and comfort and remarked:

"I am glad you feel contented: you'll probably abide here some time."

I said nothing. He glanced away from me, up under the edge of the veranda roof through the overarching boughs. My eyes followed his. I caught glints of pink from far-off flamingoes.

"Glorious birds!" Pembroke exclaimed, rapturously. "They nest on several of the low outlying keys, which, with the coral-reefs scattered between them, make it impossible for any craft bigger than a cat-boat to approach this side of the island. They have multiplied amazingly since I began shepherding them. I love them! I glory in them!"

At the word he left me, as abruptly and swiftly as after our first encounter.

Thereafter, for some weeks of what I can describe only as luxuriously comfortable and very pleasant captivity, I diverted myself by reading the very well-chosen and varied books of the villa's fairly large library, by getting acquainted with the inhabitants of the other villas, and by roaming about the lower part of the valley. The very evening of our chat Radnor had invited me to dinner, for which Fong fitted me out irreproachably, and at which I found Mrs. Radnor charming and the other guests, Conway the architect, and his wife and sister, very agreeable companions. After that I was a guest at dinner at one or another of the villas each evening, so that I lunched and breakfasted alone at my abode, but never dined there.

Once only I inspected the other village and found its neatness and the apparent contentment of its inhabitants, especially the women and children, very charming. But I seemed to divine that they felt the presence of a European or American as an intrusion: I avoided the village thereafter.

Some of the men of that village tended the trees, shrubberies, vines and gardens of the valley, and kept it a paradise, luxuriant with every sort of fruit and vegetable which could be grown in that soil and climate.

I saw nothing more of Pembroke and found that I could not approach his palace on the hill-top, for there was an extremely adequate steel fence of tall L-irons, sharp at the top, across the valley and down to the beach beyond either village, which barrier was patrolled by heavily-built, muscular guards, seemingly Scotch and not visibly armed, who respectfully intimated that no one passed any of its gates, or along either beach, without Mr. Pembroke's express permit. Very seldom did I so much as catch a glimpse of Pembroke on the terraces of his palace, but I did see on them knots, even bevies, of women whose outlines, even at that distance, suggested that they were young and personable, certainly that they were gayly clad in bright-colored silks. Near or with them I saw no man, excepting Asiatic servitors, and Pembroke himself, who powerfully suggested an oriental despot among his sultanas.

By the inadvertent utterance of someone, I forget whom, I learned that the guards had a cantonment or barrack on the other side of the island.

I enjoyed rambling about the valley, as far as I was permitted, for both the variety and the beauty of its products were amazing.

Still more amazing to me was the number of ever-flowing ornamental fountains. The Bahamas are proverbially hampered by scanty water supply. But here I found, apparently, a superabundance of clear, pure, drinkable water. There was a fountain near the village, where a seated bronze figure, seemingly of some Asiatic god or saint unknown to me, held in each hand a great serpent grasped by its throat, and from the open mouth of each snake poured a spout of water into the basin before the statue. There were other fountains, each with a figure or group of figures of bronze, in the formal garden by the village of villas. And beyond it, set against the scooped-out flank of one of the range of enclosing hills, was a huge concrete edifice of basins and outstanding groups of statuary and statues and groups in niches, more or less reminiscent of the Fountain of Trevi. I was dumbfounded at the flow of water from this extravagantly ornate and overloaded structure. There were many jets squirting so as to cross each other in the air, even to interlace, as it were. But midway of the whole construction, behind the middle basin, was a sort of grotto with, centrally, an open entrance like a low doorway or manhole, on either side of which were two larger apertures like low latticed windows, filled in with elaborately patterned bronze gratings, through the lower part of which flowed two streams of water as copious as brooks, which cascaded into the main basin.

Beyond this rococo fountain was a plot of ground enclosed by a hedge, serving as garden for a tiny cottage of one low story. In it lived an old Welsh woman, spoken of by the inhabitants of the village as "Mother Bevan." She always wore the hideous Welsh national costume and hobbled about leaning on a stout malacca walking-stick with an ivory cross-head topped with gold bosses.

She cared for and delighted in a numerous flock of snow-white geese which somehow seemed thriving in this, one would suppose, for them far too tropical climate. Among them was a large and very handsome gander, which reminded me of my childhood's pet. The flock spent much of its time swimming and splashing in the basins of the enormous grotto-fountain.

When I asked Radnor about the abundance of water and its apparent waste, he said:

"No mystery there nor any secrets. Pembroke could spend anything he pleased on wildcat artesian drilling and had the perverse luck to strike a generous flow just as his drillers were about to tell him that no humanly constructed implements could drill any deeper. It's no spouting well, though, and a less opulent proprietor than Pembroke could not afford to pump it as he does. The power-station is on the other side of the island, near the harbor. It uses oil fuel of some kind. There is never any stint of water for any use and the surplus is made to do ornamental duty, as you see."

I was interested in the old Welsh woman and in her tiny cottage, so oddly discordant with the Italianate concrete fountain near it and the spacious villas not far off. Except the Asiatics of the village and the barrier-guards I had found affable every dweller on the island; most of them sociable. I accosted the grotesque old crone, as she leaned over her gate and discovered in her the unexpected peculiarity that all her answers were in rhyming lines, rather cleverly versified, which she uttered, indeed, slowly, in a measured voice, but without the slightest symptom of hesitation. Her demeanor was distinctly forbidding and her words by no means conciliatory. I recall only one of her doggerels, which ended our first interview:

> "Man fallen out of the sky.
> "God never intended us to fly.
> "It's impious to ascend so high.
> " 'Twas wicked of you ever to try.
> "No lover of reprobates am I."

Except for this queer old creature I encountered no unfriendly word or look from any of my neighbors. I enjoyed the dinners to which I was invited and liked my fellow-guests at them; indeed I disliked no one with whom I talked; but, on the other hand, I was attracted to no one, and, while I felt entirely welcome wherever I was invited and altogether at my ease, and pleased to be invited again later, at no household did I feel free to drop in at odd times for casual chat. I found many congenial fellow-diners, but no one increasingly congenial, no one who impressed me as likely to be glad to have me call uninvited.

Therefore, as I always loved the open air, as I somehow felt lonely on my own veranda and nowhere intimate enough to lounge on any other, I took to spending many hours of the morning, before the heat of the midday grew intense, out in the shade of the little park, to which I was attracted by many of its charming features, especially by the pink masses of flowering bougainvillea here and there through it. I always carried a book, sometimes I read, oftener I merely gazed about at the enchanting vistas, overhead at the uncountable flamingoes, or between the trees out to seaward at the dazzling white heaps of billowy cumulus clouds, like titanic snow-clad mountains, bulging and growing on the towering thunder-heads forming against the vivid blue sky out over the ocean.

I think it was on my second morning in the park that I caught a glimpse of Mother Bevan crossing a path at some distance. Later I caught other glimpses of her crossing other paths. Each morning I caught similar glimpses of her. On the fifth or sixth morning I suddenly became conscious of an inward impression that she was, again and again, making the circuit of the park, circling about me as it were, like a witch weaving a spell about an intended victim.

Next morning I affected an absorption in my book and kept an alert, and I was certain, an imperceptible watch in all directions. I made sure that Mother Bevan was indeed perambulating the outer portions of the park, stumping along, leaning heavily on her cross-headed cane, and I made sure also that after she had completed one circuit about me she kept on her way and completed another and another.

I was curious, puzzled, incensed; derisive of myself for so much as entertaining the idea of anyone, in 1921, attempting witchcraft; concerned for fear that my wits were addled; and, while unable to rid myself of the notion, yet completely skeptical of any effect on me and unconscious of any.

But, the very next day, seated on the same marble bench, by the same fountain, among the same pink masses of bougainvillea in flower, I was aware not only of Mother Bevan circumambulating the outskirts of the park, but also of her numerous flock of noisy, self-important, white geese waddling about, not far from me, and indubitably walking round and round me in ever lessening circles, the big gander always nearest me. At first I felt incredulous, then silly, then resentful. And, as the gander, now and then honking, circled about me for the fifth or sixth time, I became conscious of an inner impulse, of an all but overmastering inner impulse, to seek out Pembroke and to tell him that I was willing to do anything he wanted me to do; to pledge myself to do anything that he wanted me to do.

I took alarm. I felt, shamefacedly, but vividly, that I was being made the subject of some sort of attempted necromancy. All of a sudden I found myself aflame with resentment, with hatred of that gander. I leapt to my feet, I hurled my book at him, I ran after him, I threw at him my bamboo walking-stick, barely missing him. I retrieved the walking-stick and pursued the retreating bird, and threw the cane at him a second time, almost hitting him.

The geese half waddled, half flew towards the beetling atrocities of the ornate rococo hill-side fountain; I followed, still infuriated. There was, along the walk before the fountain, an edging of lumps of coral rock defining the border of the flower-beds. I picked up an armful of the smaller pieces of angular coral rock, chased the geese into the big main basin of the fountain and pelted that gander with jagged chunks of coral. He fled through the central manhole into the grotto and hissed at me through one of the gratings, behind which he was safe from my missiles.

Suddenly overwhelmed by a revulsion of shame and a tendency to laugh at myself, I beat a retreat to my veranda. There I sat, pondering my situation and my experiences.

I recalled that, at every dinner to which I had been invited, there had been, practically, but two subjects of conversation: the boredom of life on tropical islands in general and on Pembroke island in particular; and the worth, the fine qualities, the charm, the perfection of Pembroke himself.

I watched a chance to find Radnor at leisure, to waylay him, to entice him on my veranda. When the atmosphere of our talk seemed auspicious, I said:

"See here, Radnor! I know you said you meant to elude any queries I might put to you, but there is one question you'll have to answer, somehow. Why are all these people here?"

"That is easy," Radnor laughed. "I have no objection to answering that question. They are here because Pembroke wants them here."

"I didn't phrase my question well," I said, "but you know what I mean. No one I have met really likes being here. Why do they stay?"

"That's easy, too," Radnor smiled. "Almost anyone will stay almost anywhere if lodged comfortably and paid enough. Pembroke provides his hirelings with an overplus of luxuries and is more than liberal in payment."

"That does not explain what intrigues me," I pursued. "I haven't yet hit on the right words to express my idea. But you really understand me, I think, though you pretend you don't. All the inhabitants of these villas are not merely uneasy, they are consciously homesick, acutely homesick, homesick to a degree which no luxurious surroundings, no prospective savings could alleviate. They are pining for home. What keeps them here?"

"Put it down," said Radnor, weightily, "to the unescapable charm of the island. That keeps them here."

"Did you say witchery or enchantment?" I queried, meaningly.

Radnor was emphatic.

"I said charm!" he uttered. "Let it go at that."

"I am not in the least inclined," I retorted, "to let it go at that. I take it that this is no joke, certainly not anything to be dismissed by a clever play on words. I insist on knowing what makes all these people stay here. They all declare, at every opportunity, that they are dying of ennui, that the climate is uncongenial, that they long for temperate skies, for northern vegetation, for frosty nights. What keeps them here?"

"I tell you," said Radnor, "that, like me, most human beings will do anything, anything lawful and reasonable, if paid high enough."

"The rest aren't like you," I asserted. "You and Mrs. Radnor impress me as free agents, doing, for a consideration, what you have been asked to do, and what you both, after weighing the pros and cons, have agreed to do. All the others, Europeans, Americans and Asiatics, except Mother Bevan, appear like beings hypnotized and moving in a trance, mere living automatons, without any will of their own, actuated solely by Pembroke's will; as much so as if they were mechanical dolls. They impress me as being mesmerized or bewitched. I seriously vow that I believe they have been subjected to some supernatural or magical influence. They are as totally dominated by Pembroke as if they were the ends of his fingers."

Radnor looked startled.

"It will do no good," I cried, "to contradict me or to deny it."

"I believe you," Radnor said, as if thinking out loud. He went on:

"You are right. Except Mother Bevan and me and Lucille every human being on this island is completely under Pembroke's influence, gained largely through the help of Mother Bevan."

"Why not you and your wife?" I queried.

"Lucille, because of me," he replied. "Pembroke found out, by trying Melville here and Kennard, that, after being put under his influence, while retaining surgical skill, a physician loses all ability to diagnose and prescribe. He had to ship Kennard and Melville back home, and pension them till their faculties recovered their tone."

I looked him straight in the eyes. He forestalled my impending outburst by saying:

"As far as I can discern, Pembroke's influence over his retainers does them no harm, physical or mental. Kennard and Melville have as large incomes and as many patients and are as successful and prosperous, as popular and prominent among their fellow-physicians as if they had never sojourned here. Except in their enthusiasm for and admiration of Pembroke every human being on this island appears to me as healthy as if not under any influence of any kind."

"Even so," I blurted out, "you ought not to abet any such deviltries."

"I don't admit," said Radnor, hotly, "that any deviltries exist on this island or that there is any approach to deviltry in what you have partly divined. Also I abet nothing, as I ought, but, as I also ought, I conceive that I am under obligations not to thwart Pembroke in any way. I am the island's resident physician and his personal physician; I am here to treat injuries, cure maladies, relieve pain, and do all I can to keep healthy every dweller on this island. I live up to my conception of my duty. Don't attempt to preach at me."

"I am impatient," I said, "at my enforced stay here, and revolted at the idea of succumbing to Pembroke's influence."

Radnor laughed.

"You are," he said, "the only human being who has reached the island, since Pembroke bought it, uninvited. You'll get away by and by. And you are most unlikely to be affected by anything he or Mother Bevan may have in their power to do. Neither Kennard nor Melville ever suspected anything, or grew suspicious. You alone have half seen through the situation here. You are Mother Bevan's most refractory subject, so far. Have no fear."

He went off, whistling Strauss' Blue Danube Waltz.

I had frequent recurrent fears, but I dissembled them. I think, among all the terrors which haunted me during the remainder of my sojourn on the island, that I came nearest to panic and horror within an hour after Radnor had left me. Hardly was he gone when Pembroke, arrayed precisely as before and reminding me of a stage-frog in a goblin pantomime, sauntered up and seated himself by me.

I sweated with tremors of dismay, I was ready to despair, when I found myself, however I tried, unable to utter a word to him concerning the gander, Mother Bevan, or my suspicions; unable even to allude to the subject in any way, although he asked me bluntly:

"Have you anything to complain of?"

"Only that I am here," I replied.

"I had nothing to do with your coming here," he retorted. "You came uninvited, of your own accord, or by accident. I trust I have been a courteous host, but I have not tried to pretend that you are welcome. I am endeavoring to arrange that your departure shall not entail upon me any inconvenience or any danger of disadvantageous consequences. Believe me, I am doing all I can to expedite your return to your normal haunts. Meantime you'll have to be patient."

I was most impatient and very nearly frantic at finding myself, no matter how I struggled inwardly, totally unable so much as to refer or allude to what lay heaviest on my mind.

We exchanged vaguely generalized sentences for awhile and he left as abruptly as before, left me quivering with consternation, dreading that my inability to broach the subject on which I was eager to beard him was a premonition of my total enthrallment to Pembroke's influence.

As the days passed I became habituated to stoning that uncanny gander, chasing him into the basin of the fountain and having him hiss at me from behind one of the gratings; I became indifferent to the glimpses I caught of Mother Bevan hovering in the middle distance. I had a good appetite for my meals: in fact, the food set before me at my abode would have awakened the most finicky dyspeptic to zest and relish, even to voracity; while the dinners to which I was invited were delectable.

But from night to night I slept less and less, until I was near insomnia. And, from day to day, I found it more and more difficult to absorb myself in reading, to keep my mind on what I read; even to read at all.

Again I waylaid Radnor. I described to him my progressively worsening discomfort and distress.

"I am now," I said, "or soon shall be, not merely in need of your help, but beyond any help from you or anybody. If you don't do something for me I'll go crazy, I'll do something desperate, I'll commit suicide."

"I have been pondering," he said, "how to help you, and I have almost hit upon a method. Your condition does not yet justify my giving you anything to make you sleep. As yet I do not want to give you any sort of drug, not even the simplest sedative. Honestly try to get to sleep tonight. Before tomorrow I think I'll hit upon an entirely suitable prescription, salutary for you and yet avoiding any appearance, any hint, of my antagonizing Pembroke."

I did try to sleep that night, but I was still wide awake long after midnight. So tossing and turning on my comfortable bed, I heard outside in the moonless darkness someone whistling a tune. As the sound came nearer I made sure it was Radnor. Also I recognized the tune.

It was that of "The Ballad of Nell Flaherty's Drake."

The tune brought to my mind the words of the song's refrain:

> "The dear little fellow,
> "His legs were so yellow,
> "He could fly like a swallow and swim like a hake!
> "Bad luck to the tober,
> "The haythen cashlober,
> "The monsther thot murthered Nell Flaherty's drake!"

All of a sudden I conceived that this was Radnor's method of intimating to me by indirection what he did not dare to utter to me in plain words. I thought I knew what he meant as well as if it had been put into the plainest words. I rolled over, was asleep in three breaths, and slept till Fong ventured to waken me.

After breakfast I went upstairs again and rummaged about in the closet where Fong had deposited what I had worn when I came under his care. I found there everything I remembered to have had about me. My automatic was well oiled and in good working order and its clip of cartridges was full. My belt, with the extra clips of cartridges, was as it had been when I last put it on. I put it on, over my feather-weight hot-weather habiliments; I strapped on my automatic; I strolled out, intent on somehow coming within speaking distance of Pembroke.

Chance, or some unconscious whim, guided my footsteps to the beach and, in spite of the rapidly intensifying heat of the sun rays, along it to the remaining fragments of my wreck, barely visible under a great accumulation of beach foam, left by the breakers, hurled shorewards during the thunder storm which had raged while I slept.

Not far beyond those vestiges of what had been an aeroplane, approaching me along the beach, I encountered Pembroke.

I found I had now no difficulty in speaking out my mind.

"Pembroke," I said, "I'm outdone with confinement on this island of yours. I'm irritated past endurance. If you don't promptly speed me on my way elsewhere the tension inside me is going to get too much for me. Something inside me is going to snap and I'll do something desperate, something you'll regret."

He looked me straight in the eyes, handsome in his fantastic toggery; calm and cool, to all appearance.

"Are you, by any chance," he drawled, "threatening to shoot me?"

"I haven't made any threats," I retorted, hotly, "and I have no intentions of shooting you or anybody. I realize that this island of yours is part of the British Empire and that in no part of it are homicides or murderous assaults condoned or left unpunished. But, since you use the word 'threat,' I am ready to make a threat. If you don't soon set me free of my present captivity, if you don't soon put me in the way of getting home, I'll not shoot you or any human being, but I will shoot that devilish gander; and, I promise you, if I shoot at him I'll hit him and if I hit him I'll kill him. I fancy those are plain words and I conjecture that you understand me fully, with all the implications of what I say."

Pembroke's expression of face appeared to me to indicate not only amazement and surprise, but the emotions of a man at a loss and momentarily helpless in the face of wholly unexpected circumstances.

"You come with me!" he snapped.

I followed him along the beach to the village, and, as we went, wondered to see him apparently comfortable in his tight-fitting suit and bare headed beneath the fierce radiance of the merciless sun rays, while I rejoiced in my flimsy garments and at being sheltered under the very adequate Panama hat I had chosen from the headgear Fong had offered me.

We passed the end of the steel picket fence, the two beach guards saluting Pembroke, and, I thought, suppressing a tendency to grin at me. Just around the point was a wide aviation field with a long row of hangars opposite the beach. I marveled, for I had caught no glimpse of any avion in the air over or about the island.

A half dozen Asiatics, apparently Annamites, rose as we approached and stood respectfully, eyes on Pembroke. He uttered some sort of order in a tongue unknown to me and two of them set wide open the doors of one of the hangars. In it, to my amazement, I saw a Visconti biplane, one of the fastest and most powerful single-seaters ever built.

"What do you think of that?" Pembroke queried.

"I am astonished," I answered. "I was certain that no specimen of this type of machine had ever been on this side of the Atlantic."

"This is the first and only Visconti to be set up on this side of the ocean," he replied. "The point is; could you fly it?"

"I think I could," I said, "and I am sure I could try."

"Try then," Pembroke snapped. "I make you a present of it. The sooner you're off and away the better I'll be pleased."

He spoke at some length, apparently in the same unknown tongue, and strode off towards his palace.

I spent that day and most of the next going over that Visconti biplane, with the deft, quick assistance of the docile Annamites. If there was anything about it defective, untrustworthy or out of order I could not find it. On the third morning (I had dined at Radnor's both evenings), equipped admirably by Fong, who instantly provided me with whatever I asked for, I rose in that Visconti biplane, and, contrary to my fears, reached Miami in safety. But I was so overstrained by anxiety that it required six weeks in a sanitarium to make me myself again. During those, apparently, endless hours in the air I had been expecting every moment that something cunningly arranged beforehand and undiscoverable to my scrutiny in my inspections and reinspections, was going to go wrong with my conveyance and instantaneously annihilate me. The strain all but finished me. However, all's well that ends well.

Azrael

My nurse-maid used a cruel plan,
   To curb her charges' play,
By tales about the Bogy-Man,
   Who carried you away.

I used to waken when I dreamed
   And, in the inky night,
I sat up in my bed and screamed
   With childish fear and fright.

I dreamed about a lovely land
   And there a girl and I
Were faring forwards hand in hand
   Beneath a sunlit sky.

Then, as we went, the sky grew dark,
   The shadows thickened round,
I seemed to palpitate and hark
   For some approaching sound.

On the unstable verge of sleep
   I swayed, appalled and numb;
I knew the Bogy-Man, to leap
   On one of us, had come.

o o o

My Love, your finger wears my ring,
  My heart is in your keep;
Our lives are at their perfect spring,
  Our harvest yet to reap.

Let us be happy for a span
  Together, while we may;
For, all too soon, the Bogy-Man
  Will carry one away.

The Ghoula

Because my mate did not return,
    And since my little ones must eat,
I sallied forth alone to learn,
    Myself, to win my children meat.

Whatever man upon my way,
    Hunter or villager robust,
I met alone and marked for prey,
    My smile would lull his first distrust;

My beauty touched his heart at length,
    And in my form he could not guess
A hint of that titanic strength
    Which even female ghouls possess.

At dusk, at sundawn, or at noon
    I lured him from ravine or road
To where the ruins are. And soon
    We feasted in our dim abode.

Men's flesh is best. If none came near,
    I caught some bullock, sheep, or goat,
Or, waiting at a pool the deer,
    Leapt like the panther at its throat.

Three days, and to my younglings' cries
    I brought but pilfered scraps of food.
I saw the famine in their eyes
    And hunted in no gentle mood.

Next day above the desert plain
    Our Persian sky arched blue and clear.

The Ghoula

From the lookout where I had lain
  I saw a figure drawing near;

An Englishman who strayed alone,
  Careless of nomads, ghouls, or spells,
To beat the waste of sand and stone
  For hares or bustards or gazelles.

He spoke our homely Persian tongue;
  I found him nowise hard to fool;
And yet, he was so tall and young,
  I wished that he had been a ghoul.

My hunting had engrossed my mind,
  Since of my mate I was bereft.
Now, staring through the months behind,
  I felt how lonely I was left.

My starved mouth watered at the view
  Of pink cheeks, tender, plump, and nigh,
And yet it seemed a pity too;
  He looked too comely for to die.

As by my side he idly paced,
  Before the ruins we had neared,
Between two boulders on the waste,
  Some distance off, a doe appeared.

He raised his rifle and took aim.
  Then, as I watched to see her spring,
He stopped and said: "It seems a shame
  To kill the pretty, dainty thing."

It startled me to find this youth,
  So heedless, hale, and lithe of limb,
Felt for his game the selfsame ruth
  Which I had felt at sight of him.

She stood and stared before she ran.
  "What good to us that she should roam,"

I said: "Best shoot her while you can,
   We have no meat at all at home."

His bullet missed. The creature fled.
   He flushed, surprised, chagrined, and vexed.
Then, smiling cheerily, he said:
   "I may do better with the next.

"That lean doe was not worth regret,
   You may get meat some other way."
I answered, with my purpose set,
   "Indeed, I rather think I may."

            ✿ ✿ ✿

How cool the shadowed archway smelt,
   Pleasant and softly lit inside!
His arm went round my waist. I felt
   My young would not have long to bide.

They cowered huddling in our lair,
   Their pangs I knew they would endure
In silence, rather than to scare
   Quarry of which I was not sure.

Inebriated with my charms,
   He held me closely, unaware
That he was helpless in my arms
   As is a rabbit in a snare.

Time after time our lips had met;
   His curly head to mine I drew,
A kiss upon his throat I set—
   And bit the windpipe through and through.

            ✿ ✿ ✿

The Ghoula

Firm flesh to eat, clean blood to drink,
   Fitted to make my dear ones thrive.
And yet, since then, I often think—
   He was so handsome when alive.

Who knows, but for my darlings' need
   I might have softened, let him go?
I find it in my heart indeed
   To wish that he had shot the doe.

Edward Lucas White on Dreams

"Preface" to The Song of the Sirens (extract)

A DAY-DREAMER I have been from boyhood, haunted, no matter what my task, by imaginations, mostly approximating some form of fictitious narrative; imaginations beyond my power to banish and seldom entirely within my power to alter, modify or control.

Besides, I have, in my sleep, dreamed many dreams which, after waking, I could remember: some dimly, vaguely or faintly; others clearly, vividly or even intensely. A majority of these dreams have been such as come to most sleepers, but a minority have been such as visit few dreamers.

Sometimes I wake with the most distinct recollection of a picture, definite and with a multitude of details. Such was the dream, on the night of February 17th, 1906, in which I saw the vision on which is based the tale of "The Song of the Sirens"; saw it not as a painted picture, but as if I had been on the crosstrees of a vessel under that intense blue sky, gazing at the magic islet and its portentous occupants. The dream was the more marvelous since there is nothing, either in literature or art, suggesting anything which I beheld in that vision of the two living shapes.

Often I wake with the sensation of having just finished reading a book or story. Generally I can recall the form and appearance of the book and can almost see the last page: size, shape, quality of paper and kind of type; with every letter of the last sentences.

Such a dream was that from which I woke shuddering, tingling with the horror of the revelation at the end of "The Flambeau Bracket," with the last three sentences of it, word for word as they stand in the story, branded on my sight. Yet I was not able to recall in its entirety the tale I had just read; for, in the dream, the whole action took place on the window-sill, and what was done and said there disclosed all that had gone before and implied, unmistakably, all that was to come after. This superlative artistry I could not attain to in writing the tale.

"Afterword" to Lukundoo and Other Stories (extract)
Eight of the stories in this book I did not compose. I dreamed them, and in each the dream or nightmare needed little or no modification to make a story of it. . . .

"Lukundoo" was written after my nightmare without any manipulation of mine, just as I dreamed it. But I should never have dreamed it had I not previously read H. G. Wells' very much better story, "Pollock and the Porroh Man." Anyone interested in dreams might relish comparing the two tales. They have resemblant features, but are very unlike, and the differences are such as no waking intellect would invent, but such as come into a human mind only in a nightmare dream.

The others are paragon nightmares.

"The House of the Nightmare" is written just as I dreamed it, word for word, since I had the concurrent sensations of reading the tale in print and of it all happening to me in the archaic times when all motor-cars were right-hand-drive and with gearshift-levers outside the tonneau. The dream had the unusual peculiarity that I woke after the second nightmare, so shaken that my wife had to quiet and soothe me as if I had been a scared child; and then I went to sleep again and *finished the dream*! Its denouement came as a complete surprise to me, as much of a shock as the climax of "The Snout" or of "Amina."

It will be easy to realize that anyone dreaming such narratives as "The Picture Puzzle," "The Message on the Slate" and "The Pig-skin Belt" just had to write them into stories to get them out of his system.

A CATALOG OF SELECTED
DOVER BOOKS
IN ALL FIELDS OF INTEREST

A CATALOG OF SELECTED DOVER BOOKS IN ALL FIELDS OF INTEREST

ABC BOOK OF EARLY AMERICANA, Eric Sloane. Artist and historian Eric Sloane presents a wondrous A-to-Z collection of American innovations, including hex signs, ear trumpets, popcorn, and rocking chairs. Illustrated, hand-lettered pages feature brief captions explaining objects' origins and uses. 64pp. 0-486-49808-5

ADVENTURES OF HUCKLEBERRY FINN, Mark Twain. Join Huck and Jim as their boyhood adventures along the Mississippi River lead them into a world of excitement, danger, and self-discovery. Humorous narrative, lyrical descriptions of the Mississippi valley, and memorable characters. 224pp. 0-486-28061-6

ALICE STARMORE'S BOOK OF FAIR ISLE KNITTING, Alice Starmore. A noted designer from the region of Scotland's Fair Isle explores the history and techniques of this distinctive, stranded-color knitting style and provides copious illustrated instructions for 14 original knitwear designs. 208pp. 0-486-47218-3

ALICE'S ADVENTURES IN WONDERLAND, Lewis Carroll. Beloved classic about a little girl lost in a topsy-turvy land and her encounters with the White Rabbit, March Hare, Mad Hatter, Cheshire Cat, and other delightfully improbable characters. 42 illustrations by Sir John Tenniel. A selection of the Common Core State Standards Initiative. 96pp. 0-486-27543-4

THE ARTHUR RACKHAM TREASURY: 86 Full-Color Illustrations, Arthur Rackham. Selected and Edited by Jeff A. Menges. A stunning treasury of 86 full-page plates span the famed English artist's career, from *Rip Van Winkle* (1905) to masterworks such as *Undine, A Midsummer Night's Dream,* and *Wind in the Willows* (1939). 96pp.
0-486-44685-9

THE AWAKENING, Kate Chopin. First published in 1899, this controversial novel of a New Orleans wife's search for love outside a stifling marriage shocked readers. Today, it remains a first-rate narrative with superb characterization. New introductory note. 128pp. 0-486-27786-0

THE CALL OF THE WILD, Jack London. A classic novel of adventure, drawn from London's own experiences as a Klondike adventurer, relating the story of a heroic dog caught in the brutal life of the Alaska Gold Rush. Note. 64pp. 0-486-26472-6

THE CARTOON HISTORY OF TIME, Kate Charlesworth and John Gribbin. Cartoon characters explain cosmology, quantum physics, and other concepts covered by Stephen Hawking's *A Brief History of Time*. Humorous graphic novel–style treatment, perfect for young readers and curious folk of all ages. 64pp. 0-486-49097-1

A CHRISTMAS CAROL, Charles Dickens. This engrossing tale relates Ebenezer Scrooge's ghostly journeys through Christmases past, present, and future and his ultimate transformation from a harsh and grasping old miser to a charitable and compassionate human being. 80pp. 0-486-26865-9

CRIME AND PUNISHMENT, Fyodor Dostoyevsky. Translated by Constance Garnett. Supreme masterpiece tells the story of Raskolnikov, a student tormented by his own thoughts after he murders an old woman. Overwhelmed by guilt and terror, he confesses and goes to prison. A selection of the Common Core State Standards Initiative. 448pp. 0-486-41587-2

Browse over 10,000 books at www.doverpublications.com

CATALOG OF DOVER BOOKS

DOOMED SHIPS: Great Ocean Liner Disasters, William H. Miller, Jr. Nearly 200 photographs, many from private collections, highlight tales of some of the vessels whose pleasure cruises ended in catastrophe: the *Morro Castle, Normandie, Andrea Doria, Europa,* and many others. 128pp. 0-486-45366-9

DUBLINERS, James Joyce. A fine and accessible introduction to the work of one of the 20th century's most influential writers, this collection features 15 tales, including a masterpiece of the short-story genre, "The Dead." 160pp. 0-486-26870-5

ETHAN FROME, Edith Wharton. Classic story of wasted lives, set against a bleak New England background. Superbly delineated characters in a hauntingly grim tale of thwarted love. Considered by many to be Wharton's masterpiece. 96pp. 0-486-26690-7

FLATLAND: A Romance of Many Dimensions, Edwin A. Abbott. Classic of science (and mathematical) fiction — charmingly illustrated by the author — describes the adventures of A. Square, a resident of Flatland, in Spaceland (three dimensions), Lineland (one dimension), and Pointland (no dimensions). 96pp. 0-486-27263-X

FRANKENSTEIN, Mary Shelley. The story of Victor Frankenstein's monstrous creation and the havoc it caused has enthralled generations of readers and inspired countless writers of horror and suspense. With the author's own 1831 introduction. 176pp.
0-486-28211-2

THE GARGOYLE BOOK: 572 Examples from Gothic Architecture, Lester Burbank Bridaham. Dispelling the conventional wisdom that French Gothic architectural flourishes were born of despair or gloom, Bridaham reveals the whimsical nature of these creations and the ingenious artisans who made them. 572 illustrations. 224pp.
0-486-44754-5

HEART OF DARKNESS, Joseph Conrad. Dark allegory of a journey up the Congo River and the narrator's encounter with the mysterious Mr. Kurtz. Masterly blend of adventure, character study, psychological penetration. For many, Conrad's finest, most enigmatic story. 80pp. 0-486-26464-5

THE HOUND OF THE BASKERVILLES, Sir Arthur Conan Doyle. A deadly curse in the form of a legendary ferocious beast continues to claim its victims from the Baskerville family until Holmes and Watson intervene. Often called the best detective story ever written. 128pp. 0-486-28214-7

HOW TO DRAW NEARLY EVERYTHING, Victor Perard. Beginners of all ages can learn to draw figures, faces, landscapes, trees, flowers, and animals of all kinds. Well-illustrated guide offers suggestions for pencil, pen, and brush techniques plus composition, shading, and perspective. 160pp. 0-486-49848-4

JANE EYRE, Charlotte Brontë. Written in 1847, *Jane Eyre* tells the tale of an orphan girl's progress from the custody of cruel relatives to an oppressive boarding school and its culmination in a troubled career as a governess. A selection of the Common Core State Standards Initiative. 448pp. 0-486-42449-9

JUST WHAT THE DOCTOR DISORDERED: Early Writings and Cartoons of Dr. Seuss, Dr. Seuss. Edited and with an Introduction by Rick Marschall. The Doctor's visual hilarity, nonsense language, and offbeat sense of humor illuminate this compilation of items from his early career, created for periodicals such as *Judge, Life, College Humor,* and *Liberty.* 144pp. 0-486-49846-8

THE LADY OR THE TIGER?: and Other Logic Puzzles, Raymond M. Smullyan. Created by a renowned puzzle master, these whimsically themed challenges involve paradoxes about probability, time, and change; metapuzzles; and self-referentiality. Nineteen chapters advance in difficulty from relatively simple to highly complex. 1982 edition. 240pp. 0-486-47027-X

Browse over 10,000 books at www.doverpublications.com

CATALOG OF DOVER BOOKS

LINE: An Art Study, Edmund J. Sullivan. Written by a noted artist and teacher, this well-illustrated guide introduces the basics of line drawing. Topics include third and fourth dimensions, formal perspective, shade and shadow, figure drawing, and other essentials. 208pp. 0-486-79484-9

MANHATTAN IN MAPS 1527-2014, Paul E. Cohen and Robert T. Augustyn. This handsome volume features 65 full-color maps charting Manhattan's development from the first Dutch settlement to the present. Each map is placed in context by an accompanying essay. 176pp. 0-486-77991-2

THE METAMORPHOSIS AND OTHER STORIES, Franz Kafka. Excellent new English translations of title story (considered by many critics Kafka's most perfect work), plus "The Judgment," "In the Penal Colony," "A Country Doctor," and "A Report to an Academy." A selection of the Common Core State Standards Initiative. 96pp. 0-486-29030-1

THE ODYSSEY, Homer. Excellent prose translation of ancient epic recounts adventures of the homeward-bound Odysseus. Fantastic cast of gods, giants, cannibals, sirens, other supernatural creatures — true classic of Western literature. A selection of the Common Core State Standards Initiative. 256pp. 0-486-40654-7

THE PICTURE OF DORIAN GRAY, Oscar Wilde. Celebrated novel involves a handsome young Londoner who sinks into a life of depravity. His body retains perfect youth and vigor while his recent portrait reflects the ravages of his crime and sensuality. 176pp. 0-486-27807-7

PRIDE AND PREJUDICE, Jane Austen. One of the most universally loved and admired English novels, an effervescent tale of rural romance transformed by Jane Austen's art into a witty, shrewdly observed satire of English country life. A selection of the Common Core State Standards Initiative. 272pp. 0-486-28473-5

RELATIVITY SIMPLY EXPLAINED, Martin Gardner. One of the subject's clearest, most entertaining introductions offers lucid explanations of special and general theories of relativity, gravity, and spacetime, models of the universe, and more. 100 illustrations. 224pp. 0-486-29315-7

THE SCARLET LETTER, Nathaniel Hawthorne. With stark power and emotional depth, Hawthorne's masterpiece explores sin, guilt, and redemption in a story of adultery in the early days of the Massachusetts Colony. A selection of the Common Core State Standards Initiative. 192pp. 0-486-28048-9

SKETCHING OUTDOORS, Leonard Richmond. This guide offers beginners step-by-step demonstrations of how to depict clouds, trees, buildings, and other outdoor sights. Explanations of a variety of techniques include shading and constructional drawing. 48pp. 0-486-46922-0

TREASURE ISLAND, Robert Louis Stevenson. Classic adventure story of a perilous sea journey, a mutiny led by the infamous Long John Silver, and a lethal scramble for buried treasure — seen through the eyes of cabin boy Jim Hawkins. 160pp. 0-486-27559-0

WORLD WAR II: THE ENCYCLOPEDIA OF THE WAR YEARS, 1941-1945, Norman Polmar and Thomas B. Allen. Authoritative and comprehensive, this reference surveys World War II from an American perspective. Over 2,400 entries cover battles, weapons, and participants as well as aspects of politics, culture, and everyday life. 85 illustrations. 960pp. 0-486-47962-5

WUTHERING HEIGHTS, Emily Brontë. Somber tale of consuming passions and vengeance — played out amid the lonely English moors — recounts the turbulent and tempestuous love story of Cathy and Heathcliff. Poignant and compelling. 256pp. 0-486-29256-8

Browse over 10,000 books at www.doverpublications.com